FUTURE SHOCK

FUTURE
SHOCK

ELIZABETH BRIGGS

ALBERT WHITMAN & COMPANY
CHICAGO, ILLINOIS

For my mother, Gaylene,
who never gave up hope.

Library of Congress Cataloging-in-Publication
data is on file with the publisher.

Text copyright © 2016 by Elizabeth Briggs
Published in 2016 by Albert Whitman & Company
ISBN 978-0-8075-2682-8

Printed in the United States of America
10 9 8 7 6 5 4 3 2 1 BP 24 23 22 21 20 19 18 17 16 15

Cover artwork by Paul Stinson
Design by Jordan Kost

For more information about Albert Whitman & Company,
visit our web site at www.albertwhitman.com.

WEDNESDAY

I can already tell this is one of those moments I'll later wish I could forget. But like everything else, it will be burned into my memory forever.

"Elena Martinez, correct?" The pasty-white manager looks over my application with a frown. I stare at a piece of lint on his hunter-green polo shirt and shift in the hard wooden seat.

"Yes." *Remember to smile*, I think and force my mouth to curl up. A dusty, round clock ticks overhead. 3:56 p.m. Two minutes faster than the watch on my wrist.

A waitress in a red skirt the size of a belt heads to the table next to us. If they hire me, I'll be wearing that uniform too. Ugh. But I'll take whatever job I can get at this point.

As the waitress takes the couple's order, the woman's high-pitched voice slices through the restaurant noise. "Can I get the bacon cheeseburger, without mayo but with mustard…" She goes on for another thirty seconds, replacing and adding so many items that she might as well make up her own menu item.

"How old are you?" the manager asks me, even though my age is right there on the form.

"Seventeen." His eyebrows shoot up, and I quickly add, "But I turn eighteen in two months."

He drums his fingers on the table and glances over my application again. My stomach growls at the smell of fried food wafting from another table. I haven't eaten anything since the free lunch at school.

The air-conditioning kicks on overhead with a loud rumble, blasting cold air down on me. I rub my arms, wishing I'd worn a shirt with long sleeves. I would have if Los Angeles wasn't in the middle of a freaking heat wave in the beginning of March, and if I had time to go home and change after school. No way was I spending the entire day in long sleeves, sweating all over myself. Besides, this is the nicest shirt I own.

The manager notices my movement and stares at my arms, his eyes narrowing at the sight of my tattoos. Definitely should have worn a different shirt. Why didn't I bring an extra one to change into? Or a sweater?

"Have you ever stolen anything?" he asks.

"No," I lie. Memories flicker through my head. At thirteen I stole five dollars from a foster mother's purse to pay for food. At ten I took a chocolate bar from a different foster mother's secret stash. At eight I swiped my father's bottle of whiskey and threw it in the trash. But this manager doesn't need to know any of that.

"Have you ever done drugs?"

"No." This isn't a lie. I don't mess with that stuff.

He stares me down, like he doesn't believe me. "Do you have any restaurant experience?"

"No." Yet another pointless question. It's all on my application—a big, fat zero. This is *not* going well. I can't afford to screw this interview up. I force another smile. "But I can learn."

He frowns but doesn't answer. I start to fold my hands on the checkered tablecloth but stop when I see how greasy it is. At the next table, the couple laughs. The sound gets under my skin, like they're laughing *at* me, even though I know that's ridiculous.

The manager finally stands up and offers his hand. "Thank you for coming, Ms. Martinez. We'll let you know."

Yeah right. I stand up and shake his warm, wet hand. He has a limp handshake. My father would call him a pendejo. But Papá is in prison for life, so what does he know?

The manager pulls his hand away and that's it. Another job interview over. I grab my backpack and start to walk toward the exit. I pass the other table and they laugh again. Maybe they *are* laughing at me.

What am I going to do now? I've been all over the city and have spent every free minute after school applying for jobs. No one wants to hire an underage, inexperienced, tatted-up Mexican girl. Even McDonald's turned me down. If I don't find something soon, I'm screwed.

In two months I'll be kicked out of foster care, forced out of my current home, and most likely will have to drop out of school. My time's running out fast, but I refuse to end up like some of the other foster kids I've known who aged out of the system. Living on the streets. Knocked up. Hooked on drugs. Sent to prison. *Dead*.

Screw that. I'm going to make it on my own. I'm going to college. I'm going to be free.

But I need a job, fast.

I swallow the tiny amount of pride I still have left and turn back to the manager. "Look, I really need this job. Please. I'll wait tables. I'll wash dishes. I'll do anything you want. Just give me a chance."

"I'm sorry," he says, crossing his arms. "We're not hiring right now."

Oh sure. Except for the NOW HIRING sign on the window outside. Rage flares inside me and I clench my fists. No one will give me a chance. Is it my age? My tattoos? My brown skin? What the hell is *wrong* with me?

The manager takes a step back, and I see a flash of fear cross his face. He's scared of me, of the anger in my eyes, of the ink on my arms, of the way my fists ready for a fight. I know I can take him, easy.

And the worst part is, I want to.

I'm jerked out of the moment when the woman at the other table raises her voice. "This is *not* what I ordered."

The waitress looks at the plate and then back at the woman, as though the words don't translate. "Bacon cheeseburger with coleslaw, right?"

"Yes, but this burger is *completely* wrong. Where are my onion rings? And my salad?"

"I'm sorry, what did you order?"

The woman huffs. "I *ordered* a—"

The words pour out of me before I can stop them: "A bacon cheeseburger without mayo, with mustard, no tomatoes, Swiss cheese instead of cheddar, extra avocado and bacon, onion rings instead of fries, and an extra side of coleslaw. Plus an order of the mixed green salad with no tomatoes, and a Diet Coke with no ice." I stop to take a breath, and then I add, "And he ordered the blue cheese burger with a Sprite."

Everyone's staring at me now—the manager, the waitress, and the couple at the table. Even a few people across the restaurant. Eyes wide, mouths open, suspicion and shock creasing their brows. I know these looks. I've seen them before.

My face burns, and I wish I could take back everything I said, redo the entire moment. I spin around and head for the exit before they can say anything.

A blast of heat and sunshine hits me as I step outside. I wanted to show them I could do this job just as well—if not better—than they could. But like a pendeja I let my anger get the best of me and proved to everyone in there what a freak I am. And the worst part is, I'll never forget this moment either.

Because I never forget anything.

✳ ✳ ✳

The doorbell rings at 8:34 p.m. I stare at the green numbers on the clock, while Katie reads out loud from her homework. The doorbell doesn't mean anything. It could be a salesman or a neighbor. But I know better. Sudden arrivals in a foster home are never a good thing.

"Elena, you're not listening," Katie says as she looks up from her Spanish textbook.

"I am." I tear my gaze away from the clock and force a smile. "You're going to the 'discoteca.' Keep reading."

We're huddled next to a flimsy desk light because the bulb overhead is out and no one's bothered to change it yet. Not that there's much to see—two twin beds crammed into a room not much bigger than a closet with one dresser between them. It's obvious our foster mom once put some effort into decorating it with lavender walls and fluffy, pastel pillows, but a steady stream of rotating kids has worn the place down. At least with the light out it's harder to see the stains in the carpet, the fraying edges of the sheets, or the peeling paint around the windowsill. Still, I've lived in worse places. And I only have to survive this one for another two months.

Katie though, she's only fourteen. She has a long way to go before she gets out. I don't know who will take care of her when

I'm gone. Not the Robertsons, that's for damn sure. They try, but they're stretched thin enough as it is. Not the other girls living here, who pick on Katie for being tiny and having hair so pale it's almost silver. Or they used to, anyway. I took her under my wing when she came here a month ago, after her mom OD'd on drugs. No one messed with her much after that.

Katie's kind and smart, and the system hasn't worn her down yet. I pray it never does, but who am I kidding? It gets to us all in time.

But once I get out, maybe I can help her. Or if not her, then other foster kids like us. Sometimes that thought is the only thing that keeps me going.

She starts reading again, and we work on conjugating the verb "to go" for her homework. I ignore the heavy feeling in my gut until my foster mom calls my name from downstairs.

Katie chews on her pen and looks up at me. "You should go see what she wants."

"I know." I sigh and drag myself off the bed. "Start working on the next section."

It has to be a social worker. No one else would come to the house looking for me. But I only have two months until I turn eighteen. They wouldn't make me move now, would they? I don't want to leave Katie, and even though this house is cramped and rundown, the Robertsons treat us pretty well and always have food in the kitchen. That's more than I can say for some of the homes I've lived in. But where I live has never been up to me. If they say I have to go, then that's that.

"There's a woman in the dining room who wants to speak with you," my foster mom says when I get downstairs. Her eyes are rimmed with dark circles and she's wearing one of her ridiculous aprons. This one is pink and says, *Life is precious, handle with prayer.*

The TV in the living room isn't blasting sports at full volume, so my foster dad must be working late again. He's been doing overtime more and more these days.

From what I've gathered, the Robertsons couldn't have children of their own and thought they would do some good by taking in foster kids. A worthy goal, but they got in over their heads and now they're barely keeping it together. They're overworked and under-paid and have no idea how to deal with six kids who've all been through hell and back.

Once we turn eighteen, they're done. The instant the checks stop coming, we'll be out on the street. Everyone here knows it, and there's nothing we can do. The Robertsons are doing the best they can, just like the rest of us. It's the system that's messed up.

One of the other girls living here races through the hallway and up the stairs, followed by another one who yells, "Give that back. It's mine!"

Mrs. Robertson pinches the bridge of her nose and sighs. "Go on. I'll make sure no one bothers you."

"Thanks."

I hold my breath as I head to the dining room, steeling myself for what's coming. It has to be a social worker, even though our weekly meetings are always scheduled in the afternoon. But who else would come to see me?

A woman in a sleek, black pantsuit waits inside, examining my foster mom's collection of tiny elephants. Her silky, brown hair has blond highlights, and she carries a slim, leather briefcase. After years in the system I'm an expert on social workers, and this woman isn't one of them. Her clothes are too nice, and she doesn't have that world-weary look in her eyes.

"Elena Martinez, I presume?" The woman extends her hand,

with perfectly white-tipped nails. She has a firm handshake. "My name is Lynne Marshall. I'm from Aether Corporation."

I raise my eyebrows. Aether Corporation is one of the biggest tech companies in the world. My hand-me-down cell phone is made by them, along with the ancient computer in the office we all have to share. I can't think of a single reason why would someone from Aether Corp would want to speak with me.

Lynne sits in one of the rickety, wooden chairs and sets her briefcase on the scratched-up table. I hesitate in the doorway, still trying to figure out what this woman could want, before finally sitting across from her.

"I'm sure you're wondering why I'm here, so I'll get right to it," she says, as she opens her briefcase and pulls out some papers. "As I said, I work for Aether Corporation. My company has set up a special program with the state of California to help children in foster care transition to adulthood, whether that means going to college or getting a job and finding a place to live."

"What kind of program?" I've been turned down for every transition program I've applied to so far, thanks to my record. I don't want to get my hopes up, but I need a break so bad, even if this already sounds way too good to be true. I wait to hear what the catch is.

She lays the papers on the table and folds her hands over them. "We've had our eye on you for some time. Your grades are good, especially considering how often you've changed schools. Many teachers have remarked on your near-perfect test scores."

Near perfect. Only because I realized when I was younger that I got too much attention when my answers were perfect. Teachers got suspicious when I did *too* well on tests. Other kids teased me for being a know-it-all. And foster parents freaked out when I recited facts and details back to them.

"In fact, we had your school run a few basic tests on your entire class so we could confirm our suspicions. Your results stood out." A slow smile spreads across her lips. "We know you have an exceptional memory."

My throat tightens. They've been watching me? *Testing* me? How much do they know?

"It's truly amazing what you can do. Perfect recall is a rare gift." She leans close, like we're two friends sharing a secret. "Don't worry, we haven't told anyone else about your unique talent, including your foster parents."

I'm tempted to bolt out of the room like I did at the job interview today. I've worked so hard to hide my freaky memory over the years, but they *know*. Yet Lynne doesn't look at me like I'm a freak. Instead, she eyes me like I'm a piñata and she's waiting to see what kind of candy falls out of me. I'm not sure I like that any better.

She waits for me to say something, but when I don't respond she sits back and continues. "I'm told you tutor some of the younger girls here. Why is that?"

Her question catches me off guard, but I'm glad for the change in topic. "No one else will."

"I see." She looks down at the paper in front of her. "Your record shows you've been in quite a few fights during your time in foster care, including a bad one two years ago. Want to tell me what happened?"

My stomach clenches at the memory. It's still fresh in my mind, as vivid as when it happened. Those girls deserved it, but I hate thinking about that day. It's one of those moments that make me wish I didn't have a perfect memory. "No."

She gives me a smile, which I can tell is fake. I've seen that kind of smile before on social workers, teachers, and foster parents. The smile they put on when they're trying to be patient with a kid who doesn't want to cooperate. "Do you like to fight?"

"No," I say again. "But I will if I have to."

"Good, good." She seems pleased with my answer, which sets off little warning bells in my head. But before I can question that, she continues. "We'd like to make you an offer to join our program."

I sit up straighter and hope floods my veins like a drug, but I try not to show anything on my face. I don't want her to know how desperate I am. "What do I have to do?"

"We're recruiting a small group of extraordinary teens to participate in a short research project, which will take place tomorrow at one of our facilities near here. We'll pick you up in the morning and bring you home in the evening, so you'll only miss one day of school. The project is confidential, so I'm afraid I can't disclose any other details at this time." Her smile widens, her teeth perfect and white. "What I *can* tell you is that this is a once-in-a-lifetime opportunity, and you will be greatly rewarded for participating."

Her offer is tempting, so very tempting. But I don't like going into anything blind. I study Lynne's expensive clothes and her fancy nails, trying to imagine what kind of "research project" Aether Corp could be doing with foster kids. From her questions, I'm guessing it's some sort of focus group. Watching movies, answering surveys, that sort of thing. Or maybe they're doing a study about "gifted" teens and want to ask us questions, have us solve puzzles, stuff like that. But then, why was she so pleased to hear I could fight? And why are the details confidential?

"We've already obtained permission from your legal guardians." She slides forward a stack of papers, the top one signed by my foster mom and some government authorities. Below it, there's a blank line with my name under it. Waiting for my signature. "Please read over the contract and let me know if you have any questions."

I'm tempted to just sign the thing, but I'm not that stupid. I scan the first page—and freeze when I see the amount of money they're offering. My God. No freaking way. That has to be a typo or something. There are way too many zeroes there. "Is this number correct?"

"It is."

I stare at the number and my head spins with all the possibilities. It's more money than I've ever dreamed of in my entire life. That much money means freedom. Safety. Independence. And a real home for the first time in years.

That much money means a future.

I quickly read through the rest of the document. There's a confidentiality agreement, and a paragraph about medical exams and tests both before and after the research project, *including, but not limited to, a physical exam, blood tests, and an MRI scan.* The last page of the contract has a waiver for any injuries we might sustain. Definitely not videos and surveys then.

My head snaps up. "What's this about medical exams? And injuries?"

"We'll be conducting a routine medical exam to make sure it's safe for you to participate in the project. It's nothing to worry about."

"But it says there are some risks involved."

"Oh, the legal department always adds lines like that to our contract. It's standard language for every project we do. The risks are minimal, I assure you."

She hands me a pen and her smile never wavers. I roll it between my fingers, staring at the words *not liable for any injuries, trauma, or permanent damage sustained during the duration of the research project.* I want to sign, *need* to sign, but there's so much she isn't telling me.

"Elena, you're going to be eighteen in two months. You'll be on your own with no money, no home, and no job. You have the grades to go to college but no way to pay for it." She taps the edge of the paper with a shiny fingernail. "We can find you a job. We can get you into college. And we're offering enough money for you to do whatever you want with your life. All you have to do is help us with this project. A few hours of your time, that's all we ask."

My pen hovers over the blank line. Everything she said is true. I *am* desperate, and they're offering a lot of money for one day of work. More money than I could ever expect to make on my own in a lifetime. Especially since no one is willing to hire a freak like me. If I turn this down, I'll regret it forever.

There might be risks involved—but what other options do I have? No one else is going to help me. I'm on my own. And my time is running out.

I sign my name on the line.

THURSDAY

A fancy black car picks me up early in the morning. I ride in the backseat in silence, like all the times I was chauffeured from one house to the next by one of my social workers. He always had me sit in the back too, like I was a criminal in a police car. And I always felt the same mix of uncertainty and fear swirling in my gut, along with the slightest trace of hope. Just like I do now.

We travel over an hour east of Los Angeles, to where civilization begins to give way to the desert. When there's nothing around us but rocks and dirt, the car approaches a five-story building surrounded by a high fence with a security checkpoint. It's the only thing in sight for miles and looks like a generic office: light gray exterior, shiny tinted windows, and perfectly trimmed trees breaking up the concrete sidewalk.

The driver drops me off in front of the glass doors, where Lynne is already waiting. She wears another smooth, black pantsuit, and her highlighted hair is pulled back in a tight ponytail. "Welcome to Aether Corporation, Elena. Please follow me."

The lobby is bright, with floor-to-ceiling windows and light-colored hardwood floors, probably bamboo or something expensive.

A frizzy-haired receptionist sits at a modern desk made of the same wood as the floor. The wall behind her displays the Aether Corporation logo in silver letters.

Both Lynne and the receptionist stare at me with wide smiles while I sign in at the front desk. We're the only three people in the room, but I feel like I'm standing alone on a stage with an entire audience watching, waiting for me to screw up.

The receptionist hands me a badge with my name on it, which I attach to my shirt. Lynne leads me into an elevator with walls so shiny I can see our reflections in them. "We're excited for you to get started," she says. "But first we have to do some quick, routine medical tests."

I say nothing as we ride up to the third floor. My palms are sweaty and I wipe them on my jeans. I still have no idea what I've signed up for. As I tried to fall asleep last night, I couldn't help but wonder if I was making a big mistake. But every time I thought about backing out, I remembered the money. No matter what the research project involves, it only lasts a few hours. I can survive *anything* for a few hours. It will all be over by the end of the night— and I'll be a whole lot richer. No more worrying about where I'll live or if I can get a job or whether or not I can afford to college. I'll be set for life.

We get off the elevator, and I follow Lynne into an exam room, complete with a hospital bed and a tray full of medical equipment. "Please wait here," she says. "A doctor will be with you shortly."

She shuts the door behind her and I stare at the bed. It has one of those pink hospital gowns on it, the kind where your ass hangs out the back. No way am I putting that on.

Someone knocks on the door, but it opens before I can answer. A dark-skinned man in a lab coat enters the room and closes the door behind him. His hair is black with little tufts of gray above his ears. "Ms. Martinez? My name is Dr. Kapur. Please, sit down."

I sit on the edge of the bed, the paper cover crinkling under me, and fight the panic building inside my chest. The door is right behind me. I can run if I need to. And just because he's an older man and we're alone doesn't mean he'll do anything to me. This is just a routine medical exam, nothing more.

He looks down at his clipboard. "I'm going to ask you a few questions before we start the tests. First, are you on any medication?" I shake my head. "Have you ever taken any drugs?"

"No."

"What about alcohol?"

I stare at the linoleum floor and push back the memories that threaten to flood my mind. "No."

"No, I suppose not, with your history."

I glance up sharply. He *knows*. He probably has my entire life story there, written on his clipboard. I've never felt so naked before.

He eyes me like I'm a specimen he's about to dissect. "Have you ever had any migraine headaches or blackouts?"

"No."

"Have you ever had any suicidal thoughts or tendencies?"

"What? No!" What kind of questions are these? Do they really need to know this kind of stuff?

"I'm going to check your blood pressure now." He opens the cuff with a loud Velcro rip and places it on my arm. I try not to flinch at his touch. He smells like the overpowering fake lemon of cleaning products, and every instinct tells me to get away from him. Logically, I know he isn't going to hurt me. He's a doctor and Aether Corp wants me for their "project." I agreed to this exam. But that still doesn't stop the familiar terror from rising up.

He removes the cuff and pauses, studying my face. "Do you need me to get a nurse?"

"I'm fine." I realize my fists are clenched at my sides and force my hands to relax. "Let's just get this over with."

*　*　*

The physical exam is quick, but then I'm taken to other rooms for more testing. Blood work. X-rays. Brain scans. I'm not even sure what half of the tests are for. My suspicions grow with every minute that passes, but no one will tell me anything.

When the tests are finally over, a nurse dumps me in a freezing-cold conference room with chairs arranged in two rows and a long table covered with food and drinks. I lean against a wall and study the four people already inside, all about my age. Three of them bear the scars of a life in the system: a don't-mess-with-me attitude combined with guarded eyes and clothes that have worn through or don't quite fit.

But one guy stands out. Black hipster glasses, crisp blue jeans, and a plaid button-down shirt that fits perfectly—this is no foster kid. His dark hair is slightly tousled and he's tall and lean, not exactly muscular yet not scrawny either. He gives the others a smile, his face friendly and without suspicion. I can tell he's never gone hungry before, never flinched from an adult, never gotten in a car with no idea where he'd sleep next. The badge on his shirt reads *Adam O'Neill.*

He picks at the cheese and crackers and turns to the two guys standing there, who eye him like a piece of meat. "So, what are you guys in for?"

The biggest guy in the room gets right up in his face. "Is that some kind of joke?"

Adam adjusts his glasses, clearly surprised. "Sorry, I didn't mean—"

"You think you're funny?"

The third guy moves closer, like a shark drawn to the scent of blood. "Yeah, you think you're better than us?"

"No, I don't think that." Adam holds up his hands and attempts another smile. He's outnumbered, and the first guy has to be double his size, but he doesn't back down. I respect him for that, even if he has no idea what he's gotten himself into. "Just trying to make conversation."

"Yeah, I know your type," the big guy says. He's black, with a shaved head and large, muscular arms with a couple of tats. "I saw the way you were looking at us. You think you're so fucking smart."

He shoves Adam in the chest. Not hard but enough to make him stumble back a step. The look on Adam's face is priceless, like he's shocked anyone would ever pick a fight with him. He's obviously unprepared to handle what's coming next.

"You know what we do with smart guys like you?" the big guy asks, cracking his knuckles.

This is going to end badly. I do *not* want to get involved. It's not my problem, and I haven't been in a fight in months.

But damn, I hate bullies.

"Leave him alone."

Four heads swivel to look at me. One belongs to an Asian girl with short blue hair who huddles in a chair up front. She plays with the ties of her hoodie while watching us.

The big guy sneers. His badge says *Chris Duncan*. "You gonna make me, mamacita?"

He spits the last word at me, but I've heard plenty worse. I push myself off the wall and stand next to Adam, whose eyes linger on the tattoos crawling up my arms. I'm not sure why I'm standing up for this guy, but it's too late to back down now. "If I have to."

Chris's nostrils flare and the veins in his neck stick out. I clench my fists and ready myself for a fight. He's much bigger than me. I'll have to be faster.

"No, dude. This chick's crazy," the third guy says. *Trent Walsh.* He smells like cigarettes and has long blond hair that falls in his eyes. "You were at Bright Haven, right?" he asks me.

I nod, never taking my eyes off the big guy in front of me. He could snap at any second, but I'm ready for him. You don't survive in the worst parts of LA—and in more than a dozen foster homes—without learning how to defend yourself.

"Dude," Trent says to Chris. "I heard she fought three girls at once, seriously messed them up." His eyes dart around, looking everywhere. "Besides, they'll be back any second."

But Chris isn't the type of guy who backs down. I know all about men like him. They like to hurt smaller people to make themselves feel stronger. A part of me itches to fight him. *Do it*, I think, my fists tightening. *Just try to hit me.*

"Oh good, you've all met," says Lynne at the door. Two men in lab coats stand beside her, and the three of them walk to the front of the room. "Please sit down and we'll explain the research project to you."

Chris and I glare at each other, like two dogs straining against the end of a leash, teeth snapping. Every muscle in my body wants to jump forward, but I hold myself back. Barely. I'm here for a reason, and I won't screw this up by getting in a fight.

I turn my back on Chris and sit on the edge of my chair in the front row, trying to suppress the adrenaline rippling under my skin. Adam starts to take the seat next to me, but I narrow my eyes at him. I don't want him to get the idea that we're friends or something. He sits two chairs down instead.

Chris finds a seat in the second row with his buddy, Trent. I'll have to keep an eye on him over the next day in case he tries to start something. A sick part of me hopes he does. I should be relieved that Lynne stopped the fight before anything happened, but instead I'm disappointed. And I hate myself for feeling that way.

Once we're seated, Lynne's gaze sweeps over the five of us. "Thank you all for coming and for your patience. As you know, I'm Lynne Marshall, the project leader. I believe you've all met Dr. Rajesh Kapur, our lead medical doctor, and I'd like to introduce Dr. Bob Walters, our lead physicist. Welcome to Project Chronos."

She says the last words like they carry a certain weight, but they mean nothing to me. After a moment, she continues. "At Aether Corporation we pride ourselves on being at the forefront of technology. Our company has been behind some of the biggest innovations in history and our products are used by millions of people all around the world, yet we're always looking for ways to expand our reach. You've each been selected for your special skills and talents to help us further this goal."

"Get to the point already," Chris mutters behind me.

She continues as if she didn't hear him, with a wide smile on her lips. "Dr. Walters will explain the project to you, but please keep in mind that everything we go over today is highly confidential."

"Thank you, Lynne." One of the men in lab coats steps forward. He's probably in his fifties, with a full head of gray hair and wrinkles around his eyes. "We've developed an accelerator that creates a rift in the space-time continuum, allowing us to open a temporal aperture that will send you forward."

I don't have the slightest clue what he is talking about. I focus on the words that make sense. "What do you mean, forward?"

"The aperture can send five people to the future for a short period. Due to the time dilation, only twelve minutes will pass in the present, but twenty-four hours will pass for those in the future."

"Like…a simulation?" Adam asks.

Dr. Walters looks to Lynne, then clears his throat. "No, not exactly."

"Wait, are you saying…" My voice trails off. The words are too big, too impossible to speak out loud. "That we…The future…"

"Yes," Lynne says. "You will all be traveling to the future."

I sit back in my chair with a *thump* as a hush falls over the room. No, I don't believe it. This has to be a test, to see how we react to something so completely unreal. Or maybe they mean it all as a metaphor. Envisioning ourselves in the future, something like that. Any second now, they'll explain and it will all make sense—'cause they can't seriously mean what I think they mean.

Adam raises his hand. "How does this accelerator work?"

Dr. Walters smiles, clearly pleased to have a star student. "The accelerator increases the atoms inside it to nearly the speed of light, causing time around them to slow down and—"

"The details are not important," Lynne interrupts. "And before we go to questions, I want to make it clear that each of you can back out now, but this will be your last chance. Please remember that all of the information you have seen today is confidential, and that if you leave, you will be in breach of your contract."

In other words, if we back out now we won't get the money and assistance that Aether Corp is offering us. No one speaks, but no one gets up to leave either. Chairs creak as the others trade uneasy looks. Adam's dark brows are pulled together behind his glasses. The blue-haired girl bites her black fingernails. Chris rubs his chin, his eyes narrowed, while Trent leans forward, mouth open. I don't know what any of them are thinking, but no matter how impossible this sounds or how risky this may be, it's the only chance I have for a future. There's no way I'm walking out that door.

Lynn's smile grows wider. "Very good. I'm pleased you've all decided to stay."

Adam raises his hand again. I have to give it to the guy. He is definitely persistent.

Lynne purses her lips. "Mr. O'Neill, you have a question?"

"How far into the future are we going?"

"We believe you will arrive ten years from now," Dr. Walters says.

"Ten years?" I blurt out. They're serious about this. They're actually sending us into the future. I think I might throw up. I just…I can't even…

"That's correct," Lynne says. "Once there, we want you to take notes on the technology you find and bring back whatever you can. We also want your general impressions of the future, including news about the world, in particular related to—"

"Hold up," Chris says. "Can we go back to the part where we're going into the *future*? Is this shit for real?"

"Yeah, this must be some kind of joke, right?" Trent asks.

"I promise you, this is very real," Lynne says. "In a few hours you *will* be in the future. Amazing, isn't it?"

Lynne and the scientists smile like they expect applause. Instead, the five of us sit in stunned silence. I feel like someone hit me with a truck and left me lying in the road, bleeding all over the asphalt.

"What about the grandfather paradox?" Adam asks.

The what? I want to know if the accelerator is safe and what kind of risks we'll face in the future and what exactly they want us to do there—and he's asking questions about *grandfathers*?

"Ah yes." Dr. Walters nods at the question. "For those of you who don't know, the grandfather paradox states that traveling to the past is impossible because any changes made would change the future. The famous example is that if you visited the past and killed your grandfather as a child, you would no longer exist, thus causing a paradox. But you won't need to worry about any of that. Since we will be opening the temporal aperture on our end in the present, the grandfather paradox does not apply. You simply have to make sure you return to the location of the aperture at the correct time to go through it."

"But how do you know we won't appear in the future in the middle of the ocean or stuck inside a wall?" Adam asks. *A much better question*, I think.

"Aether Corporation owns this building," Lynne says. "We've already made arrangements so it remains in our possession over the next ten years. When you get to the future you'll likely be greeted by Aether employees who will be happy to assist you." She gives a tiny laugh. "You might even see a future version of me."

This is all happening so fast and it sounds way too easy. There has to be something they aren't telling us. Am I the only one who sees the warning signs?

I don't bother to raise my hand like Adam did. "What kind of risks can we expect in the future?"

Dr. Kapur speaks for the first time since we got here. "There should be very few risks. We've already performed trial runs with the aperture, such as sending inanimate objects and small animals to the future. They all returned unharmed."

"Yes, it's perfectly safe," Lynne says. "You're the first people to visit the future, so we're not entirely sure what the future will be like, but if you compare the world now to the world of ten years ago, not as much has changed as you might think. Technology and pharmaceuticals have made great advances, but most aspects of our culture remain the same. We still use the same money, speak the same language, and use the same roads. The risks should be no greater than walking outside your own house today. We'll also be providing you with supplies and money in the unlikely event that someone from Aether Corporation is not there to greet you."

Dr. Walters looks like he wants to say something, but Lynne continues. "If there are no further questions at this time, we'll break for lunch. After that, you'll be heading to the accelerator and we'll go over a few more details there."

"I got a question," Chris says, crossing his arms. "When do we get paid?"

"As soon as you return from the future and finish your debriefing." She smiles and heads toward the door. "Now if you'll all follow me..."

As we stand, I overhear Trent ask Chris, "Dude, do you really thinking we're going to the future?"

Chris snorts. "No way in hell."

I hate to admit it, but I agree with them. What Lynne and the scientists are proposing, this "temporal aperture," it's impossible. It has to be. And if it *is* possible, there's no way they'd choose us for it. They'd use scientists or people in the military. Not foster kids.

But my God, if it is true? We'll be going to the *future*. My mind races just thinking about the possibilities. Ten years is a long time. I'll be twenty-seven years old. Maybe I'll be married with a kid or two. Maybe I'll be serving a life sentence in prison like Papá. Or maybe I'll be a social worker, helping other foster kids like myself. With Aether Corp's money, that dream doesn't seem quite as impossible as it did a few days ago.

No matter what the risks are, I'm all in. I mean, who *wouldn't* want to see the future?

* * *

Lunch is served in a cafeteria where employees probably spend their breaks, except today it's cleared out. I grab a tray and load it up with food—lasagna, salad, some sort of fancy chicken dish, french fries. They even have a frozen yogurt machine. Throwing this much food in front of foster kids is almost cruel. I eat pretty well at the Robertsons', but that wasn't always the case.

Out of the corner of my eye, I spot Trent grabbing a roll out of the basket and slipping it into his pocket. Food hoarding. I've seen other foster kids do that. He must have gone hungry a lot when he was younger. Chris catches me watching Trent and sneers at me. I roll my eyes and grab a slice of cake.

They've set up a long table for us so we can all sit together. Guess we're supposed to be bonding or something. No thanks. Chris and Trent take a different table and I sit at another one, by myself. If I'm lucky it'll stay that way.

The blue-haired girl, whose badge I finally see—Zoe Chang— hovers between our tables with her tray. She's tiny, probably not even five foot tall, and with her bright bob, she looks like a pixie or something. She studies Chris and Trent, who eat in silence, hostility rising off them in invisible waves. She must figure I'm a safer bet because she finally joins me. Of course.

"Thanks for your help earlier," Adam says, as his tray hits the table. He sits across from us. There go my plans for a quiet lunch.

I give a curt nod and avoid making eye contact. Maybe if I don't answer he'll leave me alone.

"This is unbelievable, right? This time travel stuff?" He doesn't touch his food, and instead folds and unfolds his napkin over and over. Must be a nervous tick.

I ignore him and shove food in my mouth. After living with many other kids for years, I'm in the habit of eating quickly, and I don't want to talk to this guy anyway. I'll be spending the next twenty-four hours with him, which is more than enough time already. I'm not here to make friends. I just need to make it through this day so I can get on with my life.

"Here." Adam shoves something across the table toward me. His napkin, folded in the shape of a dog or something. No, a horse. With a horn.

An origami unicorn.

"You made this?" It's a dumb question since I just saw him make it, but I'm so thrown off by his gift that I don't know what to say.

"Yeah." He shrugs and pokes at his food with his fork. "Sorry it's not very good. It would be better with the right kind of paper, but all I had were these flimsy napkins."

I slide the origami unicorn closer to me, rubbing my fingers over the precise folds of the napkin. People don't make things for me. Not like this anyway.

"Thanks." I meet Adam's eyes for the first time. Bright blue and intelligent, shining out from behind his black-rimmed glasses. The kind of eyes that never miss a thing. He smiles and I quickly look down at my food.

"No, thank *you* for earlier," he says, lowering his voice. "What was that all about anyway? Did I say something wrong back there?

He must be talking about the fight. I don't want to answer him, but he should probably know. "Your question pissed them off. They've probably spent time in juvie."

"Juvie? I had no idea."

"You're not a foster kid, are you?"

"No…" His voice trails off. "Are you?"

"Yeah. And my guess is the other three are too." I look to Zoe for confirmation and she nods, her eyes locked on her plate.

"Oh. I didn't realize…" Adam adjusts his glasses and studies me. "What did Trent mean by Bright Haven?"

I stab my food with my fork. "It's a group home."

He probably wants more from me, to hear what happened there, but he won't get it. I don't talk about the past. Especially not that day.

We eat in silence for a few minutes, and when he's distracted I steal another glance at his face. There's something about his strong jaw, dark eyebrows, and perfectly messy hair that make my eyes want to linger on him. He's better looking than I originally thought, in that geeky cute way a lot of girls find attractive. I'm not one of them. Guys like Chris are more my type.

But I can see the appeal.

"Cool hair," Adam says to Zoe.

"Thanks," she says, keeping her eyes down. "I, um, I like your unicorn."

These are the first words I've heard from her. I was beginning to wonder if she spoke at all.

"Thanks. It's something I picked up when I was bored." He's so friendly, and a part of me wants to smack that smile off his face. A guy who has time to learn origami has no idea how cruel the real world can be.

"Is that your, um, talent?" she asks. I can't tell if she's serious or not.

"Origami? No." He laughs—an easy laugh, like he does it a lot. "I'm not sure what my talent is. I guess I'm a fast learner."

"Don't be modest, Adam," Lynne says from behind us, where she's been watching us eat. She raises her voice so we can all hear. "Adam is a genius. He graduated from high school at fourteen and recently graduated from UCLA with double degrees in biochemistry and molecular biology."

Trent snickers, and Chris glares at our table with a deadly look in his eyes. Adam stares at his plate, a frown on his lips. Is Lynne *trying* to get the guy beat up? And if Adam is so smart, why is he here? What is Aether offering him?

Lynne smiles at each of us like a proud parent. "I'm sure you've all wondered why you were selected for this mission. In our early tests, we discovered that electronic equipment of any kind short-circuits when it goes through the aperture. You can still bring back technology from the future, but we're also interested in sketches and notes on how it all works, along with your general impressions of the world. With this goal in mind, you were each chosen because of your unique talents. With your help, we'll be able to glimpse the future and bring about a new era of prosperity and progress."

This must be why they picked me, since I'll remember everything I see in the future perfectly. If Adam is such a genius, it makes sense they'd want him too. My gaze travels from Zoe to Chris and Trent. What are their special skills?

* * *

Once we've finished eating, Lynne explains that they have clothes for us to wear in the future so we won't stand out too much, no matter what the fashion trends are in ten years. I'm sent to the exam room from before to change and given a plain black T-shirt, dark blue jeans, a hooded jacket, and basic walking shoes. There's also a watch with tiny silver hands and twenty-four hours on it instead of twelve. I put it on my arm above my mother's watch, which rarely leaves my wrist.

Now that I'm alone and have a second to think, too many questions race through my head. In a few minutes, we'll be going to the future. Everything is moving so fast, and they did little to prepare us for whatever we'll face.

Lynne's explanation of why they chose us rings hollow in my ears. I know my perfect memory is rare, but I'm sure they could find someone over eighteen with the same skill. So why are they using foster kids? And what was with all the medical tests? Is the accelerator really safe—or did they pick us because we're expendable?

I'm supposed to wait here for Lynne to get me, but I'm too antsy. I pace back and forth, my blood racing along with my brain. It's about a million degrees, so I remove the jacket they gave me, tossing it on the bed. I examine everything in the room, but there's nothing of interest, just the same medical supplies you'd find in any doctor's office.

After twenty minutes I can't take it any longer. I need answers, and if no one will tell me anything, I'll have to find them myself—somehow.

The hallway is quiet and empty. I head toward the elevator, but I'm not sure where to go after that. Maybe I can find an empty office where I can browse someone's computer or riffle through their file cabinet. My plan sucks, but I can't just wait around doing nothing anymore.

At the end of the hallway, I hear male voices. I jerk to a halt and try to peer around the corner without getting caught. Two men in lab coats stand outside one of the exam rooms. Dr. Kapur and Dr. Walters.

"How do you know it won't happen again?" Dr. Walters asks.

"It won't. These kids are young enough."

"What if they're not?"

There's a pause. I flatten myself against the wall, trying not to breathe. What are they talking about? What are they worried will happen again? And what did they mean by young *enough*?

"Then we'll have to go younger," Dr. Kapur says.

"Younger? It was hard enough getting five eighteen-year-olds. We can't get anyone younger! And if we do, they won't be able to bring back the kind of data we need!"

"It doesn't matter," Dr. Kapur continues. "It won't happen this time."

They're talking about *us*. Does that mean there were *other* times?

"I hope you're right," Dr. Walters says with a sigh.

"I've done the analysis and run the tests multiple times. We won't have any problems," Dr. Kapur says. I hear movement, the sound of clothes rustling. "It's almost time. We need to get to the accelerator."

"Yes, Lynne is waiting, and I need to check the calibrations before we start."

Padded steps come toward me and I bolt down the hall, tracing my steps back to my exam room. They're about to turn the corner. I won't make it in time.

I knock on the nearest door and it opens—Adam! He looks surprised, but I push him back into his room before he can speak. The door shuts behind us with a soft click.

"Elena, what—"

I cover his mouth with one hand and listen. My other hand grips his arm, holding him in place. Adam stares at me with wide eyes, but he doesn't move and doesn't speak. I count the seconds in my head. One minute. Two.

When the danger has passed, I realize how close we are. Our bodies are pressed together and my hands touch his lips, his bare arm. He isn't wearing a shirt and his chest is toned, with a trace of dark hair trailing into his jeans. The heat of his skin burns through my thin shirt, and his eyes never leave mine. He's only a few inches taller than me, the perfect height for a kiss.

And then I realize I'm alone in a room with a guy I don't know. Who probably thinks I came here for a booty call. Terror briefly flashes in my chest, but I shove it aside. I release him and take a quick step back. "Sorry."

"Elena, what's going on?" Adam sounds more confused than aroused. Good. If he tries to kiss me, I'll punch him.

I turn toward the door, but I'm not sure I want to go out there yet. The scientists might still be lurking, and I don't want to have to explain why I'm in Adam's room. But if I stay here I'll have to tell Adam something.

I fumble for an explanation. "I wanted to grab a snack before our trip."

His dark eyebrows pull together. He's not wearing his glasses. "But why did you run in here like someone was chasing you?"

I glance at the door again. I can return to my room and pretend this never happened, but something makes me want to tell him what I heard. He's a genius, so maybe he can make some sense out of the scientists' words. But still I hesitate.

Adam pulls on a shirt and sits on the edge of the hospital bed. His room is identical to mine, with the crinkly paper and the untouched pink, backless robe. He puts on his glasses and studies me with those piercing blue eyes, as though trying to solve me like a math problem. "Is everything all right, Elena?"

I think of the origami unicorn he made me, currently sitting in my exam room with my other things, and make my decision. "I overheard two of the scientists talking near the elevator."

"Right now?"

"Yeah. I heard Dr. Walters say, 'How do you know it won't happen again?'"

Adam listens in silence while I recite the conversation for him, word for word. When I finish, he asks, "Are you sure that's what they said?"

"Yes." I'm not sure if I should reveal my secret to him. But I figure we'll all learn each other's "talents" eventually. "I remember every word they said. I have an…eidetic memory." It's weird to say it out loud after keeping it a secret for so long. Feels like I'm stripping off my clothes in front of him.

Adam sits up straighter. "Really? That's amazing."

I don't want to talk about it. I switch back to the topic at hand, which is far more important anyway. "When they finished talking, they started walking toward me. I didn't want them to know I'd overheard them, but I didn't think I'd make it to my room in time."

"So I was just a convenient escape?" he asks with a hint of a grin.

"Something like that." I rub my arms, which have grown cold. "Do you have any idea what they were talking about?"

"No, but it's probably nothing. I'm sure it doesn't have anything to do with us."

"Are you kidding me? They mentioned the five of us. And it sounded like they'd done this before." I pace back and forth in the small space. "And next they want to use little kids!"

"I highly doubt a company like Aether Corporation would send children to the future."

"But it all makes sense now. Why else would they use foster kids? They know we won't be missed if something happens to us!"

"They chose us because of our abilities. And we're not all foster kids."

"No, you're the only one who isn't." I stop pacing and stare at him. "So why *are* you here?"

"I…" He shakes his head and looks down. For a minute there is only silence, and I realize that's his answer.

I turn away. We may have to work together, but we're strangers. It was stupid to think I could trust Adam. And he's right—he's *not* one of us.

"Forget it," I say, opening the door. "Just forget I said anything."

* * *

I return to my exam room. As I wait, I replay the scientists' conversation in my head a dozen times, trying to understand it. My only guess is there was another group of people who went to the future before us and something bad happened to them. Now the scientists are worried the same thing might happen to us. But that doesn't explain why they need teenagers or kids even younger than us.

I'm tempted to run away from this place as fast as I can. But if I do, I'll be exactly where I was before Lynne recruited me, looking for jobs and trying to figure out how I'll survive once I turn eighteen. And I'll miss a once-in-a-lifetime opportunity—the chance to see the *future*.

No, I can't back out now.

Lynne collects the five of us and takes us down to the basement level of the building. In the elevator, the tension in the air is almost tangible. Zoe chews on her black nails. Trent leans against the wall with his eyes closed. Chris glares at everyone. Adam keeps staring at me, opening and closing his mouth like he wants to say something. I avoid looking at him and hope he gets the hint.

The elevator doors open to a vast concrete room filled with computer panels and scientists in lab coats. In the center stands a domed enclosure covered in thick metal tubes that hug the machine, wrapping around it and leaving only one gap for a small door. This must be the accelerator.

"What, no TARDIS?" Adam asks. "I was hoping for a DeLorean, personally."

I stare at him, wondering how he can make a joke at a time like this, especially after everything I told him. But he just grins at me and follows after Lynne.

She herds us through the room, a mother hen smiling at everyone we pass. Dr. Kapur and Dr. Walters bend over a computer, talking about something on the screen. Four other scientists type on keyboards or work on different parts of the accelerator, but they stop to take a good look at us as we walk by.

Soon we'll be stepping inside that thing, facing whatever fate awaits us. After the conversation I overheard, I suspect it might be something dangerous. I know it's a long shot, but I have to do something. I have to talk to Lynne about my concerns. The trick will be making sure I don't reveal what I know.

"I have some questions," I say to Lynne, keeping my voice low.

"Yes?"

"Are we really the first ones to go to the future?"

She hesitates for the briefest moment. I almost miss it. "You are. Isn't it exciting? You'll be the first people to see the world ten years from now."

"But how do you know it's safe? Shouldn't you have someone else go first before sending in five teenagers? Why not send scientists or people who work for your company?"

"Don't worry, Elena. We've tested it thoroughly. You don't have anything to worry about." She gives me another of those big smiles she likes to throw around. "Now please excuse me. We're about to get started."

Well, that was no help at all. If anything, I'm even more suspicious now.

She leaves me at a table with five large backpacks, each labeled with one of our names. Chris grabs his, purposefully slamming into

Adam's side as he walks past. Trent follows at his heels, snickering. Zoe snatches her backpack and clings to it, glancing at the elevator like she might bolt at any second.

I grab mine and sit in a chair against the wall, while the scientists work on the accelerator. Lynne steps aside with Dr. Walters, but they speak too low for me to hear them. What are they discussing? Is Lynne telling him about our conversation? Or am I just being paranoid?

Adam sits beside me. The last person I want to talk to. "I spoke with Dr. Walters, and he said everything is fine."

"You talked to him?" I whisper, looking around to make sure no one else is listening. "What I told you was private!"

"I didn't tell him what you heard. I just asked him some questions. They've used the accelerator before with different objects and animals. They've done lots of tests. It's totally safe."

"Yeah, well, I asked Lynne some questions too, and I'm pretty sure she wasn't telling me everything."

He studies me for a long moment. "Are you going to back out?"

"No." I sigh. "I need this."

"Me too. But it's going to be okay, really." He lightly places his hand on my forearm, but I flinch before I can stop myself. He looks surprised by my reaction. "Sorry, I didn't mean—"

"It's fine. I'm just nervous." It's not a complete lie.

He gives me a lopsided grin. "Hey, whatever happens in the future, I'll be there to protect you."

"My hero." I roll my eyes. More like I'll be the one protecting *him*.

But the strange thing is, a small part of me does feel better knowing he's on my side. There's something about Adam I can't help but like. Or maybe he's just a better option than the other people on our team.

Lynne finishes conferring with Dr. Walters, and she claps her hands to get our attention. "We're just about ready to begin."

The five of us—in identical clothes, with heavy backpacks and coats that are much too warm for this time of year—shuffle toward the dome. The metal tubes that encase it begin to hum, and the floor under us starts to vibrate. My breath hitches. Is it too late to back out?

"We have one final thing to go over before you enter the accelerator," Lynne says. "When you're in the future, it's very important that you do not look up any information about yourself."

"What?" The word slips from my lips before I can stop it. The others gasp and mutter too, so I guess I'm not the only one who wants to know what happens to me. We all signed up for this research project to make sure we had a future—and now we can't even check if we do?

Dr. Kapur holds up a hand as though to silence us. "We realize it will be tempting to find out what will happen to you in the next ten years. However, we believe this knowledge could send you into a state of shock, permanently damaging your brain."

Hmm. His warning could be a line they're feeding us to keep us on track, but I doubt any of us would risk brain damage to find out. The temptation is strong though. It's impossible to not be curious about your own fate.

"And whatever happens, do not—I repeat, *do not*—interact with your future self," Dr. Walters says. "Doing so would not only send you into a state of shock, but could also create a temporal paradox."

A temporal paradox? What the hell is that? Adam must have the same question, because he asks, "What do you mean?"

"Our research shows that meeting a future version of yourself would disrupt the space-time continuum, preventing you from returning to the present."

Damn. I definitely don't want to get stuck in the future, no matter how curious I am about my future self. Ugh, this sucks. I run my fingers through my hair, trying to get a grip. Okay, we can't look into our own futures, but we'll still be *in* the future for twenty-four hours. That will be enough.

Dr. Walters opens the door on the side of the dome. "Please set your watches now. You need to be sure to return to this location in exactly twenty-four hours." I adjust my watch, twisting the knobs so the hands start at the number 24, while Dr. Walters continues. "The temporal aperture will only remain open for sixty seconds in the future, so you must be there early. Whatever happens, do not miss that window. Now please, step inside."

This is it. Go time. But I'm frozen in place. I don't know what will happen when I go into that thing. Maybe the accelerator will take me to the future. Maybe it will kill me. There's no way to know.

What I *do* know is that I don't have much of a future here.

I walk through the door before I can change my mind. The others follow, and the room is just big enough for the five of us. Once we're all inside, Lynne closes the door with a heavy thud. I swallow hard, my throat suddenly dry. No turning back now.

"Sequence initiated," a voice says from above us. And then it starts counting down. "Five."

The metallic walls of the dome vibrate. We cluster at the center, only inches apart. I hear Trent's ragged breathing beside me, echoing my own.

"Four."

The noise grows louder and buzzes through my bones. I grip the straps on my backpack, hard. Cold sweat drips down my back under the heavy jacket. All I can think is, *My God, this is really happening.*

"Three."

The vibrations turn into a minor earthquake. The five of us stumble around as the ground shakes, trying to regain our balance. Zoe nearly falls, but Chris catches her arm and steadies her. The metal walls rattle around us like we're in a giant tin can someone is shaking.

"Two."

The noise stops and the vibrations end. The dome begins to fill with a strange golden light. I can't tell where it's coming from. It simply appears around us, as though the air is full of tiny specks of pure gold. Is this the aperture?

"One."

I meet Adam's eyes, and he looks just as scared as I feel. He grabs my hand and I don't recoil this time. As our fingers intertwine, the walls of the dome fade. The entire world turns black, except for the five of us, still bathed in a soft golden glow.

And then the light goes out.

00:00

Darkness swallows me, the claustrophobic, crushing kind of pitch-black oblivion that makes your skin crawl. I can see absolutely nothing, not even the faintest trace of light. The air has a dank, musty odor, and a chill creeps over my bare skin. Everything is silent, except for the sound of my heart pounding in my ears. My first instinct is to run, to find a corner or somewhere safe to hide, but I don't know where I am or which direction to turn. But I'm holding Adam's hand, so I know I'm not alone.

The others start talking all at once.

"What's going on?"

"Is this the future?"

"Why is it so dark?"

"I can't see anything!"

My head spins and I want to tell them all to shut up so I can think. Someone's whimpering softly to my left. I think it's Zoe.

"It's okay," Adam says and squeezes my hand. I don't know if he's talking to me or to the group. "Just stay calm and we'll figure this out."

"Calm?" Chris asks. "How are we supposed to stay *calm*?"

"Maybe there's a flashlight in the backpack they gave us," says Trent.

"No electronics, dumbass."

"Oh. Right. Hang on."

I hear the sound of movement, of rustling clothes. With a scraping *click*, a flame flickers on. Trent holds up a lighter. "Good thing I didn't pick this week to quit smoking, eh?"

The flame faintly illuminates each of us. I quickly drop Adam's hand and step away from him before anyone notices. We're all standing together except for Zoe, who's kneeling, her hood pulled over her head, her arms wrapped around herself. Adam crouches beside her and puts a hand on her back, whispering softly.

From what I can see in the dim light, we're in a wide-open space with cement floors, like the room with the accelerator. Only there's nothing here but us.

Trent's flame flickers out and we're plunged into darkness again. My breath catches, but a second later he clicks it on again.

"Where are we?" he asks. "*When* are we?"

I look around again, but I can't see anything beyond our small circle of light. "Pick a direction," I say.

Adam helps Zoe up and we start walking. The room is so cold my breath makes little clouds in the air. Maybe it was good they had us wear these heavy jackets.

With each step I grow more confident we're still in the basement of the Aether facility. The place matches up with my memory of the room, but the accelerator isn't here. The scientists, the computer equipment...all gone.

"I think we're in the same room," I say. "It's just...empty."

"Wait, where's the time machine thing?" Trent waves the lighter around to get a better look, but all I see is darkness and empty space. "How will we get back?"

"Oh my God, are we trapped here?" Zoe asks, grabbing Adam's arm.

"No, the temporal aperture opens from the present," Adam says. "We'll be able to get back as long as we return to this spot in twenty-four hours."

"The elevator's over here," Chris says from the edge of the light. When he pushes the button, nothing happens. Same thing when we find a light switch and flick it up and down. The building has no electricity.

"Dude, what happened to the power?" Trent asks. "And to the scientists who were supposed to meet us?"

No one answers. But I know what we're all thinking—something isn't right here.

There's nothing to do but continue on. "The stairs must be nearby," I say.

We cluster around the flickering flame and follow the walls until we find the door to the stairs. We climb them in the dark in a strange procession, the only sounds our heavy breathing and shoes pounding against metal steps. Trent leads the way with his lighter, and I try not to think about what might be lying in wait in the darkness around us.

We emerge in the lobby, which isn't completely pitch-black for a nice change. Traces of sunlight filter into the room through boarded-up windows. The walls look dirty, and the floor is covered in a thick layer of dust. The receptionist desk I saw yesterday is gone, as is the Aether logo.

"What happened here?" I wrap my arms around myself to fight off a chill creeping into my bones that has nothing to do with the cold air.

Adam traces a finger in the dust, while Chris peers out of a crack in the window boards. Zoe stands near him in the brightest spot in the room. Her face is pale, but she isn't whimpering any longer. I should say something—I've known many foster kids who were scared of the dark—but I can't think of any comforting words right now.

"No one's been here for a long time," Adam says, wiping his hands on his jeans.

"No shit," Chris says, pacing back and forth. "Five minutes into the mission and it's already gone to hell."

My watch says it's actually been twenty-three minutes since we got here, but I don't correct him.

"Okay, let's think this through," Adam says. "Aether told us they own this building and believed there would be scientists in the future to meet us. But we're alone and this place is abandoned, so something must have gone wrong between our present and whenever this time is." He pauses to study the room. "We should look around, try to figure out what happened in those years."

"Screw that," Chris says. "What happened is they lied to us. There's no one here and we're on our own." He stabs a finger toward the front door. "We don't even know if we're in the future or not. We need to see what's outside this building."

Adam moves in front of the door. "No, we need more information first. It might not be safe. You can't go out there—"

Chris takes a step toward Adam with fire in his eyes. "Get out of my way."

Here we go again. I raise my hands to stop him. "Aether will want to know why this place is abandoned. We should look around quickly."

I can practically see smoke coming out of Chris's nose. But after a long, tense moment, he steps back. "Ten minutes, that's it. Then I'm going outside."

Adam nods. "We can split up to cover each floor faster."

"We'll take the top two floors." Chris gestures for Trent to follow him. "Let's get this over with."

They head to the stairs while Zoe bites her fingernails. "It's okay," Adam says to her with a warm smile. "We can search the other rooms together."

I'm not sure if I'm included in that "we," but I prefer to work by myself anyway. "I'll take the third floor. Alone."

Before Adam can answer, I spin on my heels and pound up the stairs. The third floor is where they did the medical exams, but it's dark and empty now. I wish I had a lighter like Trent, but there's just enough sunshine coming through the windows for me to get by. I take a moment to look outside, but the glass is so caked with dirt and dust that it's hard to see much. The sun hangs low at the horizon, and based on the position, I'd guess it's just after dawn. We got in the accelerator after lunch, yet now it's morning again. Another clue that we're not in our time anymore.

I move quickly, darting from one room to another. Exam rooms with no tables or beds. Medical labs with no equipment. Empty offices with no desks or chairs. Nothing has been left behind, not even a scrap of paper or a stray paper clip. It's creepy as hell, wandering these empty rooms alone. I keep imagining that at any second someone will pop out at me, like in a horror movie. But there's no one here and no clue as to what happened. Or what year this is.

As I'm about to head back to the stairs, something flashes in the corner of my eye. Sunlight glints off an object sitting on a windowsill. I approach it cautiously, and when the sun is no longer in my eyes I see it.

An origami unicorn.

00:32

I pick the unicorn up carefully, holding my breath. It's made of silver paper, with not even a speck of dust on it. I slide my fingers across the folds of paper, like I did with the origami unicorn from earlier today.

I know one thing for certain: Adam made this.

"Elena?" he calls from the stairway. "Are you all right?"

"Yeah!" I shove the unicorn in my backpack before he can see it. I don't know what it means yet, and I need more time to figure it out.

Adam and Zoe wait in the stairway. She stands close to him, like she might grab his arm at any second. I doubt she'd let him out of her sight, not with her hands shaking like that. And if they were together the entire time I was on this floor, there's no way he could have placed the unicorn there.

Not *this* Adam, anyway...

"Find anything?" he asks.

"No." If the future version of Adam put that unicorn there, he did so knowing I would search the third floor alone. He wanted me to find it—and *only* me.

We return to the lobby, where Chris and Trent are already waiting. "Like I said, nothing here," Chris says. "Total waste of time."

Adam sighs, adjusting his glasses. "We need a plan."

Chris crosses his arms. "The plan is we go out there, find shit to bring back to Aether, then we come back. Just the bare minimum so we can get paid, and nothing more."

"We don't know what's out there. It could be dangerous."

"Dangerous?" Zoe asks, her eyes wide.

"What if it's not just this building that's been abandoned?" Adam asks. "There could be radiation or—"

Chris shakes his head. "Hell no. I'm not gonna spend the next twenty-four hours holed up in this building. And I need that money."

"He's right. We can't stay in here," I say. Someone must have been inside the building recently to leave the origami unicorn upstairs. "Maybe there's another way out."

Chris pulls on the front door handle, but it's locked. "The doors are glass. If we find something to break them, we can pull off the boards."

"Hang on." Trent pulls some little metal sticks out of his backpack. "Lockpicks!"

That's a weird thing for Aether to put in our backpacks. I narrow my eyes. "How did you know those were in there?"

"I got bored and went through my bag while we were searching the place. There's all sorts of stuff inside—food, water, and these lockpicks. You probably got them too."

I kneel down and unzip my backpack. Inside, I find granola bars, an apple, a sandwich, and a full water bottle. There's also a wallet full of more cash than I've ever had at one time before, a blank notebook, a map of Los Angeles, and a compass, which I don't know how to use.

While Trent starts working on the door, I check the remaining pockets on my backpack. No lockpicks, but one has a first aid kit, which I really hope we won't need. I also find a handful of condoms. Guess they wanted to prepare us for *everything*.

Another pocket has a gun.

I freeze, staring at the black metal. I've never held a gun before. I can't tell if it's loaded, but I don't see any bullets in my bag, so I assume it is. Is the safety on? I have no idea. Sure, my tattoos make me look tough and I've been in plenty of fights, but I've always tried to stay out of trouble as much as I could. I thought Aether knew that. Why would they pack a gun for me? Did they expect us to run into trouble?

I raise my eyes to study the others, who are all going through their own backpacks. Do they have weapons too?

Is the gun in my backpack to protect the group—or to protect me *from* the group?

I zip the backpack closed before anyone sees the gun. If the others have weapons, they aren't announcing that to the group. And if they don't, it's probably better that no one knows about mine. I just hope it doesn't go off in my backpack by accident or something.

Trent unlocks the front door with his lockpicks and pushes it open. "Wait!" Adam yells, but it's too late.

A cool breeze rushes through the open door, along with a dash of hazy sunshine. I don't realize how musty and old the air in the building is until I get that first taste of fresh air. I breathe it in, and when none of us falls over dead, I figure we're safe.

We gather around the door, peering outside, afraid to take that first step. The sky is cloudy, with tiny drops of moisture in the air that hint of rain to come. The fence around the research facility has barbed wire and is covered in "No Trespassing" signs that weren't there before. Beyond the fence I see buildings and signs instead of rocks and dirt. Aether's facility is no longer in the middle of nowhere.

On the other side of the fence, a car drives past—at least I think it's a car. It's black but shaped like a sideways egg, sleek and shiny, with dark-tinted windows. It's hard to tell what part is the front or the back, but it has four wheels, so I assume it's a car. It zips past us and is gone.

"What was that?" Trent asks.

"Wow, cars have changed a lot in ten years," Adam says.

That's when it finally hits me. This is real. All the clues add up to one inevitable truth. "We're in the future," I whisper.

"Hell yeah!" Chris shouts, pumping his fist. "The future, baby!"

"I can't believe it," Zoe whispers, wrapping her arms around herself.

The future. It's so big, so unknown, so amazing…yet oddly familiar too. I want to see more. And now that we know for certain where we are, we can do what we came for—find technology for Aether. "We should look around. Find some stores or something."

"Finally, someone's talking some sense around here," Chris says. He strides toward the fence, and Trent and Zoe follow him. I start to go too, until I see Adam hanging back, his hands shoved in his pockets.

"Come on," I say. "There's nothing we can do here."

"I know. I just can't shake the feeling that we missed something." He looks up at the building and I follow his gaze. Every window is dark and empty.

For a brief second I consider telling him about the origami unicorn, but I remember how he brushed off my concerns earlier. The conversation between Dr. Kapur and Dr. Walters plays back in my head. They were worried about something happening "again"— did they know the facility would be abandoned when we arrived?

Considering the fully stocked backpacks, I believe it.

We catch up with the others at the fence, where Chris cuts a hole large enough for him to get through with a pair of pliers he must have found in his bag. Trent is already on the other side—he climbed over the barbed wire in the time it took us to walk over.

"What?" Trent asks, when he catches me eyeing him. "It's easy!"

Lockpicks and climbing over barbed wire...I'm getting an idea what his talent might be.

When Chris is finished, we each duck our heads and step through the jagged metal. What was once empty land is now a wide road lined with other offices and industrial buildings. Adam pulls out his map and compass and studies them, but I doubt a map from ten years ago will be much help if this area has changed so much. The others look back and forth along the road, but there's nothing to tell us which way to go.

I remember the drive here, every twist and turn stored in my brain. I know the freeway is nearby—or at least, it was in our time. There should be a mini-mart or a gas station near the exit. I start walking. "This way."

"How do you know this is the right direction?" Chris asks, catching up with me.

"You got a better idea?"

He snorts but doesn't say anything else. The five of us head down the empty road, while the rising sun struggles to peek out from the dark clouds.

Another egg-shaped car shoots past us but slows at the corner to turn right. On the back window there's a shiny red, white, and blue bumper sticker that says, REELECT NGUYEN, followed by a year. A year that makes me stop dead in my tracks.

Because it's *thirty* years in the future. Not ten.

01:06

I stare after the car, the numbers lingering in my brain long after they've disappeared from sight. "Was that…?" I can't say it. I'm finding it hard to breathe. "The car. The sticker. The *year*."

"It can't be," Adam says, his voice low. "It must be a joke or something. Like those Yoda for President stickers. There's no way…"

"Thirty. Years." Chris shakes his head. "Thirty fucking years. Not ten. Thirty. Holy shit."

All five of us are rooted to this spot in the middle of the road, gazing after a car that is long gone, hoping for answers. Zoe leans against the fence, her arms wrapped around herself, whispering, "Oh God," again and again.

Trent stands beside her with his mouth hanging open. "This is seriously messed up," he finally says.

"Okay, let's not panic," Adam says, running a hand through his dark hair. "We just need to think this through. Assuming the sticker is real, that means we're at least thirty years in the future. Or more, if it's an old sticker, although it looked shiny and wasn't peeling off or anything. Dr. Walters said they *thought* we would be going ten years forward, but maybe they weren't sure how far the accelerator would send us in the future."

"Or the machine malfunctioned," Chris says.

I think of the conversation I overheard between the scientists. "Or they lied to us."

"Why would they do that?" Zoe asks.

Adam and I lock eyes, but he gives a tiny shake of his head. He doesn't want me to tell them what I heard. Fine. It would probably freak them out even more.

"How the hell should we know?" Chris asks, saving me from having to answer. "They didn't tell us shit. Who knows what else they're hiding?"

Trent nods. "No kidding. They just went, 'Hey, guys, you're going to the future. See ya later,' and sent us on our way. Not cool."

"No matter what the date is, it doesn't change the fact that we're in the future, which is amazing," Adams says. "Yes, thirty years is further than we expected, but that just means we'll have even better things to bring back to Aether."

"But, dude. Thirty years!" Trent says, his eyes wide. "Whoa, future me must be so old. Like almost fifty. Damn."

He's right; all of us would be about forty-eight or so. I try to imagine what my life might be like at that age, but quickly push those thoughts from my head. The temptation to find out about my future is strong, but I have to resist it. We have a job to do, and we need to stick to it so we can get back to our time and get paid. That's what I need to focus on.

"Thirty years or ten years, it doesn't matter in the end," I say. "But we need to get going. The clock is ticking and we've already wasted an hour."

I start walking, and it's not long before the others catch up. After a few blocks of office buildings, we turn onto a busier street with a large strip mall and a giant parking lot. The place doesn't look much different from any other shopping center from our time— just a chain of bland, beige-colored storefronts and restaurants— except for the strange egg-shaped vehicles parked in front.

"Look at the cars," Trent says. "No one's driving them!"

A car slows as it turns into the lot, and I glimpse someone lying on their back, with their eyes closed. In the next car, two people are making out, not paying attention to the road at all. Everywhere we look, those strange egg-shaped cars whip around without anyone at the wheel, like they're possessed.

"The cars drive themselves," Adam says. "They must all be connected somehow, some sort of GPS and traffic system, along with spatial sensors…"

"This is the kind of stuff Aether wants to know about, right?" Trent asks.

"Let's get a closer look." Chris's head turns to follow each car that passes by. "I'm a mechanic, so I assume this is the kind of shit Aether picked me for."

We head into the lot and peer inside one of the parked cars. There is no driver's seat, no mirror or pedals. The dashboard, steering wheel—everything you'd use to drive the car—are all gone. It's like the inside of a limo, from what I've seen in movies anyway. Plush couches line the inside walls of the egg, with a low table in the middle.

Chris studies the car and kneels down to check under it. "It looks like the entire thing is used for passenger and storage space. There's no hood. No room for an internal combustion engine."

"But then what powers it?" Adam asks, kneeling beside him. "Is it electric?"

"I don't think so. Maybe some sort of kinetic or solar power…"

I have no idea what they're talking about, but at least they aren't fighting at the moment. They continue debating how the cars work, but I tune them out and study the stores. There's a big drugstore, along with some clothing shops, a couple restaurants and fast food places, and some others I don't recognize.

I catch Zoe drawing furiously in a sketchbook, which she must have found in her backpack. Every few seconds she takes quick glances at the stores before turning back to her page. I peer over her shoulder to get a better look. In a minute, she's sketched the shopping center and all the cars in front of us, down to the tiniest detail. Not bad. This must be her talent.

A car stops in front of us and part of it slides open. Two women step out, the door shuts, and the car drives off by itself. The first woman wears a long-sleeved dress with tiny blue lights flickering all along the edges. She has a black facial tattoo, a pretty design of swirls and flowers, curling around her left eye and along her temple. The other woman is wearing something similar, but the tattoo on her face looks like leopard print.

Are facial tattoos common in thirty years? That's a strange trend.

But as I watch, the leopard print design changes, flowing into a new pattern, and I gasp out loud. The women hear me and give our group a strange look before entering a place called Frosty Foam. Probably because we're all staring at them with our mouths hanging open.

"Did that just..." Zoe asks. "Her face..."

"I don't know, but we need to find out," Adam says.

I nod. "We should split up and check out some of these stores."

"Come on, Trent," says Chris. They take off toward a huge drugstore called Aid-Mart, leaving me with Adam and Zoe.

We check out the Frosty Foam place first. It's like a frozen yogurt shop, except that it sells sticks with foam on them in different flavors ranging from green tea to bacon to cupcake. Signs all over the place proclaim that it's a fun, low-fat treat, but it looks like a weird, frothy mess to me.

The women with the face tattoos sit in the corner with bright-purple foam sticks, but there's no one else inside. Instead of a counter with a cash register and someone to take your order, there's just a wall of screens with a menu on each one. There's also a TV showing the news, with a headline about supply problems with the Mars base and an ad on the side for cloning your pets. The date and time are displayed on the bottom, confirming our suspicions. We're exactly thirty years in the future, even down to the day.

For a minute, our eyes remain glued to the TV screen, taking it all in, absorbing that this is really happening. I set my mother's watch to match the current time: 8:13 a.m.

"Thirty years," Adam says, shaking his head. "And there's a colony on Mars now? Awesome."

"I want to try one of these foam things," Zoe says. She taps the screen for a coffee-flavored stick, but it flashes an error message: ID NOT FOUND. She tries again with no success. "Am I doing it wrong?"

"Maybe that one is broken," Adam says. He tries the next machine, pressing a few buttons, and the screen reads, "Thank you." Part of the wall opens up, and a light-brown foam stick slides out.

"Thanks," Zoe says, grabbing it. The wall closes back up again a moment later. She takes a mouthful of foam and laughs, wiping at her lips. "It's good! But weird at the same time. Like eating flavored bubbles."

Adam examines the spot where the opening was. "This place must be all automated."

"What about the food?" I ask. "Someone has to be preparing it, right?"

He finds a breakfast menu on the screen and orders some hash browns. They pop out of the wall within seconds. "Doesn't look like it."

I grab one and take a bite. Tastes normal. "How did you pay for these?"

"I'm not really sure." Adam stares at the screen. "It didn't ask for payment or anything. Just said 'complete your order' and then gave us the food."

"Hmm. Strange."

We leave Frosty Foam and walk into a store next door called Smartgear. This place does have people working here, each with one of those facial tattoos. The salespeople stand around display cases while videos play on the walls behind them, showing a woman applying something that looks like a clear Band-Aid to her temple.

"Welcome to Smartgear!" a man says. His facial tattoo is of a dark-blue geometric pattern. The collar of his shirt reads *Smartgear* in twinkling white lights. "Can I help you?"

"Um, yeah." I stare past him at the video, where the Band-Aid thing on the woman's face morphs into one of those tattoos. The screen reads *Fully Customizable* and shows the tattoo-thing changing shape and color. Ahh, that makes a lot more sense than everyone going around getting ink all over their faces.

Zoe is silent except for the scratch of her pencil against her sketchbook as she captures the store on paper. Beside me, Adam watches the video with his mouth hanging open. "We want to see one of those," he says to the sales guy.

"Certainly. This is the newest model, the SG17 flexi." He gestures to the table next to him, where thin, see-through patches are displayed on little stands. "We've improved on the augmented reality and the integration with household objects from the previous version."

"Oh. Great." I have no idea what he's talking about. He picks one up from the display and hands it to me. The patch is flexible and curved to fit on the temple around the eye. It's completely clear and feels like smooth plastic—it reminds me of when I got glue all over my hands as a kid and would peel it off. I pass the patch to Adam.

"How do they work?" he asks while he examines it.

"They're simple. Flexis have microscopic sensors that read brain waves, allowing you to access the Internet using only mental commands. No more clunky glasses or heavy tablets to carry around. And the flexis are so thin and light, you won't even know you're wearing one. They make a great fashion statement too." As he says this last line, the tattoo on his face—the flexi—changes colors from blue to purple. "See?"

"Wait, so the Internet is in your *brain* now?" I ask before I can stop myself.

He blinks at me, but quickly recovers with a smile. "Yes, and it's all connected to everything else. For example, you can control your smartclothes with a flexi. Although...you don't seem to be wearing any."

Damn Aether and their matching outfits. We're way too obvious and dated, and my stupid mouth blurting out questions isn't helping. *Think, think, think.* "Um, our parents are really old-fashioned," I say. Which makes no sense, since the three of us are clearly not related.

But Adam picks up the slack immediately. "Yeah, we go to this superconservative school with no technology." He rolls his eyes. "Parents."

"I see," the salesman says, but his smile drops. "Will they, uh, let you buy anything?"

"Oh yeah, not a problem," Adam says. "So can we see a

demonstration of how they work?"

"Certainly." The salesman still looks suspicious, but he takes the flexi and begins fitting it to Adam's face. "When you put it on, it can sync with your profile using your brain waves or your DNA."

Connecting to Adam's profile could lead to him learning about his future self. He must realize it too, because he quickly raises his hands to stop the guy. "Oh, um, I don't—"

"Don't worry. If you don't have a profile, you can easily create one. And our display models here are set up with a fake profile for you to try."

Brain waves and DNA? I shudder and turn away to examine the other displays of similar plasticky patches. The whole idea of having the Internet in your brain is just so…creepy. I don't want a computer messing around with my head. But one glance at Adam, with a spiraling pattern around his eye and a big grin on his face, and I can tell he doesn't feel the same.

On the wall, a video shows what it looks like when you're wearing a flexi. We see from the eyes of the person wearing it, and as he walks down the street, the video bounces with each step. Information swims across the screen—news headlines scroll in one corner, along with an ad for portable 3-D printers, and a message from someone named John flashes at the bottom: *Dinner at Pedro's?* Another box displays below and a message slowly appears in it, as though being typed by the user: *Sure, be there in 5.* I watch, hypnotized and horrified at the same time, as the message is sent and a map pops up in the corner of the screen, guiding the person to the location.

Adam moves beside me, still wearing the tattoo. "This thing is incredible. I can't even feel it on my face, but it's like a smartphone in my head." He laughs. "I just started watching a video of a cat riding a pig! Oh man, I wish we could take these back to our time."

"Be quiet!" I whisper, glancing around. Luckily the employees and other customers are too busy to hear us.

"Sorry." He leans close, lowering his voice. "We should buy some of these so we can study them somewhere safe."

"Won't they connect to our future selves' profiles?"

"Nah, we can just make new profiles. Let's get five of them."

"Five? Do we *all* need one?" I have zero interest in putting one of those things on.

He grins at something only he can see, while Zoe sketches one of the flexis on display. I can see I've completely lost the two of them. We'll be here all day if I don't do something.

The original sales guy is busy with another customer, so I walk up to an employee with pink streaks in her hair who can't be much older than I am. "Finding everything okay?" she asks.

"Yeah, I'd like to buy five of the SG17 flexis."

She moves to the front counter and pulls out five tiny boxes. "That'll be $980."

I pull the wallet Aether Corp provided out of my backpack and count out the money. There's $1,000 in there, so I have just enough to cover it. I try to give it to the cashier, but she looks at my hand like I'm offering her a live snake.

"I'm sorry. We don't take *cash* here." She sounds horrified. She glances at the salesman I talked to earlier, as though looking for help.

He walks over and smiles at me. "Is there a problem?"

"No." I shove the money back in the wallet and stuff it in my backpack. What kind of place doesn't take cash? And how am I supposed to pay for this stuff? Aether didn't give us credit cards, probably because there was no guarantee they'd work in the future. The way she looked at the money makes me wonder if the future has some new form of currency. "So, um, what *do* you take?"

The girl stares at me and the man frowns. I realize my question makes me look like a complete idiot, but what else can I do?

"We only accept fingerprint IDs with DNA scans," she says slowly, like I'm stupid or something. She gestures to a smooth, black surface on the counter. "You place your hand here."

"Oh. Right."

"Don't mind her. She just needs more coffee," Adam says behind me, but they don't look convinced.

I place my hand on the black surface. The fingerprints and DNA must link to a bank or something. Maybe that's how Adam paid for the food earlier. Will my future self be charged for this? If so, I'm sure I'll be understanding. After all, I'll remember this moment. Although this seems dangerously close to connecting with my future self.

The surface under me flashes red, and I jerk my hand back. The woman frowns. "That's odd." She presses something on the other side of the counter, her eyebrows pinched together.

"What is it?" the salesman asks.

"There was some sort of error. I reset the scanner." She glances up at me. "Sorry, could you try that again?"

I place my hand on the surface, and again it flashes red. Dread creeps through my gut.

"I'm sorry," the girl says, her eyes wide. "But it says you're not in the system."

"What does that mean?" I ask, heart pounding. How can I not be in the system?

"I'm not sure. I've never seen this before. It could be a glitch or something."

But somehow I know it's not a glitch. It's me.

Something is wrong with my future.

02:09

"The scanner seems to be working fine." The salesman looks up at me, and I see suspicion in his eyes. The other customers are starting to stare.

"There must be something wrong with the software," the girl says.

But the man isn't convinced. I get the feeling he'll call the cops any second now. If we aren't in the system, he probably assumes we're criminals or something. I have to save this, quick.

"That's really strange." I glance at Zoe, but she couldn't buy anything at the fast food place either. "Adam, can you get these for us?"

"Sure." Adam steps in front of me and places his hand on the counter. This time, no red flash. Instead it turns blue, and the salespeople stare at something behind the counter. They look at Adam, then back at their interface, then back at him.

"Dr. O'Neill!" the girl says. "I'm so sorry! I didn't realize...You just look so young in person."

The man is all smiles now. "I get it. This was a test, right?" He gives a little laugh. "You definitely had me convinced you didn't know how the flexis worked!"

"Um, yeah." Adam glances at me with wide eyes, but I don't

have an answer for him. All I can think of is the red flash and the woman's words: *not in the system.*

"Please accept our apologies and let us know if you need anything else," the salesman says. "This was completely our fault. Our system must be acting up, but we'll have it checked out immediately. This is all free of charge for your trouble."

"I'm so sorry," the girl repeats. She shoves the boxes in a bag and hands it to Adam, like it's an offering. "And...thank you. For everything. My grandmother..."

"That's enough, Patricia," the salesman says. Patricia bows her head.

"Um, no problem," Adam says. "Thanks."

We hurry out of there before they can realize something is wrong. Adam's fingerprints must have connected to his future self's profile. The salespeople treated him like he was a celebrity or something—and what was all that about the girl's grandmother?

We run into Chris and Trent outside—or rather, they crash into us. Before I can ask why or tell them what happened to us, Chris says, "This way. Hurry!"

He rushes past the stores and around the back, into an area behind the shopping center where deliveries are probably dropped off. I don't know where we're going or why we're running, but I'm happy to get away from Smartgear and out of sight.

Chris stops between two huge trucks that look similar to the ones in our time except they don't have a spot for drivers to sit. He and Trent check to make sure no one is following us. "Okay," he says. "There's some crazy shit going on here. The stores won't take cash, and when they scanned us, we weren't in the system."

"The same thing happened to us," I say.

That means four of us aren't in the system. Everyone is missing except Adam. The empty research facility was just the beginning of our problems. It must all be connected.

"Seriously?" Chris runs a hand over his shaved head. "How can we all not be in the system?"

"It might be related to whatever happened to Aether Corporation," Adam says, echoing my own thoughts.

"Maybe," Chris says. "All I know is, we couldn't buy anything. But Trent picked something up anyway."

"Check this out." Trent pulls something that looks like a pen from his coat. "It's like a laser that heals you. Awesome, right?"

"Wait, did you *steal* that?" Adam asks.

Trent shrugs and lights up a cigarette. "They can have it back in twenty-four hours."

Chris narrows his eyes at Adam's bag. "How'd you get *your* stuff?"

I hesitate, but they'll find out the truth soon enough. "Adam was in the system."

"What?" Chris takes a step toward Adam. "Is there something you're not telling us, smart guy?"

"No! I have no idea why I'm in the system and you're not."

"I think you're lying. I think you know *exactly* what's going on." He shoves Adam in the chest, knocking him back into the side of the truck.

Trent throws his cigarette on the ground and moves forward to join in. "Did you know we'd be going thirty years in the future instead of ten?"

I'm getting really tired of these assholes. I step in front of Chris and Trent. "Leave him alone. He doesn't know anything."

"How do *you* know that?" Chris asks. "You don't know anything about him!"

"I know he's not a thief like you two." I clench my fists, ready to fight them both. All the pent-up frustration from the last few hours bubbles to the surface, and my muscles ache to unleash it on these two. It's not their fault everything is going wrong, but they're not helping things either.

"Oh my God, stop fighting!" Zoe huddles against the truck, tugging her jacket around herself. Her eyes are wide and fearful. A memory rises up from when I was a kid, cowering under a table and scared out of my mind while my parents fought. I'm disgusted with myself as I see Zoe looking at me now with the same fear. I drop my hands and take a step back.

"She's right," Adam says at my side. "We need to work together."

"Work together?" Trent snickers. "That's hilarious."

Chris points a finger at Adam. "You're lucky your girlfriend is here to protect you. This time."

My temper flares up again. "He's not my—"

"Yeah, whatever." Chris crosses his arms and glares at us. "So what's your plan?"

No one answers. The question is too big. Nothing's gone right since we arrived in the future. Hell, we're not even in the right time period.

Maybe something bad happened to us in the thirty years between our time and now. Aether told us not to look into our futures because it could send us into shock and cause brain damage—but what if they're wrong?

Or what if that's all a lie, and they don't want us to do it because we'll discover what's *actually* going on?

I have to know why I'm not in the system. Even if it damages my brain, I need to know my fate.

"We need to find out what happened to us," I say.

"What?" Zoe asks. "But we're not supposed to look into our futures."

"Do we have any other choice?"

"Yeah," Chris says. "We figure out how this stuff works and go home. That's what we came to do."

I shake my head. "I don't know about you guys, but I signed up for this 'research project' to make sure I *have* a future. Something obviously went wrong in the last thirty years. I'm going to find out what happened and fix it."

"How do we do that?" Trent asks.

I'm not sure. But Adam answers for me. "We can use the stuff we bought to search for ourselves. We'll try to link up with our profiles. Our future selves must have Facebook or whatever the equivalent is now, right? Or a website, something we can use."

"What if we can't find anything?" asks Zoe.

"We look for other people we know. Friends, family. Or for Aether Corporation. Try to find out what happened to them."

While Chris stares off into space with a grim look on his face, Trent flicks his lighter on and off. "What about paradoxes and all that crap?" Trent asks.

"We won't actually interact with our future selves," Adam says. "We'll just look them up. That's it. We should be okay."

Zoe chews on the edge of her black nails. "I don't know..."

"Screw it. I'm in," Trent says. "We can look ourselves up *and* figure out how the technology works at the same time."

"But won't we go into shock or whatever?" Zoe asks.

"Maybe," I say. "But that's a risk I'm willing to take. I have a gut feeling something is very wrong in this future."

"This is a bad idea," Chris says, shaking his head. "If we do this, we can't let Aether know that we looked ourselves up."

"None of us will tell them." I glance at the others, and they all nod.

Adam opens the bag and passes out the flexis we bought, while briefly explaining to Trent and Chris how they work. We spread out between the two trucks. I sit against a huge tire and hold the flexi in my fingers, feeling the thin plastic membrane. The others all start to apply them, but I still hesitate. I don't want this thing poking around in my brain, but if it's the only way…

I fit it on my face, around my eye and up onto my forehead. There's a bit of tightness as it sticks to my skin, like it has tiny invisible suckers on it, and then I don't feel it at all. I remove my hand and it stays there, attached to my face.

Immediately, an image pops up in front of me, making me flinch. The message lies on top of my normal vision, but I have no trouble seeing the truck in front of me either. It has two options: *Sync* or *Create Profile*.

I might as well try syncing to see if it can find a profile for me. "How do I select something?"

"Just picture yourself touching it," Adam says. "It's all very intuitive."

I lift my hand to touch the button and it lights up. For a moment it just says *Syncing…*but then I get the message *No profile found. Create one?*

"I'm not in this system either." I click on the *Yes* button. This time I do it mentally, without my hand.

"Nope, me neither," Trent says.

"This shit is messed up," Chris says, but I hear awe in his voice too.

When it asks for my name, I create a fake one, and the letters appear as soon as I visualize them in the box. A minute later I have a fake profile connected to my brain waves and DNA, and all sorts of icons crowd my vision. I don't know what I'm doing and I somehow select one of them with a penguin on it.

Colors and images rush toward me and I try to shrink back. A second later they resolve into a game, where tiny cartoon penguins with boxing gloves slide around on ice and try to hit each other. I hear music and strange little chirping sounds coming from the penguins, and I'm hit with the smell of frost and the feel of cold wind on my face. Behind the game, I can still see the faint image of the truck, but my body is telling me I'm in the snow with the penguins.

I start to panic as the penguins move faster, the noises and colors and smells suffocating me. I can't figure out how to get out of this program. I close my eyes, but it doesn't go away. And when I turn my head, the sound and the images follow, because they're *in* my head. I can't get them out and I can't make it stop.

I rip the flexi off like a Band-Aid and feel something like a tiny electric shock in my brain. The images and sounds disappear immediately, but the feel of being in the snow takes longer to go away. Thank God it's over. I lean back against the tire, breathing heavily. No way in hell am I using that thing ever again.

Adam moves to sit beside me. "You okay?" he asks, too softly for the others to hear. They're all too involved in whatever they're seeing and hearing anyway.

"Yeah." I rub my face, trying to clear my vision. Cold sweat drips down my forehead. "Fine."

"It's a little overwhelming at first. But you'll get used to it."

I stay silent. Everyone else seems to have no problem using their flexis. Zoe has hers set to look like purple butterflies fluttering across her temple; Trent has a big, yellow lightning bolt on his; and Chris has a barbed-wire design that matches a tat on his arm. Adam's kept his flexi clear, but it's obvious he's an expert with it already. I don't want to admit that I'm the only one who can't figure the stupid thing out.

I've never been good with computers. Growing up, we never had one—couldn't afford one, I guess. Once I went into foster care I mostly used the computers at school or the library. If I was really lucky, my foster home would have one, but it was usually shared between all the kids, so I never got to use it for long. I didn't even have a cell phone until a few months ago. Many foster parents don't bother getting them for their temporary kids, but the Robertsons insisted we each have one, even if they're ancient models. Katie had to show me how to use it.

"Just try it again," Adam says. He's really persistent, but he doesn't seem to be judging me. "Take it slow this time so you can get used to it."

I stretch the flexi between my fingers, seeing how long it can get. I want to throw it into the road and never use it again, but Adam's watching me, and I don't want him to think I can't do it.

"Fine." I smooth the flexi back on my face and it connects to my new profile. This time I brace myself for the experience, and it's a little less jarring. I know more of what to expect now and I take it slower, keeping Adam's words in mind. For a few minutes, I learn how to control the device, and it starts to make a lot more sense. It really is intuitive once you have some idea what you're doing. As long as I don't go into any more games, I should be okay.

If I'm going to blend in I probably need a flexi design too. I scroll through the options until I find a basic design of five tiny, black stars scattered around the eye. Perfect—not too in-your-face, and it matches the star tattoos on my left arm.

Once that's done, I call up an Internet search. It's really strange how I can see both the search box and the truck at once, but I'm starting to like that. It means I can keep an eye on the others while doing this. I enter my name, and millions of hits pop up for different people named *Elena Martinez*. I had no idea my name was so common. I scroll through them, but there's too much info, and none of the hits seem to be me.

I don't have anyone else to search for. No real family, no friends I'm close enough to visit in the future. I could look for Papá, but the thought makes me want to throw up. Besides, if he's still alive, he'll be in prison, serving out his life sentence. No help there.

Instead, I search for Aether Corp. I find their website immediately. They're still around and have an office in downtown LA. So why was the research facility here in the desert abandoned?

"I'm not finding anything," I say. "There are too many hits for people with my name."

"Yeah, me too," Trent says. "This is impossible."

Zoe's head snaps up. "I think I found my sister! She has a website or a profile or whatever they're called now."

"Really?" Adam asks. "Is there a way to contact her?"

"Um…I don't think so. Not unless you're her friend or something. But her last status update says she's at work and her profile has the name of the place, so maybe we can go there?" Her eyes widen. "We can go talk to her. My sister, in the future."

Adam shakes his head. "You can't talk to her. She'll recognize you. Especially with your blue hair."

"I guess," Zoe says, her shoulders drooping. "But you guys could talk to her for me."

"You sure you want to risk it?" Chris asks. "Going into shock and brain damage and all that?"

Zoe chews on her nail for a minute and then nods. "I have to know."

02:53

Zoe's sister works at some place on Hollywood Boulevard called Blue Moon. We use the map program in our flexis to find a Metro station within walking distance that will take us into the city. This Metro line doesn't exist yet in our time, but now the train is packed with people commuting to work or wherever they're going in the city.

Almost everyone on board wears a flexi, some clear but most with patterns, and it's hard not to stare at their clothes that look almost but not quite normal. Many of them are made of something sleek with a touch of shine, and some have moving or flashing lights. Uniform name tags are all electronic, and one guy even has an entire advertisement for mint gum running across his chest, playing on repeat. It's as if their clothes—smartclothes, I guess—are all computerized too.

The five of us spread out so we don't look suspicious in our matching, old-fashioned outfits. I sit by myself and stare out the window. The Metro train runs aboveground on raised bridges over the freeway, where hundreds of egg-shaped cars zoom by. I rode along the same freeway yesterday on my way to Aether, but everything is different now—more cars, more buildings, more everything.

It takes two trains and about two hours to get to the Hollywood and Highland Metro exit. We emerge from the station into a sea of tourists gawking at an Elvis impersonator and checking out the gold Walk of Fame stars in the sidewalk. The place looks almost identical to the last time I was here, four years ago on a school trip. Although I guess it would be thirty-four years ago now.

The street is lined with T-shirt and souvenir shops selling random crap covered in the words "Hollywood" and "Los Angeles." Old neon signs hang below palm trees, and the air smells like piss and incense. Street entertainers and people in costumes line the sidewalk, trying to get some attention. Everything has that same dirty, fake feel I remember. The only things that stand out as different are the strange cars and the lit-up clothes people wear. And none of the tourists are taking photos—probably because the flexis have a camera app built in.

We head east, moving around the crowds and trying to stick together. Dark-gray clouds cover the sky, the air thick with the promise of rain. Adam stares down at the Walk of Fame stars the entire time, reading the celebrities' names and nearly running into multiple people in the process. "Who are all these people? I've never heard of any of them."

"Actors who haven't been born yet probably." I yank him out of the way of a guy in a Darth Vader costume. "Watch where you're going."

"Sorry. It's just so odd. It's like nothing's changed in the future until you look at the details. Like that." He points at a window display with dozens of different T-shirt styles for something called Comfortable Man. Some of them only have the logo, but others have a guy wearing typical superhero gear with a black mask and a rainbow-colored cape, along with a pink tutu. "What is that?"

"Never heard of it. Must be a TV show or movie we don't have yet." I shrug but then I nearly run into Adam, who has stopped to stare at something in front of us.

Outside the Ripley's Believe It Or Not with the T. rex on the roof, a man is completely covered in fire. The flames ripple up and down his body and shoot off the top of his head, but there's no heat from the fire. As we walk by, he hands us a ticket for 10 percent off admission, and Adam and Chris debate how the effect is done for the next five minutes.

We pass the Hollywood Wax Museum where there's a creepy wax sculpture of an older Justin Bieber, of all people, in the window. There are other wax sculptures I don't recognize, including an actress in a wheelchair. People in long coats stand on the side of the street and try to hand us things that look like little blue pills. Trent starts to take one until I give him a "don't even think about it" look.

After a couple blocks, we move away from the tourist trap and the crowd thins out. The map says we've come to the place: a plain gray building with blacked-out windows and a dark-blue door. The neon sign above it says "Blue Moon" and has an image of a woman dancing on a pole with her ass sticking out. Classy.

"Is this the place?" Adam asks.

Zoe stares at the door with wide eyes. "The address is right, but…"

"I changed my mind. I want to go in now," Trent says, grinning at the sign.

I roll my eyes. "Keep it in your pants, perv."

"C'mon, can't we all go in?"

"Shut up," Chris says to Trent. He looks back and forth between me and Adam. "You two know what to do?"

"Yeah, we got it." I take off my jacket and hand it to Zoe, leaving me in just a plain black shirt. Adam zips up his jacket. It's the best

we can do until we get some new clothes. We keep our backpacks—
I don't want the others peeking through mine and finding the gun.

While we were on the train, Chris and Adam set up our flexis so
Adam and I can record everything we see and hear while stream-
ing it to the others, so they can watch and even speak to us. From
what Chris said, it will be like they're looking through our eyes.
Personally, I think it's creepy as hell. I'd much rather be on the re-
ceiving end, but I'm stuck with the job. Zoe can't go inside in case
her sister recognizes her. Chris and Adam split up so we have a tech
guy on both ends, and none of us trust Trent not to screw this up.

"I'm turning on the camera," Adam says. "How's it look?"

"Looks good," Chris says. "We'll hang out around back. C'mon."
He waves for Zoe and Trent to follow him.

Adam opens the door, and we walk into a dark room that reeks of
beer and desperation. Loud music thumps in the background, and
two older men sit at the bar. Above them, a dark-haired girl dances
around a pole with only her underwear on. She twirls around and
stares off into the distance, her movements mechanical. Another
scantily clad girl walks around the room and stops to talk to a guy
with a long beard at a table. Otherwise, the place is empty.

"Man, strip clubs are depressing this early in the morning,"
Trent says, his voice loud in my head. I jump at the sound. It's bad
enough hearing him out loud.

"How many have you been to?" I ask.

"Um…none."

Figures. I scan the room, feeling like a creeper every time I look
at the women, and a little angry every time I see the men. But I've
been in worse places than this, so I keep my cool.

"Are any of these your sister?" I ask quietly. I focus on the dark-
haired girl, who looks like she could be Asian. "Her maybe?"

"I-I don't know," Zoe says. "I don't think so. But I'm not sure what she looks like."

"You don't know what your sister looks like?"

"It's been a while since I saw her." She sighs, and I can hear the pain in her voice. "We were kids when we were split up and put into the foster care system."

"That sucks." No wonder she wants to see her sister so badly. There were many nights growing up in foster care when I wished I had a brother or sister, someone who would stick with me through everything, who'd understand what I'd been through like no one else could. But maybe that would have been worse—to be split up from the last person you called family.

"What do we do?" Adam asks. He's been silent until now, taking it all in with a grim expression.

"No clue," I say. "I've never been to a strip club."

"Me neither."

"Get a table or something," Chris says.

We pick a spot across the room from the bearded guy. The table's surface has bright blue bubbles floating all over it, and when I touch one, it pops. Adam slides his hand across the table and the bubbles move around him, blown away by his movements but never going too far from the surface.

"This is awesome," he says, as he pops the bubbles one by one. Each time, another bubble appears in a different spot. He's probably the only guy in here more excited by the technology than the half-naked girls. "Check this out. You order at the table here."

A menu hovers over the bubbles. From it, we can order food and drinks, as well as other…entertainment.

I scan the list of names and photos of girls we can request. There are a few guys listed too. I find a way to narrow it down to only

Asian women, which cuts it down to three. Only one of them is available right now.

"That's her!" Zoe says. "Jasmine! Or I think it's her. That's not her name, but it looks like her. I just…I can't believe she works here."

I focus on the photo of Jasmine—one of the older women listed, maybe in her late thirties or early forties. She's pretty, with raven-black hair and porcelain skin, but compared to the barely twenty girls she looks almost ancient.

"Sorry, Future-Adam. Looks like you're paying for this too," Adam mutters while he orders a private room with Jasmine.

"Okay, now I really want to go in there," Trent whines.

I wish I knew how to mute him. "Now what?"

Adam orders two sodas and pops another bubble. "I guess we wait."

A minute later, the scantily clad waitress sets our sodas on the table without a word. A ring of light appears around each glass when it touches the surface, and the bubbles cluster around them.

I pick up my soda and chug it to relieve the pressure in my throat. When I set it down, windows appear above the table asking if I want to order another soda, along with suggestions for other drinks and an icon to "share with your friends." Adam leans forward to examine the options, but I shake my head and look away.

A woman with short, black hair and a ton of eyeliner comes to our table. She's well stacked, wearing a bra flashing with digital colors, a matching skirt that's smaller than some of my underwear, and a flexi that looks like fish scales. But there's something sad about her, with the fine lines around her eyes and the caked-on makeup, like she's trying too hard to be twenty again.

"You order the private room?" she asks, sounding bored.

Is this Jasmine? I glance at Adam, but he shrugs.

"That's her," Zoe says softly. "I can't believe it. She looks so…old."

"Yeah, that's us," Adam says to Jasmine, adjusting his glasses and carefully looking everywhere except her breasts. "What do we…"

"Follow me." She leads us into the side of the club, past a velvet curtain, and gestures at a purple love seat. Adam sits, but I think of all the men who must have sat on the couch and decide to remain standing.

The woman slides close to him, moving between his legs, but he holds up his hands to stop her. "Wait! We just want to talk to you."

The woman shrugs, but steps back. "Whatever. You paid for thirty minutes."

"We'd like to ask you a few questions about your sister," I say.

"My sister?" Jasmine plants her hands on her hips. "Why do you want to know about her?"

"We're, um…" We really should have planned this out better. I try to think of everything I know about Zoe. "We're doing a class project on her art. She was a great artist."

"Is this some kind of sick joke?" Jasmine cocks her head to the side, her eyebrows raised. "My sister died when she was seventeen."

05:21

I hear a sharp intake of breath in my head, and Chris starts to swear. Zoe is *dead?* That must be why she's not in the system. But if Zoe's not in the system, does that mean we're *all* dead?

No. It could just be a coincidence. It has to be.

Jasmine is eyeing me suspiciously. I need to say something. "Well, you know, art becomes more valuable after someone dies."

"Hmm." She shrugs. "I guess it *has* been about thirty years now."

Oh God. That means Zoe must have died not long after we returned from this trip to the future. It can't be a coincidence. It's all connected somehow—the conversation with the scientists, the empty building and the wrong year, and now this.

"How exactly did your sister die?" Adam asks.

"Not sure that's any of your business really, but she was murdered."

Murdered. The word hangs over us, sending chills through me. Someone starts wailing, probably Zoe. I put my hand to my forehead, feeling faint all of a sudden. I need to get these people out of my head. I need to get away from the sinking feeling that everything is going horribly wrong and there's no way to stop it.

Adam stands up and touches my arm. "Are you okay?"

"Yeah. Just give me a sec."

I push past the curtain into the main part of the club. A different girl is dancing on stage now. I dart past her and into the bathroom, which looks like it hasn't been updated—or cleaned—since my time. I stare into the mirror over the sink, trying to ignore the computerized ads that dance along the edge of it. I still hear Zoe muttering in my head, along with Chris and Trent trying to talk to her. Even in the bathroom I can't escape them. I switch off the camera feed and my head goes silent again.

Under the dim light my dark skin looks sallow, my brown eyes tired. My long hair is frizzing out. I look lost. Defeated. *Weak.*

I splash water on my face and smooth out my hair. *Pull it together*, I tell myself. *Just because Zoe's dead doesn't mean you are too.*

I use the toilet and return to our private room behind the curtain. Jasmine is leaning against the wall, examining her nails. Adam looks up at me, his face creased with worry. "Everything okay?"

"Yeah." I switch my camera back on. The other end is silent. "Do you know who killed Zoe?" I ask Jasmine.

"Nah, I was only eight when she died. I don't remember anything, except that she was shot in her girlfriend's apartment."

"No, please, no," Zoe says, with a sob in her voice. "This can't be happening. I don't believe it!"

I hear static and a thump on the other end, and then hear Chris yell Zoe's name in the background. Followed by more static.

"Zoe?" Adam asks. "Chris?"

Silence.

I dart through the curtain and into the club, while Jasmine yells, "Hey!" Adam is right behind me as we step outside.

It's raining now, and I'm quickly soaked without my coat. We rush to the back of the club where the others are supposed to be waiting. I hold my hand over my eyes to peer through the downpour, looking for any sign of them.

Farther down the street, I see Trent and Chris running down the alley, their feet splashing against the sidewalk. Zoe's in front of them and she runs like a scared child, either indifferent or completely unaware of the rain pouring down on her.

Adam and I take off after them, racing down the rain-slicked road. Zoe suddenly collapses in the middle of the alley. Is she hurt? I run faster.

I catch up to them, panting and completely soaked through, with Adam just behind me. Chris stands beside Zoe, who kneels on the ground, shivering. Trent smokes a cigarette, his hand shaking as he flicks the ash onto the wet ground.

Zoe peers up at us with haunted eyes, rain dripping down her face and mixing with her tears. "This future. I don't want it. I *hate* it."

Adam slips an arm around Zoe and helps her to her feet. "We're going to change it. All of that stuff she said…it isn't going to happen."

"Can we?" She turns to me, her eyes haunted. "Can we change it?"

I open my mouth but don't have an answer for her. Maybe this is why Aether didn't want us to look ourselves up. Nothing good can come of knowing our own fate.

We move down the alley until we find a small overhang to hide under. I rub my arms, trying to snap some warmth back into them. My hair is dripping all over me, and my thin T-shirt is soaked through. Zoe still has my jacket, but she's clinging to Adam and barely holding herself together.

"This is messed up." Chris rubs a hand over his shaved head. "What do we do?"

"We need to figure out who shot Zoe and why," I say. "And find out if the rest of us are dead too."

Trent jerks his head toward me. "You think we're dead?"

"Maybe." Probably. All of us except Adam anyway.

"But why would someone do this?" Adam asks.

"I don't know. Zoe, do you have any idea who would want to kill you?"

She shakes her head, arms wrapped around herself. She's leaning against a dumpster, sobbing quietly. I don't blame her. Not only did she see her sister all grown up and working in a strip club of all places, but she just found out she's going to be dead soon too.

Not just dead—murdered.

"What about your girlfriend?" I ask. "Would she…?"

Zoe whips her head back and forth. "No, definitely not. Never."

"What about ex-girlfriends?" Trent asks. "Or, uh, ex-boyfriends?"

She sniffs. "I have both but…I don't think any of them would want to kill me."

Adam rubs her shoulder. "It's going to be okay." He pleads with his eyes, like he wants me to help somehow. I'm not sure what he expects me to do. I'm not exactly a touchy-feely person at the best of times, and I'm barely keeping it together myself.

I lightly pat Zoe's arm. "Don't worry," I say, fumbling for comforting words. "We're going to figure this out." Man, I suck at this. But Zoe wipes her face on her sleeve and nods. Adam gives me a thumbs-up, but I didn't really do anything.

Rain thumps against the roof above and on the metal dumpsters around us. I shiver again and want to ask for my jacket, but Zoe stares into space, oblivious. I know I should say something, but the vacant look in her eyes stops me. At least she's stopped crying now.

Adam takes off his jacket and offers it to me. "Here."

"Are you sure?" I ask, and Adam nods. I slip on the jacket, which is still warm from his body heat, and pull the hood over my head to cover my damp hair. "Thanks."

"So what now?" Trent asks, lighting another cigarette. "How do we—"

"*Police!*" shouts a man down the alley. "Put your hands up!"

Through the splattering rain, I see two people who look like members of a SWAT team or something. They wear dark-blue body armor that reads POLICE along the shoulder and full helmets with clear visors. Both have heavy utility belts with large guns, more like assault rifles than handguns, and they each carry something like a baton that lights up at the top.

I raise my hands slowly. This might be a mistake. Or it might be related to everything else that's going on.

Adam steps in front of us, his hands up. "What's the problem, officers?"

"Aid-Mart reported a theft in their store. We tracked the item to this location."

That's the name of the drugstore Chris and Trent went to. Dammit, Trent! He just had to go and steal something and get us all in trouble. I could kill him myself. We should tell them we aren't with him and let him deal with the repercussions. I don't owe him anything, and Trent deserves whatever he gets for being a pendejo.

"I'm sure this is just a misunderstanding," says Adam.

The cop points his baton at Trent. "Is that a cigarette?"

Trent freezes, with the butt smoking faintly in the rainy haze. "Yeah?"

The second cop turns to the first. "Shoplifting and drug possession. That's enough to bring them in."

"Drug possession?" Trent asks. His cigarette drops to the ground.

The cops both take a step forward, and the first one raises his baton. "Don't move. You're under arrest."

Oh shit. These cops are serious. Would they really arrest Trent for *smoking*? Are cigarettes illegal now?

I'm tempted to leave him, but we can't abandon Trent, no matter how much we might want to. And we can't afford to get arrested either. Who knows how long we'd be locked up? A few hours? A day? No way—we'd miss the aperture opening again and be stuck in the future forever.

I lock eyes with Chris, and I can tell he's come to the same conclusion. I tilt my head toward the other end of the alley, and he nods. Trent's eyes widen, but I know he understands. We have to run.

Chris bursts into action, grabbing the edge of a dumpster and swinging it between us and the cops. Zoe and Trent take off running in the opposite direction, but Adam just stands there with his hands still up. I grab his arm and yank him down the alley. "Come on!"

"But—"

"Freeze!" the police yell.

Our footsteps splash against the puddles on the ground as we run, Zoe and Trent up front, Adam at my side, and Chris behind us. Adrenaline urges me on, and rain splatters against my face as my hood flies back.

We reach the end of the alley and turn onto Hollywood Boulevard. The police have gotten around the dumpster, but they're slowed by their heavy armor. We weave between people with shopping bags who gawk at us and jump out of the way. Zoe is the fastest of us, leading the way through the maze of tourists and neon signs, their bright colors now faded and blurred in the rain. I don't think she has any idea where she's going. We have no plan, no place to hide, no way to escape. Sooner or later, the cops *will* catch up to us.

Down the street, I spot a hotel with people milling in front of it. A car stops at the door with signs that read LOS ANGELES TAXI CO. Two people get out, laughing, and I dash toward the car.

"In here," I yell to the others, slamming my hand in the door before it slides shut. We pile into the car, which is empty and has no driver. That shouldn't surprise me, but it does.

Chris is last and squeezes in beside me. The door shuts. "Go!"

I glance out the back window, but can't see the cops through the rain hitting the glass. They have to be close. And the car isn't moving.

The inside of the car is oval-shaped, with vinyl seats along the edges and a table in the middle. Trent looks around the interior, his hands up. "How do I—"

"Please state your destination," says the car.

"Dude, where are we going?" Trent asks, his voice frantic.

"Anywhere!" Adam says. "Just pick something!"

"Um—"

"8411 Monroe Avenue," Chris blurts out.

"Confirmed," the car chirps. "Navigating to 8411 Monroe Avenue, Los Angeles. Estimated travel time: twenty-six minutes."

But nothing happens. "Why aren't we moving?" Chris asks.

An outline of a hand flashes on the top of the table. "Please scan payment."

"Adam, you have to do it," I say. "Hurry!"

He presses his hand to the scanner and the car glides forward. The only sound is the rain against the roof and the windshield wipers snapping. We're all breathing heavily and dripping on the yellow vinyl seats, although from the holes in them and the stuffing sticking out, they've seen worse days.

"I think we lost them," says Chris.

"They're going to track us." I stare out the window for any sign of the cops, but don't see them. "They tracked us before."

"Trent, where's that laser pen?" Adam asks.

He digs it out of his jacket. "Here."

"Throw it out!"

"What?"

"That's probably how they found us. Get rid of it!"

"Ugh. Fine."

The window opens and rain flicks inside at us, but Trent throws the laser pen out. For a full minute, I keep my eyes on the road behind us, certain that a cop car will show up at any second. Only after we've left Hollywood Boulevard do I sit back in the seat and let myself relax.

I brush damp hair off my face, feeling like a drowned rat. Adam is just as wet, yet somehow still looks put together. His black shirt is soaked through to his skin, showing the outline of his chest and arms. It's not a bad view at all, but I take off his coat and hand it back to him.

"Thanks." He doesn't put it on and instead removes his glasses to wipe water off his face. His hair looks darker when wet, making his blue eyes stand out even more.

Zoe huddles in the corner of the car, her forehead pressed against the window. Chris touches buttons on the table's screen, and a mini-fridge full of drinks opens underneath. Trent grabs two bags of peanuts and shoves them in his coat pocket.

"Where are we going?" I ask. "Whose address was that?"

"My girlfriend's place," Chris says. "I found the address while we were on the train. I need to know if I'm…"

He trails off, but I know what he means. It's time to find out if we're all dead.

06:13

The taxi stops outside a drab two-story apartment building with bars on the windows. It reminds me of places where I've lived in similar shady neighborhoods.

"You'd think they could do better in home security by now," says Adam, eyeing the barred windows as he zips up his jacket.

"You sure you're okay with this?" Trent asks Chris.

"Yeah." He shrugs. "Zoe didn't go crazy, right?"

I'm not one hundred percent sure that's correct. She's still huddling against the window of the car, her blue hair hanging in her face. But no, she only went into shock after she heard she was murdered. Aether was wrong about what would happen to us if we found out about our future selves—or they lied to us.

"Zoe, can I get my jacket back?" I ask.

"Oh." She blinks at me as if in a dream. "Yeah."

She pulls my coat out of her backpack and hands it to me. It's nice and dry, and I slip it on and yank up the hood. Like before, Adam and I will be on point, while the others wait behind and watch through our feeds.

The instant we step out of the car, we're drenched again. "A backpack full of stuff, and they couldn't pack us an umbrella?" Adam asks as he raises his own hood.

We trudge around the building through dead weeds now muddy from the rain until we find the right door. It has a smooth, black panel, which I recognize as being for fingerprint scans. Otherwise, it has no locks, knobs, or anything to open it.

"3A, right?" I ask.

In my head, I hear Chris's voice. "Right."

I knock on the door and wait. A moment later someone calls out, "Who's there?"

"Shawnda Jones?" I ask, using the name Chris gave me.

"Yeah?"

"We're, um…"

"We're old friends of Chris," Adam says. "Can we talk to you for a few minutes?"

"Chris who?"

"Your boyfriend, Chris…"

"Duncan," I supply, remembering his name badge. "Chris Duncan."

"You're too young to be friends of his," Shawnda says, her voice closer now. There's no peephole, but she must be able to see us somehow.

Adam glances at me with raised eyebrows. "What we mean is, our parents were his friends."

"They lived in the same foster home," I add.

"Right," Adam continues. "And we just have some questions about what happened to him."

"Which foster home?" Shawnda asks.

"Tell her the Lees," Chris says, and I repeat his words.

There's a long pause, and I don't think Shawnda's going for it.

No surprise. I doubt I'd open my door for some weird teenagers either. Adam looks pretty geeky in his glasses, and my tattoos are hidden under my jacket, but we're still strangers to her.

"Tell her something personal," Trent suggests.

"Yeah, tell her I used to work at Downey Automotive," Chris says. "That's how I met Shawnda—she brought in her dad's car, and I asked her out to dinner."

"Chris used to work at Downey Automotive," I repeat. "My mom said that's how you two met."

Finally, the door opens, and inside stands a black woman with braided hair and dark, suspicious eyes. She must be forty-seven or forty-eight if she's about Chris's age back in the present. She wears a moss-green uniform with her last name on the front, sparkling in digital letters, and her flexi is clear. "I've only got a few minutes before I need to head to work."

"No problem," says Adam. "Thanks."

She lets us inside, into a small living room with furniture that looks like it might have been new back in our time. I stand in the middle of the room, wondering what to do. I have no idea what to say to this woman. How do you ask someone why a guy they knew thirty years ago doesn't seem to exist anymore?

I sit on the edge of the sofa, feeling like an intruder. "So…when did you last see Chris?"

She cross her arms and stands a little away from us, mistrust clear in her eyes. "Thirty years ago, obviously."

"Thirty—are you sure?" Adam asks, adjusting his glasses.

"Hard to forget. I was pregnant at the time."

I shoot Adam a startled look. Chris didn't mention this. Maybe he doesn't know?

"Dude, what?" Trent asks in my head.

"Shut up," Chris snaps. "I need to hear this."

I notice a photo on the wall behind Shawnda of a guy who looks a lot like Chris. "Is that your son?"

"Yeah, Chris Junior. Named after his father."

"My *son*," Chris whispers.

"He looks like his dad," Adam says. "I mean, from photos we've seen."

She digs around in her purse for something. "Mmm-hmm. Now what all do you want? I need to get going."

I lean forward, anxious to get some answers finally. "We just want to know what happened to Chris."

"Some bitch shot him. What more do you want to know?"

"He—he died?" I don't want to believe it, because if he and Zoe are both dead, that means there's little hope for me. But then I process the last thing she said. "A girl shot him?"

"Yeah." She narrows her eyes at me. "Isn't that why you're here?"

"This is bullshit," Chris says in my head. "I can't be dead. No fucking way."

"Yes," Adam says, answering her question. "We just wondered if you knew any more details."

"All I know is this girl killed him and a few other kids, then blew her own brains out."

My fingers dig into the thin fabric of the couch. I knew it. We're all dead. Murdered. Shot by some girl. Maybe it has nothing to do with Aether Corporation after all. I can think of a couple of girls who might want me dead, but I don't know of any connection with Zoe, Trent, or Chris. It might explain why Adam is still alive in the future though.

Adam stares at me, his forehead creased with concern. The others are silent in my head. Maybe they're in shock. I know I should ask more questions, should try to find out as much as I can, but my tongue is frozen. Maybe a part of me doesn't want to know more. All I can do is stare at the tan carpet and think about how I'm going to be dead soon.

I don't get it. Why would some girl kill us and then kill herself? Maybe it's a setup. Aether could have framed some girl to take the suspicion off themselves. But that doesn't make any sense either.

"Do you know this girl's name?" Adam asks Shawnda.

"Listen, that was a long time ago. Why are you digging this up now?" She strides over to the door. "I think it's time for you to go."

"Of course," Adam says, jumping to his feet. "Thank you for your time."

"Ask her about my son," Chris says, his voice strained. "Ask her!"

"One more question," I ask, standing up slowly. "Can we talk to your son?"

"Is that why you're really here?" Shawnda asks, hands on her hips. "He owe you money?"

"No—" Adam starts.

"You want revenge? Just let it go. He's already in prison." She throws open the front door. "Now get out."

"What?" Chris roars. "*What?*"

I cover my ears to block out his voice, but of course it doesn't work. Trent yells, "Chris, wait!"

Oh shit, not again. Adam and I rush outside, and the door slams shut behind us. Chris stomps across the grass toward the apartment. "Shawnda!" he yells. "Shawnda, where's my son?"

"Dude, knock it off!" Trent says, grabbing his arm. Chris turns and punches Trent in the face. He falls to the ground, into the muddy weeds.

"Stop!" Zoe yells at Chris, bending down to help Trent. "Stop it!"

"Chris, get back in the car," I say, blocking his path. Adam stands beside me, but Chris towers over both of us. I dig my feet into the earth, taking a fighting stance.

"I need to find my son." Chris glares at us, his mouth twisted with rage. "Get. Out. Of. My. Way."

I raise my hands to try to calm him down. "Chris—"

He slams between me and Adam, trying to get by. The force knocks us back, but we hold our ground. I can't let Chris talk to Shawnda—not like this anyway.

I don't want to fight him. I really don't. Not anymore. Not when we might be dead in a few days. But he leaves me no choice.

Chris tries to get by us again, and I shove him in the chest. Not that it does much good—it's like shoving a mountain. But it sure makes him mad.

He takes a swing at me, but I duck, coming up under his punch. With my hands in fists, I slam a quick jab into his side. He tries to grab me, but I dart away, out of his reach.

Adam's yelling something, but my focus has narrowed to just Chris and his massive, tattooed arms. He's a big guy, but I'm small and quick. I just have to make sure he doesn't hit me.

That thought doesn't last long. Chris swings at my gut and I dodge it, only to be punched in the face a second later. Everything goes black and then I'm on my knees somehow, my vision blurry. My face throbs with heat and pain, but I see Chris standing over me.

I reach around, hands shaking, and open the pouch on the side of my backpack. Then the gun is in my hand, pointed at Chris. "Stay back!" I yell.

"What the…" Chris freezes. "Where the hell did you get that?"

"It was in my backpack." The gun wobbles in my grip, but I don't lower it. "Get back!"

"Why would they give you a gun?" Adam asks. He looks more scared of me holding the gun than he did of Chris a minute ago.

"I don't know!"

Chris stares at me, and I prepare myself in case he's about to attack again. My finger twitches on the trigger. We lock eyes for a minute, an invisible cord of tension connecting us, the threat of violence heavy in the air. Finally the moment passes and he steps back, his shoulders slumping.

"I was gonna propose to Shawnda as soon as we got paid. She told me last week she's pregnant. That's why I took this job." He stares at the ground. "I just wanted to be a good father."

I lower the gun, hands shaking. I can't hate him now that I know he's doing all this for his family. It's more than Papá ever did for me.

"We're going to stop this." I have to believe it, or I might as well turn the gun on myself right now.

Chris nods. "Sorry about…" He gestures at his face. "All that."

I struggle to my feet and he holds out a hand to help me up. I take it and then wipe my burning nose with the back of my jacket. Red blood mixes with the rain, which has slowed to a trickle now.

I put the gun away in my backpack. "I wouldn't have shot you, you know."

"No shit," he says with a faint grin.

I can't help but let out a small laugh. This whole situation is just so messed up.

The other three watch us like we're crazy, but I know something's changed between me and Chris. We understand each other now, in a way only people who have fought each other can. My face still throbs, but he didn't actually hit me that hard. I've been in worse fights. Chris turns to Trent and apologizes, and the two slap each other on the back.

"Let's get out of here," I say. Even with the rain, we're too visible, too exposed standing out in the open like this. The police might still be looking for us.

"Guys." Adam stares at the street. "The taxi is gone."

"Oh yeah," Trent says. "It asked for more money while you were in there. It probably ran out and drove off."

Back at the apartment building, I see Shawnda's face at the window, glaring at us. And then I hear the sirens in the distance.

06:34

I whip my head around, trying to gauge how close they are. We take off running, down rain-slicked sidewalks, past beat-up apartments and stores, in the opposite direction of the sirens. For a few minutes all I know is the feel of my legs pumping, my heart racing, and water splattering against my face.

"Under here," Adam says when we can no longer hear the sirens. The five of us duck under the awning of a store that's been closed down, that once sold candles or bath lotions or something. It provides shelter from the rain but not much else.

I lean against the front window, trying to catch my breath. My face still aches, and I'd give just about anything for dry clothes right now. But worst of all, everything Jasmine and Shawnda said replays in my head.

"We're all dead," Zoe whispers, tugging on the strings of her hood. "Dead, dead, dead."

"We don't know that," Trent says. He pulls out a cigarette but then shoves it back in his jacket, probably remembering what happened the last time he got caught smoking.

I take a breath and try to clear my head. "Okay, Chris and Zoe are going to be shot by some girl after we get back to the present. We need to find out more about their deaths, and also…" I pause and look at Trent, my throat dry.

"Find out if we're really dead too," he whispers, finishing the sentence for me.

I turn to Chris. "Do you know of any girl who would want to kill you?"

"Nah. Just you."

I roll my eyes. "There has to be some connection between the four of us. Maybe some previous foster home or someone we all knew."

For a few minutes, we go through all the group homes and foster families we've lived with, and list anyone who might hold a grudge against us. The only overlap is that Trent and I both lived at the Bright Haven group home, but he moved there a few months after I got kicked out, and that doesn't link Chris or Zoe to us.

"We could go to the places we were shot," Chris suggests. "Look for evidence."

Adam shakes his head. "That was thirty years ago. There won't be anything there now."

Chris grunts but lets it go. Frustration churns inside me, and I want to slam my fist into the store window. How are we going to find out more about our deaths? I gaze out at the street, watching the egg-shaped cars scroll by. The rain has started to thin out, and I can see the faint outline of the skyscrapers of downtown Los Angeles towering above us. And then I have an idea.

"We should go to the library," I say.

"Huh?" Chris asks.

"The library," I repeat. "They should have records or old news articles or something, right?

"Good idea," Trent says. "We're only a few blocks from the

Central Library." I blink at him, surprised he knows that, but he shrugs. "It's a good place to go when you have nowhere else. I used to hang out there a lot."

"Me too." It's weird agreeing with Trent on something, but I know exactly what he means. There were many times I had to escape—from Papá, from foster homes, from life in general. Sometimes libraries and the books inside them were the only places I felt safe.

"Good news, Adam," Chris says, slapping him on the shoulder. "You're not the biggest nerd here after all." Adam rolls his eyes but gives him a faint smile. The tension between all of us has vanished now that we have a common purpose: fighting for our future.

A map with directions to the library appears in my vision, sent by Chris. We pull up our hoods and venture back into the rain.

The Central Library is in the financial area of downtown Los Angeles, a beautiful oasis in the middle of a desert of sleek stone skyscrapers. The short, beige building is topped with a small pyramid in the center, covered in tiles depicting a sunburst. It's surrounded by a garden of tall, lush trees and fountains with sea serpents spraying water. The tiered steps leading up to the entrance are carved with letters in different languages, and Greek statues stand guard over the doors.

I can't believe how little has changed in the past thirty years. They finally fixed the tricky step at the front that everyone tripped on, but otherwise the library looks almost identical to the last time I was here. There's still a tiny food court to the right as you walk in, although now it looks automated like Frosty Foam was.

We pass by it and into the front lobby, where chandeliers with illuminated globes hang from mosaic-covered ceilings. The walls are lined with colorful murals, the kind you'd see in a church. I remember coming here as a kid and thinking the place was like something out of a movie. I get that same feeling now, as if I'm somewhere magical.

The building is quiet, our footsteps loud against the tile floor. People in suits walk in and out, probably on their lunch break. I check my watch. 1:27 p.m. We've been in the future for seven hours already.

Trent sucks in a deep breath of air, which still smells of old books. "I love it here."

"What now?" Chris asks.

I hesitate, unsure where to go. The library is massive, with arches and elevators leading off from this lobby, and I don't know what exactly we need to look for. Through the nearest arch, I can see bookshelves, along with cubbyholes and desks with people sitting at them.

While the others examine the murals, Trent and I walk up to the curved, wooden information desk, where a woman smiles at us. Her flexi depicts three tiny books flapping their pages and flying away, like birds.

"Anything I can help you find?" she asks.

"Yeah, we uh…" I'm not sure how to phrase it. "We're looking for old records."

"Do you have death certificates?" Trent asks.

"We do," the librarian says. "Each computer has a subscription to a genealogy program that can access those records. Is there something specific I can help you with?"

"What about old newspaper articles, like from thirty years ago?" I ask.

"Thirty years ago…We should have all of those in the computers too, and we might have some of the originals in the back."

"Thanks."

We give the others the details, and then the five of us head under the nearest arch and split up to sit in different cubbyholes. Some of the cubbies can fit two people, but I think we all want to be alone when we read about our fates.

The cubbyhole has just one big screen with the Los Angeles Public Library logo on it, and underneath it says "Touch to activate." I press my finger to it, surprised it doesn't have newer, fancier technology. Probably due to budget cuts or some crap. I'd much rather use this one anyway, since it doesn't mess with my head.

There are half a dozen different kinds of searches listed—for ebooks, paper books, videos, and so forth—but I find the one to the genealogy program. A search box opens up with different things you can input, such as name, location, date of birth or death. I'm not sure how much this genealogy site will have on me, since I'm both a foster kid and a child of immigrants, but I enter my name and birth date, and narrow the search to Los Angeles County.

But I can't hit the search button. A part of me doesn't want to know what my future holds. For this one final moment, I can pretend everything is going to be okay when we get back to the present. Aether will give me my money, I'll get my own place to live, and I'll start college in the fall. I'll have a real future. I'll be free.

I lean back to check out the others, but their faces are all intent and focused on their screens. I can't tell if they've found anything yet or how bad it is. I sigh and turn back to my screen, where the search box waits, blinking cursor and all.

I hit Search and there it is. My death certificate.

My dream for the future crumbles at the sight. I'm dead, I'm really, truly dead.

I click on the image to make it bigger. No turning back now. I have to know everything, have to see if it's true. Besides, this might be another Elena Martinez. There have to be hundreds, thousands even, in Los Angeles.

But the date of birth on the certificate matches mine, along with other things like my parents' names and my current residence with the Robertsons. It has to be me.

Then I see the date of death, and it's like someone's taken my heart and crushed it in their fist.

Friday. Tomorrow. The day after this crazy time-travel experiment. The day we return to our normal lives.

The walls close around me. I can't die tomorrow. I'm not ready. I need days, months, years to figure out how to stop this from happening. I'm not even eighteen. I can't die yet.

But the others died thirty years ago too. It has to be true.

This is the last day of my life.

When I was a kid, Mamá would tap her watch and say, "Hay más tiempo que vida." *There's more time than life.* She meant it in a life-is-short-seize-the-day kind of way, but her words take on new meaning for me now. I check her watch, touching the cool face with my finger, trying to find some comfort from the familiar habit. There's something soothing about the predictability of time. No matter what happens, there are always sixty seconds in a minute, sixty minutes in an hour, twenty-four hours in a day. For years, this watch, with its steady ticking hands, was my one constant.

In all those years, even in my darkest moments, I've never wanted more than those sixty seconds, sixty minutes, twenty-four hours.

Now I'd give anything to have more time.

But I'm not dead yet. The ticking watch, my beating heart, the smell of the musty books around me, they all mean I still have time. Not much time, but hopefully enough to stop this.

I pull myself together, brushing hair out of my face. I told Zoe and Chris that we were going to fix this, that we were going to change the future, and I have to believe we can. But to do that, I need more information.

My time of death is 11:38 p.m., a little over twenty-four hours after we return to the present. The place of death says Santa Monica State Beach. Not very descriptive, since the beach is pretty big, and I have no idea why I'd be there so late.

I scroll down, but when I see the cause of death, I have to cover my mouth to keep from crying out.

Self-Inflicted Gunshot Wound. Suicide.

I'm the girl Shawnda mentioned, the one who shoots the others and then herself.

I'm the killer.

07:17

No, it can't be. But the words stare back at me. *Self-inflicted gunshot wound. Suicide.*

No, no, no. It doesn't make sense. I would never kill the others—would I?

I know I have a temper. I know sometimes I itch to fight, to let my rage out, to show other people I'm not weak. I know I've done some stupid shit in my past—but to actually kill someone? And not just someone, but three people I'm starting to think of as…friends?

No, never. I refuse to believe it. And I'd never kill myself either. Not in a million years. It must be a setup. Aether Corp or whoever is behind our deaths did this to us and then placed the blame on me to tie it all up with a nice string.

But I'm the only one with a gun, and I would bet money the gun in my backpack is the same one that's going to shoot the others. I even turned it on Chris less than an hour ago. And despite what I told him, I would have pulled the trigger.

Oh my God, it is me. I really am the killer. I'm going to become the one thing I swore I'd never turn into: a murderer like my father.

I guess it's inevitable. It's in my blood.

My nails dig into the desk, sending sharp, shooting pains up my fingers. I can't look away from the image with my fate written on it. But if I am the killer, why would I do this to them? I can't think of any reason I'd want to kill them. Maybe I snap at some point between now and then...and afterward my grief drives me to shoot myself. But if that's the case, why do I spare Adam?

I need to know more. Maybe I can find some hint of a motive, or learn when and where the others were killed so I can stop it from happening.

I won't become a killer. I *won't*.

I close the genealogy program and open a new search for old news articles. I input my name plus suicide, and half a dozen articles show up from various local news sites. I click on the first one, with the headline: *Four Teens Dead in Apparent Murder-Suicide.*

SANTA MONICA, Calif. – Four teens, all in the foster care system, have been found dead in an apparent murder-suicide.

Three of the teens suffered fatal gunshot wounds yesterday in different locations across Los Angeles County. Coroner's assistant Edith Moore said the victims were shot multiple times. The names of the victims have been withheld.

Police suspect the final teen, Elena Martinez, 17, killed the others before taking her own life. A lifeguard discovered her body early this morning near the Santa Monica Pier, with what police believe to be a self-inflicted gunshot wound. No suicide note was found. The investigation is ongoing.

Any lingering doubt I had is gone. This is going to happen.

The other articles all have similar headlines. I go through each one, hoping to learn more, but none give any hint as to *why* I did it. Most of the articles are short—just another random murder in a big city. They don't even have pictures of our bodies or names or locations or anything I could use.

"Hey," Trent says.

I jump and twist around, using my body to block my screen. Trent's leaning back from his cubby, which is next to mine. His face looks even whiter than usual, bleached out by whatever he's learned. Does he know I'm the one who is going to kill him? If they find out, I might not make it to tomorrow. Zoe wouldn't do anything, but Chris or Trent? I'm not sure.

"Are you..." He stops and closes his eyes for a moment, but I know what he means.

"Yeah. I'm dead too." I rub my sweaty palms on my jeans and watch him for any reaction.

"Tomorrow?"

I nod. He's not freaking out at me and neither are the others, so they must not know that I'm the one who killed them. Good. But if they keep poking around, they'll find the same articles I did sooner or later. I can't let that happen.

I close the screen—everything I saw is imprinted in my memory forever anyway—and spin around. "Did you guys find anything?" I ask, loud enough for the others to hear.

"Just that I'm gonna be shot tomorrow," Chris mutters, turning away from his screen. "Like Shawnda said. What about you?"

He doesn't know. Thank God. My shoulders relax, and I tilt my head at Trent. "Us too."

We all pull our chairs close so we can talk quietly. Adam stands on the fringe of our group, silently watching our discussion. He's the only one who isn't going to be dead tomorrow. I study him for a moment, with his black glasses and rumpled brown hair, wondering why I will spare his life.

Zoe hangs her head in her hands, hiding her face. "Everything my sister told us…it's all true. It's all in my death certificate."

"Cause of death, multiple gunshot wounds," Trent mumbles, and my throat clenches up.

Chris swears and runs a hand over his scalp. "So all four of us, tomorrow?"

"Looks that way," I say.

"But why?" Zoe asks. "Why would someone do this?"

I need to think of something, quick. Otherwise they might start digging through the past for more information. "It has to be Aether Corporation."

Zoe blinks at me. "You think…you think Aether did this?"

"It's the only thing that makes sense. It's the only connection between us, other than foster care."

Chris studies me, his brow creased. "You think they killed us to keep the project secret?"

"Maybe. Or maybe we learn something in the future they don't want getting out."

"Elena might be right," Trent says. "Think about it. The empty research building. The lies about going crazy if we look into our own future. The fact that we went forward thirty years instead of ten."

"There's something else too." I wasn't going to tell them about what I heard, not after Adam dismissed it, but it might keep the suspicion on Aether and off me. And I'm still not sure they *didn't* kill all of us. "I overheard Dr. Kapur and Dr. Walters last night."

I briefly tell them everything I heard. How the scientists were worried something might happen *again*, and they might have to use younger kids next time. I leave out that I already told this story to Adam.

"You're sure? You're one hundred percent sure that's what they said?" Chris asks.

"Elena has a perfect memory," Adam says, speaking up for the first time since we got here.

"That's your talent?" Chris raises an eyebrow at me, and I nod.

"But Adam's not dead," Trent says, and every head swivels to look at Adam. "Wouldn't Aether kill him too?"

"He's right." Adam takes off his glasses and stares at them. "I'm still alive in this future. That store we got the flexis from, Smartgear—it's owned by Aether Corporation. They're still around. And"—he takes a breath—"my future self works for them."

My stomach drops, like someone's punched me in the gut. Future-Adam, working for Aether? I don't believe it. Except…a part of me does. I saw the faces of those salespeople at Smartgear when they realized who he was.

"What do you mean?" asks Zoe, her eyes wide.

"I knew you were involved somehow," Chris growls, jumping up from his chair.

Adam throws up his hands. "We don't know if it means anything. I'm just as surprised by this as you are."

I don't want to admit it, but Chris might be onto something. It would explain why Adam defended Aether when I told him what I overheard. Chris was right before—I don't know anything about Adam. I have no reason to trust him.

"Are you working for Aether now?" I ask him, taking a step forward.

"What? No." Adam looks shocked. "I was recruited by Aether for this research project just like you guys were. That's it. I don't know anything else."

Chris grabs the front of Adam's shirt and drags him close. "You're working for them, aren't you? Double-crossing us!"

"I'm not! I'm not working for Aether. I swear it!"

I don't know what to do, whether I should interfere or not. Until now I've always stuck up for Adam, but now I have my doubts too. And I can't ignore the fact that he *isn't* like the rest of us. He wasn't recruited out of foster care. We still don't know why he's really here.

A librarian approaches us. "Please keep your voices down." She looks back and forth between Chris and Adam, eyebrows raised. Chris lets go of Adam's shirt, and they both take a step back. The librarian eyes them for one tense moment and then leaves.

"Just wait," Adam says to us, and then he looks like he's squinting. "Maybe if I show you this—"

A video blares to life inside my head and I jump. It sits in a corner of my vision, a little box over the world I can see.

"What the hell is this?" Chris asks.

"Just watch."

There's an image of Adam, but an older version of him, maybe in his forties. He's standing at a podium giving a speech, while an announcer talks. "On next week's episode of *Celebrity Profiles*: Adam O'Neill. Billionaire genius…or mad scientist?"

A logo for the show flashes on the screen with the subtitle underneath. The video then shows a clip of Adam in a lab coat, looking a few years older than he does now and grinning at the camera.

"Adam O'Neill changed the world when he developed the cure for cancer at the young age of twenty-eight," the announcer continues.

I want to pause the video and ask if this is real, but it keeps switching clips—to Adam accepting an award, to images of him in hospitals standing next to people with bald heads, to shots of him shaking hands with government leaders. Everyone is smiling, crying, and hugging. No wonder the girl at Smartgear looked at him with such awe—Adam is a freaking saint.

"Once the drug became available to the public, Adam O'Neill's cure quickly decreased the rate of cancer deaths to two percent worldwide. It was hailed as a miracle, as a gift from God, and he became one of the youngest people to win a Nobel Prize for this groundbreaking discovery. And as head of the new pharmaceutical division of Aether Corporation, Dr. O'Neill later went on to develop other drugs and technologies to combat Alzheimer's and Parkinson's."

The video switches to some other scientist with a thick beard. "Adam O'Neill is without a doubt the most influential scientist of the last fifty years."

It cuts away to an older woman with white hair and paper-thin wrinkled skin. "Adam O'Neill saved my life. I had stage four cancer and only had months to live when his treatment became available." She dips her head for a moment and comes up with tears in her eyes. "And I've been cancer-free for eighteen years."

"Adam O'Neill is celebrated as a hero worldwide," the announcer says. "His discoveries have changed the face of modern medicine. But who is he really?"

The music darkens, and the screen switches to Adam staring off into space, his expression haunted. Another clip shows him rushing away from the press and into his car. "How much do we really know about this billionaire hero?"

A man in a suit speaks to the camera. "Adam O'Neill has never been married. He has no close friends or family. He's almost never seen in public. What is he hiding?"

"His experiments have grown…erratic," says a woman in a lab coat with an upturned nose. Underneath her name, it says she works for some company called Pharmateka, which I've never heard of. "There are rumors he's an alcoholic."

The video switches back to an image of an older Adam, sitting at a desk with his head in his hands. "With rumors of an alcohol problem and a dark secret in his past, the world is beginning to wonder if Adam O'Neill is an eccentric hero…or a mad scientist. It's all revealed on the next *Celebrity Profiles*."

The video vanishes, and for a second all I can do is blink as my focus returns to the room around me. "You…cured cancer?" I ask. "And won a Nobel Prize?"

Adam slowly nods. "It seems I did."

"Great," Trent mutters. "We're dead and this guy becomes a freaking billionaire."

Chris crosses his arms, glaring at Adam. "And he works for Aether Corporation in the future."

"Future-Adam is a hero," Zoe says. "I can't believe he'd have anything to do with our deaths."

Trent shrugs. "I don't know…They said he had a dark secret."

Zoe rolls her eyes. "Those shows always say that kind of stuff."

"He might be a hero then, but that doesn't mean he is now," Chris says.

"But if Future-Adams works for Aether, why wasn't anyone at the research facility?" Trent asks.

"Maybe…" Adam sucks in a breath. "Maybe we should talk to my future self."

"No way," says Trent. "I'm not causing a temporal paradox or whatever that was called."

Adam adjusts his glasses, his lips pressed into a thin line. "Aether said we'd suffer brain damage if we learned about our futures and that hasn't happened. Maybe the paradox thing was a lie too."

"I don't know," Chris says. "Looking into your future is one thing…actually meeting yourself is another."

I stay silent while they argue, trying to wrap my head around everything from the video. I have to agree with Zoe—it's hard to believe the guy who will cure cancer and save millions of lives could have anything to do with our deaths. But I'm still not sure I can trust him.

"Look, my future self has lived through all of this already," Adam says. "He might be able to tell us what happens after we get back to the present."

"And maybe he'll know how to change this future," Zoe adds, her voice hopeful for the first time in hours.

But if Future-Adam's lived through all this, then he'll know that I'm the killer. Would he tell the others about me? He left me the silver origami unicorn—was that a sign or something? Adam gave me the first one as a gesture of thanks or maybe a token of friendship. I have to hope that the second unicorn was placed there to send a similar message.

I finally speak up. "If you're wrong and the paradox thing is real, you could be stuck here in the future."

Adam meets my gaze with his piercing blue eyes. "I know."

Chris grabs his backpack. "Fine, we'll talk to Future-Adam. But I still don't trust you."

For a few minutes we discuss our next steps. We can't find Future-Adam's address, so the only option is to go to Aether Corporation's office building here in downtown LA and somehow track him down. It's risky if they are the ones who killed us, but we have no other choice.

We step outside the library and the rain's picked up again. I flick my hood over my head as we venture down the steps, taking care not to slip in a puddle and break my neck, since that's the last thing I need right now. Except I already know that won't happen, because that isn't my fate. I just hope we can find a cab or something, because this downpour will not be fun to walk in.

But when we get down the steps, there's a car waiting for us: a Mercedes that looks like it could have been from our time. It has a normal hood and trunk, plus all the side mirrors and brake lights, and its boxy shape stands out among the other egg-shaped cars driving past.

A man waits beside it, holding an umbrella with lights inside, illuminating him in a soft, blue glow. "Get in!" he yells.

He's speaking to us. He knows who we are. Is he from Aether Corporation? Have they finally sent someone to meet us?

But as we step closer, I recognize the familiar face, the knowing eyes behind the black glasses, the shape of his strong jawline and broad shoulders. The crinkle of his smile, only with a few more wrinkles at the edges. The dark-brown hair now peppered with gray.

The man standing there is Adam.

Future-Adam.

07:48

I glance back and forth between the two Adams, trying to make sense of what I'm seeing. Future-Adam must be in his late forties by now, but still looks so much like his younger self. And it's more than just how they look—it's the way they stand, their voices, the expressions on their faces. Even their flexis are the same, both clear and without decoration.

I shouldn't be surprised—*of course* Future-Adam would be here. He'd know exactly where we would be at any given moment because he'd lived it himself. But I don't know what his presence here means. Is he going to reveal my secret? Can he help us change the future?

"I heard you're looking for me." Future-Adam stares back at his younger self for a moment before sweeping his gaze across the rest of us. His eyes seem to linger on me, but maybe I'm imagining things. "Get in the car and I'll explain everything."

None of us move. Adam just stares at his older self, while Trent keeps muttering "dude" over and over.

"Well, you wanted to talk to him…" Chris says, glancing at Adam.

"I know." He adjusts his glasses, which I've noticed he does whenever he's nervous, and turns to me with questioning eyes.

For a minute I debate telling Adam and the others that we should turn around and leave. To forget Future-Adam and try to figure this out on our own. My motive for doing so is purely self-ish—I want to protect my secret, and Future-Adam could reveal it at any moment. But I need answers, and he might be the only one to give them to us. And maybe the others should learn the truth about who killed them. They deserve to know.

I'm just not sure what they'll do to me once they find out.

"You guys coming or what?" Future-Adam asks. "I know you want to get out of this rain. And don't worry about that whole paradox thing—that's obviously not true."

"It'll be fine," I say to Adam, trying to sound certain. "It's you, after all."

Adam nods, but he doesn't look convinced. We start walking toward the car, but Future-Adam holds up a hand to stop us. "Hang on," he says. "Take your flexis off and dump them in the trash over there."

"Huh?" Trent asks.

"Your flexis. The police can track you through them."

I peel the flexi off my face and feel a tiny jolt in my brain as it disconnects. Once the flexi is off, I'm free—no maps floating in my vision, no voices in my head, no videos recording everything I see and do. I chuck mine in the nearest trash bin and the others do the same.

"Damn," Chris says as he throws his flexi in last. "I'm gonna miss this thing."

Future-Adam thrusts something at Adam's chest. "Put this on."

Adam blinks at the baseball cap, but then shoves it over his head. With the rim pulled low, it's harder to see his face.

Future-Adam throws open the door to the backseat and gestures for us to get in. "It's a bit tight back there, so you'll have to squeeze in. Chris, you should probably sit up front with me."

Chris snorts, but it makes sense because he's by far the largest. The rest of us cram into the backseat, and somehow we end up with Zoe squished between me and Trent, and me on Adam's lap.

"Sorry," I say to him. I try to scoot over, but Zoe's in the way. I get that she doesn't want to snuggle against Trent, but I'm on top of Adam here.

"It's okay. Maybe I can move over." Adam tries to adjust in the seat, but that just pushes us closer together. His hand brushes against my thigh. "Sorry, sorry."

A wave of heat washes over me. I'm not sure if it's from the stuffy air in the car or from the way my body is pressed up against Adam's with only our wet clothes between us. We stare into each other's eyes, our faces only inches apart, and something passes between us—that same connection I felt with him earlier.

Future-Adam gets in the driver's seat and looks back at us with a grin, like he enjoys seeing us all squished inside. "Everyone in? Good."

"Where are we going?" Adam asks. That's the first time he's spoken directly to his future self.

"Aether Corporation headquarters." Future-Adam starts the car, and it pulls away from the curb. Unlike the other cars we've seen, this one has a dashboard and steering wheel and everything you'd expect in a normal car—although he doesn't seem to be using them.

"I got this car converted to driverless so I could use it on the road," Future-Adam says over his shoulder. "The government banned regular cars about five years ago. Now you can only actually *drive* cars on special tracks or in certain rural areas. But I had someone put in an override system because I miss driving. Check this out."

He presses a button on the center console and takes control of the steering wheel. The car speeds up and suddenly whips around a corner. I grip Adam's shoulder to keep from flying across the seat, and he puts an arm around my waist to steady me.

"Sorry." I avoid looking at him, but I don't let go. And he doesn't either.

"Man, they sure don't make cars like they used to," Future-Adam says with a laugh.

The car takes another sharp turn, tires squealing on the wet pavement. Adam holds me in place, his arm tightening around my waist. Is Future-Adam driving like a maniac just so his younger self can cop a feel on me? Then again, I'm not exactly pulling away from Adam either, so maybe I'm just as guilty.

"Sorry," I say again. I'm stuck on repeat, my brain fuzzy. Maybe because I'm burning up in this hot car. Or maybe because of the way Adam's looking at me, like he wants to kiss me. This time I don't want to punch him.

"All right, I'd better put it back in automatic before the police come after me." Future-Adam presses the button again. The car slows down and Adam releases his grip on me.

Zoe and Trent are staring at us, and I want to jump out of this car and forget this moment ever happened. I pull away from Adam and try to move off his lap to escape his eyes and his lips and the heat between us. Zoe attempts to scoot over, but she only gets an inch closer to Trent, who's already slammed up against the car door. There's nowhere for me to go.

"Comfortable back there?" Future-Adam asks. I glare at him. Oh yeah, he's definitely doing this on purpose. "Relax, we're already here."

The Aether Corporation building is impossibly tall, with black granite walls and sleek, silver windows reflecting the dark, cloudy sky. The car takes us down into an underground parking structure and parks itself in a spot labeled RESERVED: ADAM O'NEILL. The doors unlock and Future-Adam jumps out to open the door for us.

"Sorry about that," he says and offers a hand to help me out.

I ignore it and hop out of the car, giving him a look that says, "I know what you were doing there." But he just smiles and steps back so the others can get out.

Future-Adam leads us past rows of parked driverless cars to an elevator with the Aether logo. As we walk, he pulls something out of his pocket that looks like a thick metal pen, except there's a red light glowing at the end and buttons along the side. He presses one of the buttons, and the light switches from red to green.

"What's that?" Adam asks.

"It's a jammer. It blocks audio and visual recording devices within a twenty-foot radius." He hands the device to his younger self, who begins to study it.

"Why do we need that?" I ask. Isn't he working for Aether? Will they be expecting us?

"I don't want Aether's cameras recording us."

Adam examines the jammer and then hands it back. "It looks like a sonic screwdriver from *Doctor Who*."

"That's not an accident." Future-Adam grins at him. "A friend made it for me. Same person who designed the flexis."

"You were wrong," Trent mutters to Chris. "Adam is still the biggest nerd here."

"And now there are two of them," Chris says.

I shake my head as we step into the elevator. The two Adams stand side by side, the younger one sneaking peeks at his older self. It's freaky seeing them together and noticing how similar they look, except for the thirty years added to the future version.

"Why do you still wear glasses?" Adam asks his older self. "Flexis can auto-correct your vision, right?"

"A girl once told me I look cute in glasses. But you need to pay attention." Future-Adam checks his watch, and I'm surprised to see it's the same twenty-four-hour watch we all have on now. He kept it all these years.

The door opens, but he blocks us with his arm so we can't exit. "Get ready to run." He peers outside the elevator, then checks his watch again. "Wait...wait for it..."

People in suits enter in a huge group from the revolving doors and head to the front desk where a security guard is waiting. They crowd around, completely blocking our view of the desk.

"Now!" Future-Adam runs out and darts across the lobby toward a section of elevators labeled FLOORS 2–15.

I give Adam one quick glance and then we run after his older self, although I'm still not sure what the hell is going on. Our footsteps are drowned out by the chattering of the people in the lobby, who also hide us from the view of the security guard.

"Hurry up!" Future-Adam ushers us inside another elevator, his arms waving frantically. We crowd inside and the doors close. The elevator starts to rise and he turns to us with a grin. "That worked perfectly. Good thing I remembered how this all went down. I hope you're keeping track of all this," he says to his younger self.

"Um, yeah." Adam looks at me like *Is this guy for real?*

I shrug. I've given up trying to figure out what Future-Adam is doing. We put our faith in him once we got in that car, and all we can do is go along for the ride now.

"Okay, get ready to move," Future-Adam says. "Adam, keep your hat down."

The elevator opens on the sixth floor, and we quickly follow our leader down a row of offices with closed doors. Most of them have dark windows so you can't look inside. We only see two other people. They both have their heads bent low over their desks and don't seem to notice us as we pass by.

We stop at an office labeled with Adam's name, and the older version uses his thumbprint to unlock it. Once we're inside, he darkens the windows to opaque, and then his shoulders relax.

"Now we can talk safely." He rests the glowing jammer on his desk beside a Rubik's Cube that's already been solved and a silver spinning thing that floats an inch off his desk.

His office is huge, with a couple of sofas and expensive-looking leather chairs on one side of the room and a mini-fridge and bar on the other. The floor-to-ceiling window behind his desk has an impressive view of downtown and the Hollywood sign in the hills.

Chris crosses his arms. "Okay, what the hell is going on?"

"Yeah, what's with all the cloak-and-dagger stuff?" Trent asks.

"Hang on a sec." Future-Adam grabs a golf club from the corner and starts to poke at the ceiling vent above him, which bounces with each hit. "Stupid thing. I've asked them ten times to fix my air conditioner. I'd do it myself, but I'm too big to fit in the vents."

"Future you is kind of weird," Trent whispers to Adam.

Adam scowls. "Tell me about it."

Seriously, what is *with* this guy? Who cares about the stupid air conditioner? First he drives like a maniac, then he makes us run through Aether's building like criminals, and now this. Did he lose his mind in the last thirty years? Maybe that video was right about him...

"Enough messing around," I say to Future-Adam. "You told us you have answers."

"Right. Take your jackets off and relax, and then we'll talk."

He grabs each of our wet coats and hangs them on a rack in the corner, and then brings a bunch of sodas over to the table. I wish he'd get to the point already, but it is a relief to dry off a bit. We all dump our backpacks around the room and find a place to sit down. Adam picks one of the sofas, and I think about joining him but take one of the leather chairs instead.

Future-Adam sits in the other chair and watches us for a long moment. "I've been waiting for this day for the past thirty years. Now I don't know where to start."

"Start with who's gonna kill us," Chris says.

The older Adam sighs. "I don't know."

"You don't *know*?" Chris asks. "What about the girl who's going to shoot us?"

"I don't think she did it." Future-Adam's eyes flicker briefly to me. He knows. And he's trying to protect me.

"Me either," I say. I need to talk to him alone to find out what he knows and what he's hiding from the others.

Chris slams his empty soda can on the table. "Then who did?"

"I've always suspected Aether Corporation," Future-Adam says. "But I never found any evidence and the police closed the case quickly. They had their killer, and she was conveniently dead. They didn't want to look any further than that."

"No surprise there," Trent mumbles. "Like they'd care about four dead foster kids."

Future-Adam stands and walks to the window, resting his hands on the frame as he stares outside. "There's something we discovered—something you're going to discover—about what happened to the other people who went to the future. I believe Aether killed all of you to protect this secret."

"Wait—what other people?" Trent asks.

"I thought we were the first," Zoe says.

Future-Adam shakes his head. "That was a lie. Aether sent teams of scientists and other people to the future before our group. But they all came back...damaged."

I *knew* it. I knew there were others before us. "Damaged how?"

He turns back to us, his face grim. "Brain damaged."

08:25

My stomach twists. Maybe Aether wasn't lying to us about the possibility of brain damage from looking up our future selves. Could this be what the scientists were talking about when they were worried about something happening *again*?

My God, is this the reason I end up killing the others and myself?

"Hold up," Chris says, jumping to his feet. "Are we gonna be brain damaged too?"

"What does that even mean?" Zoe asks, her voice rising.

"No, we were all fine—at least while we were in the future," Future-Adam says. "And I was okay when we got back. I lied to Aether and said I didn't remember anything to protect all of us. I assume the rest of you did the same." He pauses, frowning. "Although I can't say for sure what happened to you. We were split up for questioning as soon as we returned to the present. After that, I never saw any of you again."

"You never saw us again?" I glance at the younger Adam and our eyes meet. The idea of never seeing him again bothers me more than it should.

"No," the older version says. "I heard two days later that you were all dead."

"So you don't know for sure if we were brain damaged or not?" Zoe asks.

Trent starts flicking his lighter on and off. "Maybe that's why Adam's the only one still alive now. They killed the rest of us off because we were damaged and he wasn't."

Chris glares back and forth between the two Adams. "Or maybe he's been working for Aether this entire time, and all of this is bullshit."

Adam throws up his hands. "I'm not working for them!"

"My younger self is telling the truth. I started working for Aether to find some explanation of why you were all killed. With Lynne's help, I made sure Project Chronos was shut down and buried forever. That's why the research facility was empty when you arrived. I couldn't risk anyone finding out about it."

"Do you know why we ended up thirty years in the future instead of ten?" I ask.

"I believe the accelerator malfunctioned. It's possible someone tampered with it, but I could never find any evidence of that, and I don't know why they would want to send us thirty years forward instead of ten."

My mind races, processing his words. Everything Future-Adam's told us makes a lot more sense than me killing the others and then myself. Aether must have set me up to protect their secrets. There's just one question that his story doesn't answer.

"Why did Aether let you live?" I ask.

"I've asked myself that question a thousand times over the past thirty years. I wish I had an answer for you."

His voice sounds sincere, but it's hard to believe he's telling the truth. How could he not know why he's still alive? He must have learned *something* in the last thirty years while working with

Aether. Or there must be something that set Adam apart from us, other than the foster care thing.

"So if you've lived through everything we've been through now..." Adam says. "What can we do differently?"

His future self gives him a sad smile. "We did have a plan to stop Aether and to protect ourselves, but it didn't go the way we wanted. Maybe all of you can succeed where we failed."

"What kind of plan?" Chris asks, his voice skeptical.

"Blackmail. We tried to get evidence about what Aether's been doing to make sure we had leverage against them when we got back to the present. But things went wrong, and the evidence was lost."

Trent and Chris exchange looks like they're not buying this. "But how do we get evidence?" Trent asks.

"Talk to Dr. Walters. He lives in a retirement home in the Valley." Future-Adam checks his watch. "We don't have much time, and I need to talk to my younger self alone for a moment." He opens the door and gestures toward it. "Adam?"

Adam stands up slowly. As he follows his older self into the hallway he looks like he's about to face a firing squad.

"I don't trust either of them," Chris says as the door shuts. "Do you believe any of this shit?"

Trent shoves two of the sodas in his backpack. "I don't know."

"I believe him," Zoe says.

"No surprise there." Chris turns to me. "Elena?"

I'm not sure how much to say before I talk to Future-Adam myself. His story feels right, and it matches up with what I heard Dr. Kapur and Dr. Walters say. I want to believe Future-Adam, but I still have so many questions and suspicions. I don't think we're getting the whole story.

"It could be the truth," I finally say.

The door opens and the two Adams walk back in. A short talk—I wonder what they said to each other. Adam stares at the floor, the baseball cap low so I can't see his face.

"Time's up," Future-Adam says. "You should head back to my house to change clothes and clean up before you meet Dr. Walters. You'll also need to get fake fingerprint IDs from this guy I know called Wombat. My car has all the addresses you'll need programmed into it."

"You're not coming?" Adam asks.

"No." He checks his watch again. "The police will be here any minute to arrest me."

"Arrest you?" I ask, while Trent blurts out, "What?"

"Come on." Future-Adam opens the door and slips into the hallway, disappearing before we can ask him what's going on.

We scramble to grab our coats and backpacks, then hurry after him. He's waiting at the end of the hallway in front of an unmarked, extra-thick metal door, which has both a fingerprint scanner and a keypad. But he doesn't open it.

Chris points a finger at Future-Adam, once we catch up to him. "Tell us what the hell is going on."

"The police connected my fingerprints to everything you've done," Future-Adam says, like he's explaining something obvious. He starts down the hallway again. "But it's okay because I need to be in custody when you break into this place later."

I nearly drop my backpack. "Break in? Why would we—"

"To get the evidence, of course."

"But…" Adam stares at his future self like he's crazy. "If you knew you'd be arrested, why let this happen? Why not just pick us up earlier at the building?"

"Because if I'm in police custody when you break in, then Aether won't suspect it was me. I'll just claim someone stole my identity."

He turns another corner and opens a door to a gray stairwell before we can ask him any more questions. "Take these stairs down to the parking garage and get my car. The police can't know you're here."

"But—" Adam starts.

Future-Adam presses the jammer into his younger self's hands. "Take this and make sure it's green when you don't want to be recorded. Now go!" He shoves Adam toward the stairs and nudges Zoe forward next. Chris and Trent follow, but just before I head in after them, Future-Adam grabs my arm. "Elena, wait."

He closes the door to the stairs, so we're alone in the hallway. "I'm sorry, Elena. I did everything I could to protect you."

He's thirty years older than me, but in his eyes I see the same Adam I know and feel that same connection between us. "Thanks for not telling them about…you know. But why are you helping me?"

"You know why. Or you will soon." He turns away, his face drawn. "It's painful to see you, knowing I failed to save you. The guilt, after all these years…it's still just as strong."

"It wasn't your fault. Aether did this. But we're going to change it this time."

"I don't think you can." His voice is rough, pained. "I'm sorry."

"What do you mean? You said we could get evidence—"

"I've had thirty years to go over those twenty-four hours in the future more times than I can count, to figure out what we did wrong, what we could have done differently…but all I've learned is that you can't change the future. I've tried, Elena. And I've failed."

"Then why bring us here?" I ask, stepping away from him, my temper flaring. "Why help us at all?"

"I had to do something. I just don't know…" His voice trails off. "There might be one more thing. But no—" He stops and shakes his head. "I already know you won't listen."

"I'm listening!" I practically yell at him. We have to be able to change the future. *We have to.* "What is it?"

"You need to trust me. Not me now, but...past me. Current me for you. Trust that Adam when the time comes. He's a good guy. Sort of an idiot sometimes, but he just wants to do the right thing. And...he likes you a lot."

Something flickers inside my chest. I don't know what to say to that. I had some idea that Adam liked me, although it's something else to hear his future self say it out loud. But I don't know if I can trust him. I want to, but I have so many questions, so many doubts. My instincts always tell me to trust no one but myself, but maybe this time they're wrong.

"What about the origami unicorn?" I ask. "Why'd you leave it for me?"

"Ah yes. I knew you'd find it. Open it when you're at my house, when you're alone and somewhere *safe.*"

The elevator dings and slides open around the corner. I hear heavy footsteps and someone says, "We're on the sixth floor."

"They're here. You need to go now." Future-Adam throws open the door to the stairs again. I rush through but glance back at Future-Adam one last time. I have a million more questions, but there's no time to ask them. "I hope you can prove me wrong. I hope..." He pauses, taking a long breath. "I hope you can change this future."

The door shuts with a loud thud, and I'm alone in the gray stairwell. I linger for a second, straining to hear something on the other side of the door, but there's only silence. Future-Adam should be okay—the police won't do anything to him. But if they catch me, I can't say the same for myself.

I run down the stairs, my shoes pounding on the metal. It's six flights back to the lobby level and another two down to the parking garage. The others are waiting there, their faces full of unasked questions.

"The police are here. Let's go." I keep my face blank and head for Future-Adam's car. I have nothing else to tell them.

The car opens with Adam's fingerprint, but Chris gets in the driver's seat. This time we have room to spread out, but I still end up next to Adam in the back. We both try to snap our seat belts in at the same time, and our hands brush against each other's. My eyes jump up to meet his. I can't help but wonder what Future-Adam told him.

Can I trust either of them?

09:11

The car knows where to go and needs no help from us to get to Future-Adam's house. We turn off Sunset Boulevard and pass under a sign that says BEL AIR. The car takes us up narrow roads and winding hills, driving past ornate fences and ivy-covered walls. Sometimes I get a glimpse of massive houses behind them, like the kind I've only seen in movies.

The car stops at a tall metal gate that opens automatically for us. Adam sucks in a breath as we pull into a circular driveway lined with grass so green it looks fake and perfectly trimmed topiaries of elephants, giraffes, and even a dragon. The car parks in front of a huge mansion with stately pillars and massive arches, and all I can do is stare. I knew Future-Adam is rich, but until now it never really sank in that he's *a billionaire*. This place could probably house ten families at least.

"Dude," Trent says as we get out of the car, "you're loaded."

"Yeah," Adam says, but he doesn't sound too excited about his future wealth.

I study his expression but try not to look too obvious about it. Ever since I learned he likes me, I don't know how to act around him, like I know a secret no one else does. He *shouldn't* like me. He seems like a good guy with a real future ahead of him, and I'm...I'm bad for him in every way.

It's stopped raining, but thick clouds darken the sky above us. The air smells of wet plants, and a cool breeze makes me pull my jacket around myself.

"We should go in." I need a moment alone, away from the others, so I can open the origami unicorn and find out what message Future-Adam left for me.

Adam doesn't move. Under the brim of his baseball cap, his eyes dart around, taking everything in. Beside him, Zoe has her sketchbook out and is drawing everything she sees.

"Let's go then," Chris says, nudging Adam toward the front porch.

The door has a bronze knocker in the shape of a lion, about the size of my head. Trent uses it to bang on the door, but there's no answer. "No one's home," he says. "Adam, you're up."

After a second of hesitation, Adam places his hand on a smooth, black panel on the door, like we saw at Shawnda's apartment. There's a click, and the door creaks open.

It's dark inside, but I glimpse hardwood floors covered in patterned rugs. None of us step forward. I definitely don't want to be the first one to go in. Not that I think anything bad will happen to us, but it just seems wrong to enter someone's house like this. Although I guess technically it's Adam's house—or will be someday.

Adam straightens up, visibly steeling himself, and then ventures inside. I follow, stepping on the thick rug, and wonder if I should take my shoes off or something. A light flicks on overhead, revealing an entryway with only a small wooden side table and an ornate mirror. It's warm now that we're inside and I want to take off my coat, but I don't know where to put it. Something about the house makes me feel like I should whisper and try not to touch anything, but I run my hand along the shiny, dust-free table anyway. Future-Adam probably has servants to keep the house clean, although it seems to be empty right now.

"This is your place, Adam," Chris says. "Give us a tour."

"Doesn't really seem like my kind of place," Adam mumbles as he walks farther into the house.

We step into the longest living room I've ever seen. I swear it must be big enough to fit the Robertsons' entire house inside. It's filled with what I assume is antique furniture, all lush fabric and scrolling wood, in colors like navy and burgundy and gold. Heavy curtains block out all natural light, and art that looks like it should be rotting away in a museum watches over us.

"This place is *sweet*," Chris says, flopping down on one of the love seats with little wooden feet.

He's right, but there's something sad about it too. Empty. Lonely. It looks staged, like it's all for show to prove how rich and important Future-Adam is. There are no photos anywhere. No trinkets. No clutter. No dogs running around or kids playing. It doesn't feel *lived* in.

"Dude, I'm starving," Trent says. "Where's the kitchen?"

I'm pretty hungry too, now that he's mentioned it. Our last meal was at lunch before we went to the future, but that was—I check my watch—over nine hours ago. And who knows when we'll have a chance to eat again before we return to our time.

"Didn't Aether pack us some food?" Zoe asks.

"Yeah," Chris says. "But I bet this place has something better than soggy old sandwiches."

We wander through wide hallways until we find the kitchen,

with its dark-green marble counters and shining stainless-steel appliances. The fridge looks wide enough to pack a couple bodies in. I can't imagine anyone needing *that* much food.

Chris jerks the fridge door open and a whoosh of cold air rushes out. We peer inside, but all I see are half-empty salad dressing bottles and a plastic container with something growing in it. Suddenly the idea of soggy sandwiches doesn't sound too bad.

Zoe wrinkles her nose. "I guess your future self orders in a lot…"

"Step aside. Let the master get to work," Trent says, brushing past me.

"The master?" Chris asks, crossing his arms. "You?"

Trent starts pulling things out of the back of the fridge and from inside the pantry. He checks each item and either tosses it on the counter or in the nearby trash bin. The rest of us just stare at him. I'm not sure if I'm more blown away by the fact that he's taking charge for once or that he seems to know what to do with all this food.

"What, like you've never seen a guy cook before?" Trent checks the drawers next and keeps poking around until he finds whatever he's looking for. Within a minute he's got the stove running and is throwing things in a skillet. "We're having breakfast, even though it's the middle of the afternoon. It's the best I can do."

"Hey, breakfast is always good," Adam says.

"True that." Trent points his spatula at him. "Just remember to go grocery shopping in thirty years."

"Uh…I'll try."

We ease ourselves onto bar stools perched in front of the center island and watch Trent do his thing. The skillet sizzles as he throws some bread and eggs onto it.

"Where'd you learn how to cook?" I ask as the delicious smell of frying food fills the air.

"My parents were junkies. They'd shoot up and sit around all day watching talk shows and forget they had a little kid to feed. Sometimes I'd sneak over to my neighbors' place and they'd cook for me. They were from El Salvador and made the best damn pupusas you've ever tasted. I learned a lot from them before the state took me away." His voice sounds casual, but his eyes are glued to the skillet as he talks. "After my last foster home went to hell, I took off. Been living on the streets ever since, shelter-hopping and grabbing food where I can. Cooking skills come in handy when you're on your own."

There's a long moment of uncomfortable silence, the kind that comes whenever someone ventures into TMI levels of sharing. I've heard of other kids who bailed on the foster system and went homeless. It's a tough life, but sometimes it's better than whatever they were dealing with in their foster homes. I've considered going out on my own plenty of times when things got really bad. I was just too chicken to actually do it.

"That's cool," I say, breaking the ice. Trent looks up at me with a grateful smile.

"Yeah, man," Chris says. "I wish I knew how to cook. And Adam *definitely* needs to learn."

We all laugh and the nervous energy in the room vanishes. Trent serves us French toast with maple syrup, along with some bacon he somehow managed to find. I don't know if any of it is fresh or not, but it all melts in my mouth and fills me with warmth. Turns out Trent's a pretty damn good chef.

We all sit around the island counter and eat while teasing Trent about his cooking skills and Adam about his future self's empty fridge. We don't bring up what Future-Adam told us or how we're all going to be killed tomorrow. We just stuff our faces and pretend we're five ordinary people hanging out together with our whole lives ahead of us.

But even though we laugh and smile, our fate hangs over us like a reaper's scythe. I can't forget it, no matter how hard I try. The clock never stops ticking—and I only have a few more hours to stop all of our murders.

09:40

We explore the house, going through bedroom after bedroom after bedroom. Seriously, how many guests does Future-Adam expect to have at once? There's also a library full of old books—which Trent and I both *ooh* and *aah* over—plus an exercise room, a giant office, and even a freaking movie room. We practically have to drag Chris out of this last one.

We find some extra clothes laid out in what I assume must be Future-Adam's bedroom. It's not the biggest one or the fanciest one, but it is the *messiest* one. It's the only room we've seen that actually looks lived in. The bed is unmade, clothes are piled on a chair in the corner, and there's a glass of water on the bedside table. Future-Adam is kind of a slob.

Adam walks around the room, studying everything like he's searching for clues to his own life. I can't even imagine what it must be like, standing in your future self's house, trying to piece together what happened to yourself in that thirty-year gap.

Zoe sifts through the clothes. "They look the same as what we're wearing. Bleh."

"Aw man, no smartclothes?" Chris asks. "I wanted to check them out."

"It makes sense," Adam says, pausing to examine a large mirror with a silver frame hanging on one wall. "If we went back to the present with different clothes, Aether might suspect something."

"I guess," Chris mutters as he grabs the largest shirt from the pile. He leaves the room to change, followed by Adam and Trent.

Zoe studies herself in the mirror, smoothing her damp blue hair, and sighs. "I could really use a shower."

I gesture to Future-Adam's bathroom. "There's a bathtub the size of a small pool in there—feel free."

She lets out a small laugh. "Maybe I will. What do you think of this place?"

"It's…impressive," I say as I pick out my clothes. "Except for this room anyway."

"This room's a bit messy, but Adam's still a catch."

My eyebrows shoot up. "You think so?"

"Oh yeah. If I wasn't already with someone, I would totally be into him." She picks up her new clothes, hugging them to her chest. "I'm bisexual, in case that wasn't obvious. And Adam's hot, smart, funny…and in the future he's a hero and superrich." She gives me a faint smile. "But Adam only has eyes for you anyway."

I don't know what to say. Maybe it isn't such a secret that he likes me. But that doesn't mean either of us has to act on it. We barely know each other. And we have far more important things to focus on—like staying alive.

Changing in Future-Adam's bedroom feels too personal, so we split up to find other rooms. It's my first chance to be alone and I head into a bathroom off the front entry of the house, far from the others. The bathroom has a counter you can sit at with special lights and a mirror (for putting on makeup?), plus two ivory-colored chairs in the corner and a separate room for the toilet. I can't imagine why anyone would need all this in their house. I half expect someone with a towel to pop out and ask for a tip.

I take a few minutes to change from my clothes into the dry ones Future-Adam left for us and clean myself up a bit. My hair is all stringy and has dried in a weird crunchy way, but without a brush, all I can do is run my fingers through it. I'm a mess, but at least I'm a dry mess now.

I sit at the counter on a fuzzy cushion with tassels and dig around in my backpack. The origami unicorn is a bit smashed from being stuffed inside, but the silver paper still glints in the light. I slowly unfold the paper, trying not to tear it as I unravel its intricate design. As it flattens out, I see numbers scrawled in black ink on the matte-white back: *73 21 12 37*.

Huh? I read the line again, trying to make sense of the four numbers. I thought there'd be some secret message inside, some words of wisdom, something to explain what is happening to us—but all I get are numbers? What kind of sick joke is this? I know that Adam is a genius, but these numbers don't mean anything to me.

I go over the message again. The numbers are mirrors, forming a palindrome. That must be a clue of some kind, but what? I rub my palms against my eyes. *Think.* Future-Adam wants me to understand whatever he's trying to tell me. He wouldn't make it too obscure or he'd know I would never figure it out.

I replay his words about the unicorn: *Open it when you're at my house, when you're alone and somewhere safe.* Somewhere *safe*—this could be a combination to a safe. But he didn't tell me where the safe is, and I don't have time to search this entire massive house.

No, Future-Adam would know that, so it can't be too hard to find. There's only one room that looks lived in, and that's his bedroom. He left our clothes in there too. The safe must be in there.

The hallway outside the bathroom is empty. I walk through the silent, hollow house, my footsteps echoing on the hardwood floor. I don't see any of the others, but they're probably still getting cleaned up.

I half expect Adam to be in his future bedroom, going through the dressers or something, but it's empty. I shut the door behind me and scan the room. Where do rich people hide their safes? I search around the place quickly but don't see anything that could hold a safe.

I sink down onto the bed, suddenly so tired I can barely move. It's been about ten hours since we got to the future. Even though it's only 4:41 p.m. here, to our internal clocks it's after midnight. I've never been out of California, but I bet this is what jet lag feels like. I'd love to just lie down and pass out until it's time to get back to the aperture. Let someone else figure out what's going on—I'm *exhausted*.

But there's no one else. I'm the only one who can stop these murders.

As I stand, I spot my reflection in the silver-edged mirror on the wall. That's it! The mirror. That's why the numbers were in that sequence. I rush over and peer behind the frame. There's definitely something back there.

I grab the mirror and yank it off the wall. A small metal box is embedded underneath with a keypad on it. My heart races as I enter the numbers and the safe pops open.

Inside is a thick folder. Nothing else.

I flip the folder open and find page after page of information on each of our murders. This must be everything Future-Adam collected on our deaths. Police and autopsy reports. Crime scene photos. News articles. It's all here.

I go through each page, soaking up everything like a sponge. Trent was killed first, with his time of death estimated between

3:00 p.m. and 4:30 p.m. His body was found in a dumpster, but he was killed in an abandoned building nearby where he'd been squatting. Zoe died next, between 4:30 p.m. and 6:00 p.m. in her girlfriend's apartment, just like her sister said. No signs of forced entry. Chris is the third victim, shot two blocks from the auto repair shop where he works, between 8:00 p.m. and 11:00 p.m.

I'm last in the folder. My body was found on the beach, partially submerged in salt water, which washed away both fingerprints on the gun and gunshot residue on my hands. I had some injuries, but they thought they were from fighting with the others. And one bullet to the head, from close proximity. My mother's watch cracked from the impact of the gunshot, freezing it at 11:38 p.m. That's how they knew my exact time of death.

Through blurry eyes, I force myself to look at photos of the crime scenes and of the bodies. The police reports say the gun that killed us was a Glock 9mm with the serial numbers filed off. A photo confirms it for me—it's the same gun as the one in my backpack. The police also have witnesses, fingerprints, and even strands of my hair, all tying me to the crime scenes.

The papers flutter to the floor. I slide down the wall and cover my face with my hands, trying to block out the horrible images that are now carved into my memory like into stone. All the bodies, bent at awkward angles, covered in blood. My own corpse, bloated and pale.

Any questions I had in my mind are gone. We're going to die tomorrow, and all evidence points to me as the murderer.

"Elena?" Zoe calls from the other side of the door. "Are you all right?"

"Yeah, fine." I should show the others everything in this file. They need to know about their own deaths, to know the facts about what is going to happen to us. They'll discover I'm the killer, but maybe they can figure out why I'd do this or how to stop me. And if they do something to me…well, at least I won't kill anyone tomorrow.

I start to collect the papers but pause when I see the unfolded origami unicorn on the floor, where I must have dropped it. Future-Adam told me to open it alone. He left this folder for me, and only me. Not the others. Not his younger self. *Me.*

He trusts me to be able to figure this out on my own. Or else he has a damn good reason for keeping the truth from the others. All I can do is hope that he's right.

I shove everything back inside the safe and slam it shut.

10:29

I wander around in a haze until I find myself on a wide lawn of grass trimmed with rosebushes and thick hedges. The sky has grown dark, and the sun dips into the ocean in the distance. We've run out of daylight.

There's an amazing view of Los Angeles from up here, all twinkling lights and cloudy skies. The city of the future doesn't look much different from the city I know. Downtown is wider and the buildings seem taller, but the residential areas all look the same, with a few pockets of high-rises scattered on the path to the coast. From Future-Adam's backyard I can see it all.

I sink to the ground and wrap my arms around my knees. The grass is wet on my butt and a cool wind brushes against my bare arms, but I welcome the chill. It keeps me focused. I've done enough moping around. Now I need to sort through all the data I've collected in my head if I'm going to get us out of this alive.

I hear footsteps on the brick behind me but don't turn around. I'm not in the mood for conversation. Maybe if I ignore whoever it is they'll go away.

No such luck. Adam sits next to me on the grass, facing the

view. I stiffen up, bracing myself for whatever he is going to say. I'm not ready to talk to him or to face the knowledge of how he feels about me. But for a few minutes, the only sound is the wind riffling through our hair.

"I don't want to become this person," he finally says.

"Why not?" Future-Adam didn't seem that bad to me. The others thought he was crazy, but I see now that everything he did had some meaning behind it. There was a method to his madness.

"I live in this house, but it's not a *home*. It isn't me." He rips grass out of the lawn and lets it fall between his fingers with a sigh. "I'm not married. I don't have any kids. I'm all alone…This isn't the life I want."

I open my mouth but struggle with what to say. He's rich in the future. Famous. Important. And he's good-looking even in his late forties, so I suspect he could be married if he wanted to be.

But I understand the desire for a real home. And learning you're going to spend the next thirty years alone can't be easy either. "You've done great things in the future. You cured cancer. You saved millions of lives. You won a Nobel Prize."

"But I don't even have a *dog*." His head drops, as if the thought of not having a dog in the future upsets him more than anything.

"A dog?"

"My dog, Max—I know he won't be around in thirty years, but I always assumed I'd get another one." He turns to look at me with tortured, blue eyes. "Why don't I have a dog?"

"I don't know. Maybe you work long hours now or travel a lot or…"

"And I failed," he continues, like he hasn't heard a word I've said. "I watched all of you die and was unable to stop it or find out who did it. In the future, I have to live with that. Every. Single. Day." He shakes his head. "No wonder I'm alone."

I should do something or say something, but I can't find the right words. I've never been good at comforting other people when they're upset. He's talking about his future self like he's already become that person, but he's not. He doesn't have to be. But I don't know how to tell him that and make him believe me. Instead I place my hand over his on the grass.

His gaze drops to my hand. "I'm sorry. I probably sound like a jerk whining about my problems when you're…" His voice trails off.

"You just saw your own future. That can't be easy."

"I probably shouldn't ask this, but what did he say to you? When you were alone?"

"He…" I'm not sure how much to tell him. Most of what Future-Adam said isn't for this Adam's ears, but I want to say something. I want to be honest. Finally I spit out, "He told me to trust you."

Adam's eyebrows dart up. "Yeah?"

I focus on an airplane flying overhead to avoid his gaze. "What did he say to you?"

"He told me to be careful. And…to not get too attached to you." Adam shifts his hand to grasp mine, his pale fingers tangling with my darker ones. "I don't care what he said. We're going to change this future. I'm not going to let you die."

Our eyes lock and my breath fails me. So much pain in those eyes, but so much determination too. He truly believes he can save me, and in that moment, I believe it too. My gaze flickers to his lips, and I want nothing more than to press mine against them, to forget everything except this moment. I lean into him, my face lifting to meet his. His breath flickers over my skin, and I part my lips—

"Adam? Elena?" Chris calls. "You out here?"

We jerk apart, the moment over. The outside world rushes in again. Cold grass on my butt. City lights stretched out in front of me. One day left to live. And Chris behind us on the patio, calling our names.

Adam rises to his feet. "Yeah?"

Chris eyes the two of us like he knows something is going on. "We've sat around long enough. Let's get out of here."

"Just give us a minute," Adam says.

He holds out a hand and helps me to my feet. My skin tingles as my fingers grab on to his, but as soon as I'm up, I pull away and wipe grass off myself. I avoid his eyes—I can't get sucked back into them again. It was good Chris stopped us before we kissed. There's no point getting close to Adam if I won't see him again once we get back to the present. He's better off without me. With my impending killing spree and suicide looming over me, I don't have time to get involved with Adam anyway.

Chris is right. We need to get going. Time is running out.

11:14

After some debate, we decide to get fake IDs first, like Future-Adam suggested. That way we can buy things without having to rely on Adam's fingerprints, which might send the police after us again. This time I sit in the front of the car with Chris, after practically shoving Trent out of the way. I can't sit next to Adam again. I can't even look at him. Not after our near-kiss.

Chris enters the name Future-Adam gave us—Wombat—into the car's navigation system, and we take off. The car heads north over the hill into the Valley, and the homes of the rich and famous soon give way to busy shopping areas and rows of nearly identical homes, and then to seedier parts of town.

It's dark by the time the car stops outside a rundown house with peeling paint and a broken window. A rusted old trailer with no wheels sits smack-dab in the middle of the front lawn, with weeds growing over the front bumper.

"Future-Adam knows someone who lives here?" Zoe asks. Her sketchbook is out, but she doesn't bother to draw this place in it.

Chris checks the car's navigation. "It's the right address."

"What kind of name is 'Wombat' anyway?" Trent asks.

Adam tugs his baseball cap on. "Maybe it's a code name like 'Wolverine.'"

I get out of the car and scan the road for cops. I don't really expect them to show up, but it can't hurt to be careful. Now that we're out of the safety and comfort of Future-Adam's house I'm back on alert.

My gaze flicks to Adam for a second. Yeah, I definitely got *way* too relaxed at that house.

Chris knocks on the front door and the rest of us crowd behind him. A large woman in a floral dress opens the door and grunts. No words, just a grunt.

"We're looking for Wombat." Chris says. "He here?"

"Around the back." She slams the door in his face.

Chris raises his hand like he's about to pound on the door again, but then drops it. "Nice. Real nice, lady."

"I feel better about this place already," I mutter.

We kick through weeds and past mounds of trash piled along the side of the house, almost to the roof. The woman must be a hoarder or something. Everything reeks of garbage and cat piss. Or at least I hope it's cat piss.

Music blasts from an open garage door, like heavy metal but with a pop vibe to it. Inside, tables and desks that look like they were scavenged from different garage sales fill every open space. Each one is stacked high with electronic equipment and pieces of hardware I couldn't even begin to guess at. Some of it looks futuristic; some looks like it's from our time or even earlier.

A guy around our age with an unshaved face glances up from a toolbox, and the music switches off. He wears a blue T-shirt with the Superman logo, and his flexi has a green-and-yellow pattern that looks like a circuit board. He wipes his hands on his jeans and steps around his desk. "Looking for someone?"

"You Wombat?" Chris asks.

"That's me."

"Adam O'Neill sent us. He said you can get us some fake IDs."

"Hmm." Wombat checks us out, but when he sees Zoe his eyes widen. "Yeah, I might be able to help you out."

Zoe shoots me a "What's happening?" look and I shrug. He probably thinks she's cute or something. Seems funny, since this guy probably isn't even alive yet back in the present.

"I can do it, but five IDs…That won't be cheap."

"We got cash," Chris says.

"Cash? Seriously?" The guy laughs. "How long you been hanging on to *that*?"

"About thirty years."

"Thirty years?" Wombat keeps laughing, doubling over like this is the funniest thing he's heard all day.

I should have known cash wouldn't work here after the salespeople at Smartgear turned it down. We might have to use Future-Adam's account one last time, but then the police might be able to trace us here.

Trent lights up a cigarette. "Whatever, will you take it or not?"

Wombat stops laughing and stares at Trent. "Whoa, is that a cigarette?"

Trent flicks his lighter back and forth. "Yeah, why?"

"Do you have more?"

Trent arches an eyebrow and brings the cigarette slowly to his mouth. "I might."

"Whoa, okay, wow. Cigarettes." Wombat rubs his scruffy dark beard. "I'll do the IDs for a pack."

Saved by Trent's nasty habit. Who knew cigarettes would be

worth more in thirty years than thousands of dollars in cash?

Trent pulls a new pack out of his backpack and tosses it to the guy. "Done."

"Sweet. Step into my office and I'll sort you out."

We move into the garage, although there's barely enough room for all of us to stand in it. Tools and equipment are scattered across the tables between plates with crumbs and pizza crusts. A movie plays on the wall with Batman rappelling down a wall, but I don't recognize the scene. Another remake?

Wombat pulls out a chair for Zoe and gestures for her to sit down but doesn't give the rest of us the same courtesy. He grins the entire time, making puppy-dog eyes at her. The boy's got it bad, and she has no idea.

"We need some money on our IDs too," I say.

Wombat holds up a hand. "Hey now, no one said anything about making fake accounts too. That's a whole 'nother deal." He glances at Trent. "Unless you have another pack…"

"Nope, that was it," Trent says.

Looks like cigarettes can only get us so far. And he won't take our money…but I might have an idea.

"We only need one account," Chris says. "We can share it."

"And it only has to last until tomorrow," Trent adds.

They argue with Wombat, while I slide up beside Zoe. She's sketching everything in the garage with meticulous detail, the scene practically popping off the page.

I lean close enough to whisper, "He likes you. Go see if you can get him to help us."

"What?" Zoe clutches her sketchbook to her chest. "He's kind of cute, but I have a girlfriend."

"He doesn't need to know that." I nudge her with my elbow.

"And you'll never see him again after this anyway."

She nods slowly, then pats down her short blue hair. "Wombat?"

"Yeah?" He practically leaps over to her. I move aside to give them some space and watch as she shows him her sketchbook.

"What's going on?" Adam asks me. His cap is pulled low over his face, but I can see his frown.

"Just wait." *C'mon Zoe*, I think. *You can do this.*

Wombat's head is bent low near hers, and she places a hand on his arm. The guy's face turns the shade of a lobster. He probably hasn't been touched much by a girl. Or ever. She whispers something in his ear, and he laughs. Zoe is better at this than I expected.

After a minute, he straightens up and clears his throat. He turns to the rest of us with a little lovesick smile on his face. "Okay, I'll set up the account for you. Just leave the cash here. I'll find someone who can do something with it."

Score one for Zoe. She winks at me, and there's a confidence in her eyes I haven't seen before.

Wombat weaves through the maze to get to a table in the corner. He leans over it and pokes at a smooth, black screen. "See this scanner here? I need you to each put your hand on it, one at a time."

I'm the closest, so I step up and put my hand on the screen. It makes a little beep and lights up as it scans my palm.

"All right, hang on." He touches something on the screen and then stares off into space. After a moment I realize he must be doing something on his flexi. It's creepy because he looks like he's concentrating, but it's impossible to tell what he's really doing. I hope we can trust this guy. For all we know, he could be scamming us. We don't have any proof he can actually supply us with real fake IDs. We just have Future-Adam's word to go on.

Wombat turns to something that looks like a computer printer, and a second later a thin, clear sheet of plastic slides out.

"Here you go," he says, handing it to me. There's a barely visible cutout of a thumbprint for each finger. "Put these on. They should have your new identity all set up. And whatever you do, don't lose them."

While he scans Zoe's hand, I peel off the prints, which are vaguely sticky, and put them on each fingertip. They seem to be made of the same material as the flexis and sink into my skin, almost undetectable.

He repeats the process, making IDs for the rest of the team, and then creates our fake bank account. The whole thing takes way too long, and I pace back and forth outside the garage, checking my watch every two minutes. Our time in the future is dwindling, and we still don't have any answers.

"How much longer?" I ask.

Wombat grins at me. "Hey, you can't rush genius."

I roll my eyes and turn away, practically running right into Adam. There's an awkward pause as he opens his mouth like he wants to say something, and I dodge his gaze, hoping to avoid any conversation.

"You okay?" he asks.

"Yeah," I push my hair out of my face, needing to do something with my hands. "Just ready to get going."

He continues to watch me, confusion written all over his face. But I'm saved from any more discussion when the others finally emerge from the garage. We thank Wombat for his help, and Zoe gives him a quick hug.

As we walk back to the car, I ask her, "What did you say to him?"

"I invited him to dinner tomorrow," she says and then sighs.

"He's a nice guy. I feel bad I lied to him."

"You did the right thing. We had to get those IDs." But I feel a little guilty about it too.

When we came to the future and started looking into our pasts, I had no idea our actions would affect the people living now. We were supposed to be ghosts of time, flitting in and out of the future without leaving a trace. Now the police are after us and Wombat's waiting for a date that will never happen. What other echoes will we leave behind in the future?

12:02

Dr. Walters's retirement home looks more like a five-star hotel than a place for old people to live out the rest of their days. Automatic doors slide open to marble floors, potted plants, and chandeliers. A nurse pushes an older woman past a sign that points to different rooms: cafeteria, library, game room, media room, exercise room, and medical center. Basically, everything you'd need so you never have to leave the building again.

I head to the front desk, anxious to talk to Dr. Walters and get some answers. The others crowd behind me, and a man with curly red hair smiles from behind the counter.

"Hi, we're here to see Dr.—I mean, uh, Bob Walters," I say. I wonder if his name is actually Robert and if I should have said that instead.

But the guy just nods. "Are you on the list?"

"The list?" I shoot a look at the others. Future-Adam didn't say anything about a list.

"The list of approved visitors." The guy's smile drops, and he taps the edge of a fingerprint scanner. "I'll need you to sign in here."

So much for our fake IDs. "Um, one sec," I say. The five of us retreat to the corner to talk.

"What do we do?" Zoe whispers.

Adam removes his baseball cap and runs a hand through his hair. "I'll have to scan in."

"No way," I say. "The police will be able to trace us here."

"What other choice do we have?"

"How do we know you're even on the list?" Trent asks.

"My older self told us to come here," Adam says. "He wouldn't have sent us if we couldn't get in. And I can use the device he gave us to knock out the security cameras."

Trent eyes the guy at the front desk, then checks out the doors. "I don't know. Maybe we can sneak in somehow."

Chris shakes his head. "Too risky."

I weigh all our options but don't see any other way in. And our trail ends here. Future-Adam gave us no other clues or leads after this. We have to find out what Dr. Walters knows. But I can't shake the feeling this is a really bad idea. "No, Adam's right. He's the only one who can get us in."

"What about the police?" Chris asks.

"We'll have to be fast."

Chris swears under his breath, but the others agree this is the only way in. Adam flips on the jammer and hides it in his pocket.

The guy at the front desk eyes us suspiciously as we return.

"I'm on the list," Adam says and places his palm on the scanner.

I check my watch, debating how many minutes it will take the police to get here. Ten? Fifteen? Can we get the information we need and get out in time?

The guy's head jerks up. "Oh, Mr. O'Neill! I'm so sorry. I didn't recognize you with the baseball cap on. I *just* watched your episode of *Celebrity Profiles*."

"Uh, great," Adam says. "These people are with me too."

"No problem. Go on up."

"Thanks. Um…remind me. Which room is he in?"

"Three-oh-four."

We rush into the elevator and breathe a collective sigh of relief, even though the elevator reeks of bad perfume. We find room 304 and Adam knocks. A nurse with fluffy, brown hair and blue scrubs opens the door. She peers out at us but doesn't seem to recognize Adam. Maybe she's new or not the regular nurse. "Yes?"

"Hi, we're here to talk to…Bob," Adam says.

She nods and lets us in, leading us past a living room with floral furniture and into a small bedroom. Dr. Walters lies in a hospital bed, his eyes closed. He's a frail version of his former self. His gray hair is now all white and wispy, and his wrinkled skin is paper-thin.

The nurse walks over to him and bends down close to his ear. "Bob," she says, and he blinks and looks up at her. "These kids want to talk to you. Is that okay?"

His face changes when he spots us. His eyes widen, his lips part, and his hands clutch the sheets at his waist. "You…you…"

I tense up—he must know I'm the murderer—but then I realize he's not looking at me but at all of us. Still, he probably blames me for their deaths. I have to make sure he doesn't say anything to the others about it.

"Do you want me to send them away?" the nurse asks, touching his arm.

"No." He tries to sit up. "Leave us."

The nurse props a pillow behind him. "Are you sure?"

"Go!"

She huffs and adjusts his pillow again but leaves the room with one last warning look to us. The door shuts behind her, and we all crowd around his bed. He can barely move, but seeing him like this is a painful reminder that I'll never grow old myself.

"What are you doing here?" he asks, his eyes focusing on each of us in turn. His voice is raspier now, much weaker than I remember. "This isn't the right year…"

I exchange a glance with Adam. Dr. Walters doesn't know. Maybe the accelerator *did* malfunction.

"So you remember?" Chris asks. "You know what happened to us?"

"Project Chronos. Wish I could forget."

"We were sent forward thirty years instead of ten," Adam explains.

Dr. Walters closes his eyes for a brief moment. "No wonder… I waited for you at that building twenty years ago, but you never appeared."

Adam moves closer to Dr. Walters. "The older me, the one from this time, said we should ask you about the people who went to the future before us."

Dr. Walters starts coughing, big, racking coughs that shake his entire body. He grabs a tissue and holds it to his mouth, his eyes watering. Poor guy. I briefly debate if we should get the nurse again, but he told her to leave and we don't have time to mess around.

He holds up a hand, asking us to wait, and his coughing finally settles down. "We never should have done it. All those people… and what happened to you…"

"What happened to the others?" I ask him, stepping closer to the bed.

"I guess there's no point keeping it from you now." He stares at the crumpled tissue in his wrinkled hands. "They all came back broken. Paranoia, memory loss, madness…future shock, we called it."

"Future shock?" Adam asks.

"Yes, shock from the time dilation. It proved too be too much for the human brain to handle." He shakes his head, his eyes lost in his memories. "We made changes. We warned them not to look into their own fates, which we thought might make it worse. We reduced the hours spent in the future. We sent people only ten years forward instead of thirty. The damage was lessened each time, but not enough. Dr. Kapur thought if we used teenagers, whose brains were still developing, they might be able to withstand it better."

Everything clicks into place. The conversation they had in the hallway. The reason they sent foster kids to the future instead of scientists. We were disposable.

"Did we..." I stop to take a breath, afraid to ask the question. "Did we come back broken too?"

Dr. Walters stares up at me with pale eyes. "I'm sorry."

"What does that mean, old man?" Chris asks. "Are we going to go crazy?"

"It was all my fault," the old man mutters, his eyes unfocused. "I built the accelerator...I never should have listened to Kapur."

Chris grabs on to the edge of the hospital bed. "Answer the question!"

"Yes. You were all suffering from future shock. You had no memories of your time in the future."

My heart falls to the ground and shatters. If we won't remember anything that happens in these twenty-four hours, how will I be able to save us?

Does this explain why I kill the others and then myself? Maybe Aether tricks me somehow, or I'm confused after we get back...

"How can we stop from being brain damaged?" Trent asks.

Dr. Walters shakes his head. "I don't know. I'm sorry."

"How could you do this to us?" Chris yells. "You knew this would happen, and you sent us to the future anyway?"

"We thought we were gods, trying to control time." He lets out a bitter laugh. "So arrogant. So stupid. After your mission failed, Kapur wanted to try again with younger kids. But I couldn't let him do that. I destroyed the accelerator."

"You destroyed it?" Adam asks.

"I had to. I couldn't let them hurt anyone else." He starts coughing again, his back bouncing off the pillow. When his cough settles down, he continues. "Aether couldn't build it again without me. They threatened me, but I didn't care. I was done trying to be a god."

Zoe kneels beside the bed, almost like she's begging. Or praying. "Dr. Walters, please. We need to know how to stop this. What about Dr. Kapur? Where is he?"

Dr. Walters scrunches up the sheets in his hands. "That bastard. After I quit, Aether put him on another project. Something involving memory. I didn't want to know. But karma found him, and he died in a car accident not long after."

"What about Lynne?" Trent asks. "Future-Adam said she helped him bury the project."

"She might be able to help you, although I haven't seen her in years. Adam is the only one who visits me." His gaze rests on Adam and he smiles sadly. "Such a nice boy."

"This is bullshit." Chris paces back and forth, smoke practically steaming out of his ears. "We're going crazy and we're all gonna die and there's nothing we can do? No, screw that."

"I don't feel like I'm going crazy..." Trent says.

"But would you know?" Zoe asks.

Trent shrugs. "I don't think I'm forgetting anything. And hey, what about Adam? His future self said he lied to Aether about having future shock. And he seemed to remember everything, like when we'd be at the library."

"True, and he cured cancer and all that," Zoe adds. "He can't be *too* brain damaged."

Chris steps toward Adam, his hands in fists. "Yeah, why aren't *you* going to suffer future shock like the rest of us?"

I stand up straighter, wanting to defend Adam again, even though all their words make sense. Throughout all of this, Adam has always been the odd one out. The only one not in foster care. The only one not disposable. The only one alive in the future. And now the only one who isn't going to lose his mind.

"Is it possible we were all just faking it?" I ask.

"I suppose it's possible, but…" Dr. Walters doesn't sound hopeful.

"It can't be a coincidence that the four of us who suffer future shock end up dead," Chris says. "Adam has to be involved somehow. He must have lied to us about what really happened."

"Why would he do that?" Trent asks.

"If he's working for them—"

"Guys, I'm standing right here," Adam says.

As they argue, I rub my palms against my eyes and try to think. As much as I sometimes hate my perfect memory, I can't imagine not remembering these hours of my life. I catch Adam watching me and realize that if Dr. Walters is right, I won't remember Adam either. Probably for the best, really.

"I'm sorry I can't help you more," Dr. Walters says. "You seem like good kids. Very sad how it all turned out."

Trent pulls back a curtain and peers out the window. "We should go. The police could be here any second."

"Yeah," Adam says. "Lynne's address is probably in the car. Maybe she can help us."

"Wait." I know we need to hurry, but there's one last thing I have to ask Dr. Walters. "Can the future be changed? Or is everything we've seen going to happen?"

"Somehow I'm not surprised *you* asked me this," he says. I hold my breath, fearing he'll blow my cover, but he relaxes back on his pillow and continues. "That's one thing I hoped to study with the accelerator, but I was never able to prove anything one way or another." His voice grows stronger as he slips back into the scientist role.

"One theory says everything is predetermined, which means everything you do once you return to the present will lead up to this future. Even if you *think* you're changing something, you won't be. But another theory says if you change something when you get back, the moment will split off and create an alternate timeline with a new future."

"So if we go back and change something in the present, this future might be different?" I can't even think about the other possibility—that nothing we do matters.

"Maybe. This future might still exist, but you would be living in another parallel timeline, based on the changes you made. Or maybe the future you went to, including this moment right now, would vanish entirely. It's impossible to know."

Everything we've heard from Future-Adam suggests that we're living in a predetermined loop where it's impossible to change the future. Otherwise, how would he know so much about what we're going to do? But maybe we're only visiting the timeline he's lived through, the one in which we all die. If we go back now and change something in the present, maybe our future will be different.

I know the chance is slim, but if I don't hold on to this one shred of hope, I might as well give up right now. We *have* to be able to change our fate.

We say good-bye to Dr. Walters. There's so much more I want to ask him—like if he knows why I killed the others or if he thinks

Aether murdered us—but there's no time. We rush back to the lobby, and as the automatic doors slide open, I see it's pitch-black outside and raining again. Of course. If I was smart, I would have grabbed an umbrella at Future-Adam's house, but it never rains this much in LA.

As we step into the downpour, a police car pulls up to the curb, lights flashing. A voice booms, "*Freeze!*"

12:27

For a heartbeat all I can do is stare at the car, but then my reflexes kick in and I start running. We took too long with Dr. Walters. I should have been checking my watch more and not asked so many questions. I should have made sure we got out sooner.

The car isn't far, parked in a lot next to the retirement home. But the police are already on foot, chasing after us. "Freeze!" they yell again.

We make it around the building, but then I hear Trent cry out behind me. I'm tempted to keep running, to leave him behind, but I turn around. One of the cops has hit him with a baton and brought him to his knees. While the second cop approaches, the first one smashes Trent with the baton again. He flattens against the wet cement, eyes bulging. He's frozen stiff, unable to move. The baton must be electrified or something.

Cop number two pulls out a thin pair of handcuffs. Which means we've lost Trent—maybe forever if he can't get back to the aperture in time. Unless we do something.

"Go!" I yell at the others. I leap on the first cop, surprising him, and rip the baton from his hand. I slam it into his helmet as hard as

I can and shove him against the wall. He bounces off and then hits the ground, his armor smacking against the sidewalk.

He won't be down for more than an instant, and the second cop is already reaching for his gun. They're wearing full body armor, so I'm not sure where to hit them. I know this is probably a losing battle anyway. But it feels good to fight. It reminds me I'm still alive. I grip the baton tighter in my hand.

From the ground, Trent kicks at the second cop's leg, distracting him. I spring forward, bringing the baton down on a spot between the cop's shoulder and his arm, where the armor looks weaker, probably to allow for movement. He instantly jerks and falls to the ground.

The other cop is back on his feet and smashes into me before I can react. He slams me into the wall, pinning me with his heavy armor. My forehead bangs against the concrete, hard, and for a moment everything goes dark. Pain screams along my temple and into my skull.

Instinct starts to take over. I have to fight. I have to get away, no matter what the cost. I won't be a victim ever again.

The cop grabs me, yanking my arms back. His big, gloved hands bite deep into my skin.

Big mistake.

Fear and anger, my oldest friends, explode inside me. A red haze clouds my eyes as I fight back against the cop. I yank my arms free and spin around. I kick. I punch. I bring the baton down, again and again and again.

"Elena, stop!" Arms wrap around my waist and pull me back. I struggle, ready to kill whoever is touching me now. But this touch doesn't make me flinch. The familiar voice shouts my name again and breaks through my fury.

Adam.

I blink and my vision clears. Sweat and rain cling to my face and hair. Both cops are on the ground. Neither one move.

Oh my God, what have I done? I've *killed* them.

No, they're both alive. I can see one breathing, and the other groans softly. I pray their armor has protected them from most of the damage.

Adam helps Trent to his feet, while the car pulls up beside us with Chris and Zoe in front. "Get in!" Zoe says.

We pile into the backseat. I pull my knees in close, cold and wet and horrified at what I've done. My arms tremble from the adrenaline still pulsing through me, and my hand hurts from gripping the baton so hard.

"Holy shit, Elena," Chris says as we drive away.

"Just drive!" I hate that the others saw me like that. And more than that, I hate myself for hurting those cops. I only meant to get them off Trent so we could escape. But I lost control, my rage taking over, turning me into something I loathe. And Adam saw me do it.

I haven't hurt anyone like that in years. I don't want to be that person anymore. But what if Adam hadn't stopped me? Would I have killed those cops? I saw the evidence at Future-Adam's house, but a part of me still couldn't believe I'd actually commit murder tomorrow.

Now I believe it.

I've tried to bury this part of myself for my entire life, but it's in my DNA. This is who I am. A killer.

"You're bleeding," Adam says, reaching for my face.

"I'm fine," I say, jerking away from his hand. My forehead might be bleeding, but I don't feel any pain. I'm numb, inside and out.

I turn toward the window. I can't stand the sight of him looking at me like I'm something dangerous and unpredictable. Like I might snap at any moment and hurt one of them too. But maybe it's good Adam saw the real me. Future-Adam told him to not get too attached to me, to be careful. Now he knows why.

"Elena—" he starts.

A siren blares behind us. I twist in my seat and spot the police car right behind us, lights flashing in the darkness. And even though they're right on our tail and we're pretty much screwed, I breathe a tiny sigh of relief that they're okay. I'm not a killer—not today anyway.

"This is bad," Trent says.

Lights flash on the dashboard and a robotic voice sounds from inside the car. "Police override. Your vehicle will pull over to the side. Please remain seated."

"Make that *really* bad," Trent adds.

We start to slow and veer to the right. Chris grabs the steering wheel. "What? No, don't pull over!"

The car crawls to a stop. I tug on the door, but it's locked. Even the windows won't roll down. We're trapped here. But we can't get arrested, not now, not with only a few hours left in the future. We still need to find Lynne, and if Future-Adam's right, break into Aether Corp—all with enough time to make it back to the aperture.

"What's going on?" Adam asks, leaning forward to peer at the dashboard.

"The police must have control of the car or something," Chris says. "Wait, let me try..." He presses the button Future-Adam showed us that switches to manual driving, and the car takes off again. Yet another thing Future-Adam planned for.

"There we go!" Chris yanks the steering wheel to the side and we dart into another lane. He makes a quick right, the car's tires squealing in the rain, and we speed down a smaller street. But the siren stays behind us.

With the others helping to direct him, Chris weaves us through traffic at a dangerous speed, turning down random streets. Next to him, Zoe rocks back and forth, clutching her bag. I stare out the back window, giving updates on how close the cops are. But after a couple more twists and turns, their lights vanish in the haze.

"We lost them," I call over my shoulder.

"Yes!" Chris says, pounding on the steering wheel.

The others cheer, and I relax back into my seat. "Now we can head to Lynne's and—"A siren cuts me off with a flash of red and blue.

Adam leans forward to examine the dashboard. "The car must have a tracker or something. We'll never get away from them."

"You're probably right," Chris says. "I think I can disable it, but someone else will have to drive."

"I can drive," Adam says.

"No, I might need your help. Anyone else?"

Trent and Zoe mutter that they don't know how. The sirens get louder as the police car creeps up our ass.

"I'll do it." I got my license a couple months ago, although I'm definitely not experienced enough for a car chase with the police. But there's no one else who can do it.

"Okay," Chris says. "I have to put the car back on automatic so we can switch seats, so let's make it quick."

He hits the button and the car slows down again, dashboard lights flashing. Zoe climbs in back first, squeezing between us, and then Chris takes her spot in the passenger seat. I jump into the driver's seat, grab the steering wheel with shaking hands, and hit the manual button.

"Go, go, go!" Trent yells from the back.

I slam my foot on the gas and we zoom forward, tires squealing on the wet road. Chris pulls a mini toolbox out of his backpack. He uses a screwdriver to open the screen on the dashboard, revealing the wires behind it. Adam leans forward from the middle of the backseat, and the two of them quietly discuss the inner workings of the car's computer.

I want to watch what they're doing, but I'm too busy trying to keep us on the road. Rain pounds against the windshield, and I have to squint to see anything ahead of us. Sirens blare behind us. I grip the steering wheel so hard my knuckles turn white. I don't bother trying to lose the cops. With the tracker on, there's no point. I just try to keep ahead of them, barreling down the street and darting around other cars.

"I think I found it," Chris says. "Adam?"

"Yeah, that must be it. But if you cut that, it'll kill the navigation too."

"Just do it!" I yell. The cops are gaining on us, and I don't know how much longer I can stay ahead of them.

"Give me one minute…" Chris says, using pliers from his backpack to pluck at the wires.

Adam points to something in the panel. "Watch out for the—"

"I know, I know!" Chris leans close, and a second later every screen and light on the dashboard dies. "There! Done!"

"Great…now how do I lose them?" I ask.

"Make lots of quick turns," Chris says. "Once we lose sight of them, we can turn off the headlights and hide somewhere."

I take a sharp left, and we're all thrown to the side of the car. But the cops stick right behind us the entire time. I have no idea where I'm going or what I'm doing. I'm running on fear alone right now, my limbs so jumpy I can barely hang on to the steering wheel.

"You're doing great." Adam puts a hand on my shoulder. "Just focus."

Something about his touch, or maybe his confidence in me, clears my head a little. I check the road around us and brace myself for what I'm about to do. "I have an idea. Hang on."

I jerk the car to the left, onto the wrong side of the street, straight into oncoming traffic. Zoe screams and my heart jumps into my throat, but the other cars swerve out of the way or stop before they hit us. One side of our car scrapes against another one with a shriek of metal.

"Watch it!" Chris yells.

The police hang back now, thrown off by my reckless move. It was a gamble, but I'd guessed that the computers inside the cars wouldn't let them hit us. Luckily, I was right.

While Chris guides me and Trent yells at me to go faster, I drive through streets I've never seen before. I don't know where I'm going or where we are. I'm just trying to escape the flashing lights behind us. But soon we're lost in a city that's become a stranger.

Finally Zoe says, "They're gone!"

I check my rearview window but don't see anything through the rain. We take another few turns to be safe, and then Chris points ahead. "Quick, pull in there."

I speed into the parking lot for a storage facility wedged underneath a freeway overpass. We drive around back so we're blocked from the view of the street by the large building. I shut the car off and we crouch down in our seats, waiting in the darkness. Listening to rain drum against the roof. Straining to hear sirens.

After the longest five minutes of my life, we peek our heads out and look around. No one yanks the doors open. No one yells at us to freeze.

We've escaped. Barely.

13:05

I stare out the front window at the downpour. Now that my pulse is slowing and we're out of danger, my earlier thoughts crash back into me. Memories flash of everything I did to those cops. Of the crime scene photos showing what I'm going to do. And the knowledge of what I am and what I'm going to become. The others talk around me, but it's almost like they're in another room, their voices muted and distant.

"But the navigation is dead—how will we find Lynne's house?" Zoe asks.

Chris inspects the open panel on the dashboard. "I can probably fix it, but it might take me a few minutes."

"Wake me up when you're done," Trent says, pulling his hood over his head.

The warm air in the car suffocates me. I can't be with these people for one second longer. I throw open the door and jump out into the rain and the darkness.

"Elena, where are you going?" Zoe calls after me.

"I need some fresh air." I shut the door and walk away. My shoes splash through deep puddles, soaking my socks. Water trickles down my hair and into my jacket. I'll probably catch a cold, but what does it matter? I won't be alive after tomorrow anyway.

Once I'm on the other side of the building, out of sight, I slouch against the wall. I close my eyes and try to block out all thoughts but the sound of the torrent around me. I try to forget what's going to happen tomorrow. I try to forget that we might be brain damaged soon. I try to forget what I did to those cops. But of course I can't. I remember every single second. Every tiny detail.

Right now, future shock doesn't sound so bad. I'd do anything to wipe these twenty-four hours from my brain.

I finally understand why I'm going to kill myself. I'll never be able to escape the memory of killing the others or the guilt. How could I live with myself after that?

I pull the gun out of my backpack, the metal heavy and cold in my hand. I should pull the trigger now and save the others' lives. What exactly am I living for, anyway? There's no one who would miss me. Even if I live, I won't have much of a future. Not a monster like me.

Footsteps approach and I shove the gun into my backpack. Adam stands in the rain, dark hair clinging to his face, wet clothes clinging to his tall, lean frame. His eyes find mine through the downpour. I don't want him to see me like this, but it's too late.

"You're still bleeding," he says. "Let me look at it."

Am I? I touch my face and find a trace of blood mixed in with the rain. Not enough to worry about.

He moves closer and opens his first aid kit. I want to tell him not to bother, to leave me alone, but my throat aches and I can't summon the energy to speak. I keep my eyes to the side, unable to look at him as he cleans my wound. He works quickly but his touch is gentle. I feel the heat rising off his body and his breath on my cheek.

When he's done, he brushes damp hair out of my face, his fingers trailing lightly across my skin. "Are you okay?"

His touch makes me feel things I can't allow myself to feel right now. I pull away. "I'm fine."

"Elena, you can trust me."

My breath catches at his words. Is this what Future-Adam meant when he told me to trust Adam when the time came? Is this *that* moment?

Adam's blue eyes study me from behind his glasses, and they're so sincere I want to tell him the truth. I want to spill everything I know, to have someone else to talk to about it. But I don't want him to look at me like I'm a killer. I shake my head.

But he doesn't leave like I'd hoped. Instead he leans against the wall and pulls something out of his pocket. Silver origami paper.

"Where did you get that?" I ask.

"From my house. My future house, I mean. I figured my older self wouldn't mind me taking some paper."

I can't believe he's doing this right now. But as he creases and folds, I find I can't pull my eyes away, hypnotized by his long fingers patiently working on the paper.

In a minute he's made a tiny origami boat. He offers it to me. "Hold this."

"What...?" I take it, resting the silver ship on my palm. It looks sort of like a triangular party hat. It's pretty cute, but it's not as impressive as the unicorn he made me (twice).

"My mom's the one who first taught me how to make origami." He whips out a sheet of gold paper and begins to fold another boat for himself. "I was about seven or eight. She found me crying on the back porch, sitting in the pouring rain, because some kids had beat me up at school again. She folded an origami boat out of paper and said, 'Put all your troubles into this.' Then she placed it in one of the puddles and let it float away with the rain."

His voice is filled with so much love that it sends pangs through my heart. I touch my mother's watch, a wave of longing and grief washing through me. I'm honored he shared this memory with me, even If I doubt an origami boat can actually help ease my troubles.

He bends down and sets his golden boat adrift in one of the larger puddles, where it spins in a circle. "Your turn."

I feel silly, but I place the silver boat in the puddle next to his. The two race around, chasing each other, then dip into a little stream and drift away toward the street. And as they vanish into the darkness I do feel lighter somehow.

"Why did you make me a unicorn before?" I ask.

He shrugs. "It's from my favorite movie, *Blade Runner*."

"Never seen it."

"It's old but still good. We should watch it together when this is all over."

I can't believe he still wants a future with me, even after what he saw me do. He needs to know the truth.

"I would have killed those cops," I say. "If you hadn't stopped me."

"That's not true."

"You don't know." A single tear breaks through my defenses and slides down my face, getting lost in the rain. "You don't know what I've done. What I'm going to do."

He takes my hand, his fingers entwining with mine. "Tell me."

"I'm the one who kills the others."

As soon as I speak the words, everything else pours out of me. Everything I learned at the library. Everything Future-Adam told me. Everything I saw in the safe. I don't hold anything back.

Adam looks shocked at first, but he doesn't let go of my hand.

With each confession, I'm sure he'll turn on me, sure he'll look at me like I'm a murderer and run away. But he doesn't.

"They set you up," he finally says. "It's the only thing that makes sense. You're not a killer, Elena."

"I am." I close my eyes and lean back against the wall. I have to tell him everything. "Remember how Trent mentioned Bright Haven, the group home? And how I messed up three girls?"

"Yeah."

"I lost control then too." I've never told anyone about this. I've buried the memory as best I could, but I can't deny this part of me anymore. "There was this one girl there, Nina. She was small for her age and real dainty, like a doll. But there was something off about her too. She didn't talk much, and she'd just stare at you with these big brown eyes, like she had no idea it was rude.

"She'd wear her clothes inside out and she'd walk around with a huge stack of books balanced on her head. She didn't bother anyone, but the other kids thought she was weird. They picked on her a lot. I saw it, but I didn't do anything, 'cause I didn't want to get involved. I just wanted to keep my head low and get through my time there. But it got worse and worse, and the taunts turned to bruises…"

My voice breaks, and I have to stop a moment to breathe against the rush of painful memories flooding me. "One day I heard moaning from another room. I knew someone was in pain, and I had to check it out. There were these three girls, really nasty girls who pushed everyone around, and they had Nina. She was on the floor, and…and they didn't even need to hold her down anymore. They'd beaten her within an inch of her life and covered her in lighter fluid. I walked in right when they were about to light her up. And when I saw her—broken, lying there, unable to protect herself—something within me snapped. I turned on those girls and I hurt them. By the time someone stopped me, none of them could move."

"They would have killed her." Adam squeezes my hand. "You saved her life."

"But I nearly killed them. I *wanted* to."

"Elena, don't you see? Both times you lost control you were trying to protect someone else. That girl and then Trent…and the cops weren't even that injured. You're not going to kill the others or yourself."

"But what if I lose control again? What if something happens and…"

He puts his hands on my shoulders, staring into my eyes. "You won't. I know you, Elena. You're not a killer."

I want to believe him. But there's one more thing I haven't confessed, one thing I've held back. My father. And even though I've told Adam everything else, I can't tell him that being a killer is in my blood. He'll turn away from me, and I want him to keep looking at me like he is now, like he wants nothing more than to kiss me.

But he doesn't kiss me. He waits for me to make a move, always patient, always understanding. Adam is too good for me, and I'm…I'm a mess.

I pull away from his touch and turn my back to him. "You should stay away from me."

"Elena…"

"Please. Leave me alone."

For a long second he doesn't move. But then he sighs. I hear his footsteps heading back toward the car. Something tightens in my chest at the sound.

I don't understand how I can have feelings for someone so different from me, someone I've known for only a day. Someone I'm completely wrong for. And yet…

"Adam, wait!" I sprint into the rain, catching up to him.

This time I don't hesitate. I don't think. I slide my hands up to his neck and pull him toward me. My lips press against his and he responds immediately, wrapping his arms around my waist. Our kiss is desperate, intense, like we know this might be our only chance. He holds me close and his body is warm against mine, igniting something inside me. As water pours down on us, together we're a bonfire in the middle of a storm. And as I cling to Adam, suddenly, more than ever, I want to *live*.

13:28

The others don't say anything when we get back in the car, but from the looks they give us, I can tell they know something's changed. Chris has fixed the car's navigation, and once we punch in Lynne's name, the car starts forward again.

Adam sits in the backseat with me, and every time I sneak a glance at him, he gives me a hint of a smile. I don't know what this thing is between us now, but opening up to Adam has unlocked something inside me, freeing something I didn't know was caged. I'm not in this alone anymore. Together, we'll change our future.

I slide my hand down my leg until it brushes the back of his thigh. He tenses, but then I feel his fingers wrap around mine. We stare forward with our hands secretly locked between us, the rest of the car oblivious to the fire racing up my arm and spreading through my entire body.

It's finally stopped raining by the time we reach Lynne's house in Malibu. Her place is at the end of a little cul-de-sac that butts right up against the ocean. It's not as big as Adam's house, more like a large beach cottage with a sandblasted look, as though the wind and salt water have worn the paint down to almost nothing.

The door opens the second we pull into the driveway, like she's been waiting for us. Lynne stands on the porch, and you can barely tell any years have passed from the Lynne of our time. Her hair is almost exactly the same—maybe a little shorter but with the same blond highlights. She has wrinkles around her eyes but not as many as you'd expect considering it's been thirty years. I wonder if she's had some work done.

"Oh my God." She covers her mouth with her hand, shock etched on her face. "Adam said it was today, but I guess I never truly believed it until now."

"He told you we were coming?" I ask.

"Yes. I've been waiting all day for you." She stares at each of us in turn, like she can't believe she's not in a dream. "I always knew the accelerator worked, but to see real proof right in front of me…I'm sorry. Please, please come inside."

We follow her into a brightly lit living room that smells faintly of cinnamon, with a view of the beach from her floor-to-ceiling windows. Seeing the dark water crash against the shore only feet away brings back the image of my body lying on the sand, half submerged by the waves. I shudder and turn away.

"Can I get you anything?" Lynne asks. "Something to drink or eat or…?"

"Coffee would be nice," Trent says with a yawn.

"Of course. You poor things, you must be cold and exhausted. Just give me a minute."

She disappears into her kitchen, and we spread out around her white-and-blue furniture. She's taken the beach theme a little far, with seashells on the table and a dolphin sculpture in the corner. Even her flexi has a little orange starfish on it.

There are framed photos all around the room of a pretty blond who looks a lot like Lynne. At her graduation. At her wedding. In doctor's scrubs giving a thumbs-up. With her husband and two kids at Disneyland.

One larger frame catches my eye, and I move closer to get a better look. It's a collage, with a bunch of photos of the girl when she was younger, ranging from baby photos to prom photos. In some of the earlier ones she's in a hospital bed, like she was sick a lot, but she's always smiling.

"My daughter," Lynne says behind me. She's returned with a tray full of steaming mugs and sets it down on the table. "She's a pediatrician now."

We each take a mug, and after one sip I already feel a lot warmer. I don't drink much coffee, but I'm so tired I can barely think. We've all been awake for way too long, and we're running on nothing but fumes and adrenaline at this point. But there's no time to sleep—so coffee it is.

"We need your help," Adam says, right when I say, "We have some questions."

"Of course." Lynne looks back and forth between us. "What can I do to help?"

I look at Adam and he nods, letting me go ahead. I briefly tell her everything we've learned about our deaths and about future shock. I leave out any mention of me being the killer and hope she gets the hint not to bring it up.

"Future shock…" She bows her head. "It was horrible, what happened to those other people, but Aether wouldn't stop the program. From the brief hints we got from the other test subjects, we knew the aperture was working. The accelerator was sending people thirty years in the future and bringing them back. We just needed to find a way to keep them sane. We decreased the time to ten years instead of thirty, but that didn't remove all of the problems. That's when Dr. Kapur suggested we use teenagers."

"So you knew when you recruited us that we might go crazy?" Chris asks, leaning forward, fists clenched like he's about to jump out of his seat and attack her.

"Dr. Kapur promised us that none of you would suffer from future shock. He showed us studies of teenage brains…" She sighs and stares at her hands folded in her lap. "I didn't like it, but it wasn't my call. And we all thought you were going ten years forward, not thirty. I had no idea you went so far ahead until Adam told me many years later."

"If you didn't like it, why didn't you quit?" Chris asks. "Or expose what they were doing?"

She stares into her coffee mug. "You have no idea how hard it is to be a single mom trying to pay the bills. Especially one who desperately needs health insurance for her kid. I *couldn't* quit." She sucks in a long breath. "But after what happened to you, not a day goes by that I don't wish I'd done something to stop it. That's why I helped Adam bury the project—so Aether could never send people to the future again."

I like her excuses and apologies about as much as Chris does, judging by the look on his face, but there's nothing we can do about that now. "We know Adam lied about losing his memories, but what about the rest of us?"

"I'm not sure," she says. "At the time, we believed you had all suffered from future shock. It's hard to say if that was true or not, especially since you were all killed only hours later…"

"Is there anything we can do to protect ourselves from future shock?" Chris asks.

"Not that I know of. I'm sorry."

"There has to be *something*," Trent says.

"The only thing would be to stay here in the future, I suppose. Dr. Kapur thought that the act of traveling back to the present was what triggered it, although he couldn't ever prove it."

Chris shakes his head. "Staying here is not an option."

I don't know. Staying in the future doesn't sound too bad. I could live out the rest of my life here and never kill the others or myself. Although staying here would mean giving up my dream of going to college, plus there's that whole problem of having no identity here and the police being after me…I doubt they'd let me off lightly for beating up two cops. No, staying in the future isn't an option.

"There's one more thing you need to know," Lynne says. "A few hours after you got back, I overheard Dr. Kapur arguing with Dr. Walters about sending younger kids to the future. He said something like, 'It will work if we purge this round of test subjects and erase any evidence they were involved. Then we can start over with a new group.' A day later, you were all dead."

"So you think Dr. Kapur had us…purged?" I ask. A tiny spark of hope flickers in my chest at hearing this could all be a cover-up. That would mean I'm not really the killer after all. And now we have a real person at Aether to pinpoint this all on. A person we can focus on stopping.

Lynne nods. "That's always been my suspicion, but I never found any other proof."

"Dr. Walters never mentioned any of that," Zoe says.

"Of course he didn't," Trent says. "He was in on it the whole time!"

"That son of a bitch," Chris growls. "I'll kill him!"

"Maybe there's another way." Adam leans forward, setting his mug on the table. "My older self said we could get something to blackmail Aether with, some sort of evidence. Do you know anything about that?"

Lynne tilts her head, considering. "There might be something you could use in the old files we kept from the project. They're all locked away in Adam's lab in the Aether building."

Adam exchanges a look with me. "My future self was right. We *do* need to break into Aether Corporation."

Lynne glances back and forth between us, her brow furrowed. "Break in?"

"Hold up," Chris says. "If Future-Adam knew we'd need evidence, why not just get it himself?"

"Adam isn't allowed in his lab anymore," she says. "I'm surprised they let him in the building at all."

"How could he not be allowed in his own lab?" I ask.

"Adam's on…well, they call it a 'personal leave' but he's actually been suspended. The board of directors are calling him unstable, but really it's because of genicote." At our blank expressions, she continues. "Genicote, the cure for cancer? Adam created the cure many years ago, but he needed funding and distribution and factories that could make it in bulk. He came to me for help, and I convinced Aether to start a pharmaceutical division for him with me as the director. We both knew there were risks working with Aether, but I thought if I helped him, I could protect him from them. And for many years I did."

"What do you mean, protect him?" Trent asks.

"There's a…problem with the cure. When used by people with cancer, it's a miracle drug. With just a few treatments they're completely cured for life. But if used by someone who doesn't have cancer, it causes massive mutations that quickly result in death."

Adam's jaw drops, his face horrified. "And I could never get rid of this problem?"

"No. You said it wasn't possible, due to the way the cure works to manipulate DNA. Naturally, the drug had to be tightly controlled to make sure it was never in the wrong hands. That's one reason it took so long for genicote to be approved and distributed—the risks were too high." She stares out the window at the crashing waves, lost in the memories.

"Together, Adam and I made sure the truth about genicote remained under wraps, and for years it worked. Until Aether had a few rough years and got greedy. They wanted to sell the drug to the military to use as a weapon. Adam wouldn't back down, and he's too well respected and influential for them to ignore. Instead, they're trying to discredit him. Telling the world he's a mad scientist so no one will listen if he goes public with what they're doing."

"He *did* seem a bit mad," Zoe says. "No offense, Adam."

"Yeah." Trent nods. "They say there's a fine line between madness and genius, right?"

Adam rolls his eyes. "Again, standing right here."

"I can assure you, Adam is perfectly sane," Lynne says. "But unfortunately he can't get into his lab anymore, and neither can I. They demoted me to a useless project, managing statisticians." Her mouth twists like she's tasted something sour. "I used to oversee some of the most cutting-edge projects in the world that saved millions of lives, and now I work with a bunch of math nerds."

Chris drums his fingers on the coffee table. "But if you and Adam can't get in, how are we supposed to get into the lab?"

"I don't know. Without the code for the keypad, there's no way in."

"Keypad?" I repeat. Memories of our time in the Aether building rush back to me. "The heavy door we passed down the hall from Future-Adam's office—was that his lab?"

"Yes, that's the one."

"Adam wanted us to see that door," I say as all the dominoes fall in my head. "He made sure we'd walk by it, and he gave us the device to disable the cameras. And—the air conditioning! He was showing us everything we'd need to break into the place."

Chris nods quickly. "You're right. There must be a way to get to his lab through the ventilation ducts."

"But what about the lobby?" Adam asks. "He must have had us run through it for a reason."

"Good point," Chris says. "Maybe he wanted us to know there were guards there."

"You're *actually* planning to break in?" Lynne asks, her voice rising. "No, definitely not. I can't let you do that. There are too many guards, too much security—you'll get caught for sure."

"Not if you help us," Adam says.

She shrinks back against her couch. "Me? No. No, I can't risk it."

"And what, lose your job?" Chris asks. "We're going to *die*. You owe us for this."

"I don't know…" She bites her lip and turns to Adam, almost like she's asking him for permission. Maybe because they're friends in the future she probably trusts his judgment more than the rest of us.

"You can make this right," he says. "No more guilt."

"Okay, okay," Lynne says with a sigh. "I can let you in the building, in case they've blocked Adam's access, but that's it. And you'll have to go very early in the morning to make sure the building will be empty. No one can see me helping you."

That would only give us a few hours before the aperture back to the present opens—but we'll make it work. We have to.

"Thanks, Lynne," Adam says. "What else can you tell us about the lab?"

She takes a moment to compose herself, taking a long breath. "The door can only be opened with a numeric code and a finger-print—even from the inside—and there's always a guard stationed behind the door."

Chris runs a hand over his head. "I could try to take the keypad apart or something, but it might be too advanced…Or what about explosives? We could blast our way in."

I blink at Chris. "You want to blow a hole in the wall?"

"Sure, why not?"

"Um, because it will bring every cop in the area to investigate, not to mention the guards in the lobby?"

Lynne shakes her head. "No, that wouldn't work anyway. The doors and walls are reinforced."

"You got any other ideas?" Chris asks.

"I do," Adam says. "But we'll need to go shopping first."

14:36

We develop a plan to break into Aether Corporation and make a shopping list of everything we'll need for the perfect heist. I have no clue if we'll be able to pull it off, but for once we're actively trying to change the future and I'm anxious to get started.

We say good-bye to Lynne—she'll meet us at Aether later to avoid suspicion—and take the car to the nearby Aid-Mart, a huge drugstore like the one Trent stole from earlier in the day. It's mostly empty at this hour, and we split up to quickly get everything on the list. Zoe and I head to the toy section to pick up some kneepads for her upcoming crawl through the air ducts. She's the only one of us small enough to fit inside.

"I don't know if I can do this," she says.

We pass under some way-too-realistic-looking pterodactyl toys that fly up and down the aisle on their own, letting out random shrieks. I'm a tiny bit worried they might actually attack us, but we make it by unharmed.

"What do you mean?" I ask. She didn't seem nervous about the plan earlier when we were going over it. Maybe she feels more comfortable talking about it now that the guys are gone.

"It's just a lot of responsibility." She tugs on a strand of blue hair. "What if I mess up? Like, what if I get lost in the ducts and can't get to the lab? Or what if I can't start the fire or…"

"You won't mess up. And Adam will be right there the entire time in case there's a problem."

She nods, but she bites on the edge of one of her black fingernails. "The rest of you are just so smart and talented. You and Chris can fight. Adam's a genius, and Trent's basically a ninja…but I'm just a girl with a sketchbook."

Okay, she is *way* overestimating Trent's skills. I stop and turn to face her. "You are *not* just a girl with a sketchbook. You helped us with Wombat, remember? We wouldn't be able to buy any of this stuff now without your help. And you're the only one who can fit in the air ducts."

I feel like I should say something else and try to imagine what Adam would do in this situation. I give Zoe a light hug, unsure where to put my arms. Hugging doesn't exactly come naturally for me. "You're going to do great."

"Thanks, Elena," she says, hugging me back.

We find the aisle with the skateboarding kneepads and grab some that look like they'd fit her. Then Zoe sees something and skips down to the next aisle.

"Look!" She holds up a walkie-talkie headset for kids. "We can use these to keep in touch."

"Good idea. See, you're making the plan better already." I grin at her and we throw six of them in our basket. "Let's grab some ice and see what kind of trouble the guys are getting into."

We track down Chris and Adam in the aisle with the household cleaners, where they're loading the cart with rags, latex gloves, bleach, and God only knows what else. Trent joins us a minute later with some flashlights and one of those laser pens he stole earlier, and then we head to the checkout. There's nobody working in the store—just a self-checkout—which saves us any awkward questions about why we need so many cleaning products.

I check my watch. It's 9:16 p.m. "We have about six hours before we're meeting Lynne. Maybe we should get something to eat."

"We'll need some time to get all of this ready," Adam says. "But yeah, we should probably eat first."

"And a nap wouldn't hurt either," Trent adds. "Don't want to be tired when we break in."

"Shh!" I glance around quickly, but no one's close enough to hear him.

He shrugs, and we bag all our stuff and head back to the car. Once we're driving along the Pacific Coast Highway with the dark ocean to our right, Chris asks, "Where should we eat?"

As the white spray splashes against the shore, I think back to my body again. I still don't know why it ends up on the beach or why I'll choose that spot to kill myself. But I have a few hours to find out. "Let's go to the pier."

15:16

We stroll under the arch of the Santa Monica Pier sign and onto the rickety wooden walkway heading toward the ocean. The beach stretches to our left and right, the sound of the waves mixing with laughter from farther down the boardwalk. The clouds have thinned out now, and a soft moon peeks over the twinkling dark water and the bright lights of the Ferris wheel.

The pier is another classic Los Angeles landmark, and like Hollywood Boulevard or the Central Library, this one hasn't changed much in the last thirty years. The most obvious difference is that there are more roller coasters at the end of the pier now, jutting out over the waves and curling into the sky. I stop and take a long breath of the salty air as memories of happier times come back to me, mixing with the creeping dread of seeing the spot where I might die in a few hours.

"What exactly are we doing here?" Chris asks.

"Getting something to eat," Adam says with a shrug.

"Yeah, but there are a hundred restaurants between Lynne's place and here. We could have stopped at any of them."

"I just thought we should have some fun," I say, thinking quickly.

I can't tell them the real reason we're here. "Tomorrow might be our last day alive, and we've spent all of today running from the cops and searching for clues. That's not really living."

Zoe nods. "She's right. We should enjoy every minute we can."

"Sounds good to me," Trent says, grinning.

Adam flashes me a warm smile, and it rekindles all those feelings from when we kissed. I pushed them deep down while we were with Lynne, but now they bubble to the surface again. We hang back a bit from the others, walking close and sometimes brushing shoulders, but otherwise not touching.

We pass by shrimp shacks, an old-fashioned arcade, and tourist shops with *Los Angeles* or *Santa Monica* written all over mugs, sweatshirts, and random tchotchkes. Most of them look like things you could buy back in our time, except for a snow globe with a miniature version of the pier inside, complete with moving roller coasters and Ferris wheel, seagulls flying overhead, and crashing waves. It looks as real as the pier we're standing on, yet fits in the palm of my hand and has no glass surrounding it. I turn it upside down and sparkly lights appear instead of snow, dancing around the tiny pier. They vanish the second they hit the "ground." The birds continue to fly in circles, and when I touch the water, it's cool and wet. Incredible.

The icy wind whips my hair and I shove my hands in my pockets. A few tourists pass by, some wearing shorts and looking surprised that Los Angeles could get this cold. There are a few locals too—couples on dates or people who got off work and are heading for a bar. But for the most part the pier is empty. People in LA just don't go out when it rains.

We stop to check out a group of balloon animals for sale that seem to be alive, twisting into different shapes and colors as we watch. One forms a dachshund that barks out loud, tail wagging. Another becomes a big, round happy face, smiling at us while it changes colors every few seconds. There's also a dolphin that seems to leap through the air, a bird that flies back and forth, and a T. rex that roars and stomps around. The last one is my favorite.

"They're all programmable," the vendor says. "You pick the shape and whatever you want it to do or say from dozens of options."

Zoe buys a butterfly that flits around her head, shifting between different sparkling colors, while Trent gets a black cat that curls up on his shoulder and purrs. They can't take them back to the present with us, but at least they can enjoy them for the next few hours.

There are lots of restaurants on the pier, including a Mexican restaurant that's been there forever, but we decide to eat at one of the little food stands outside. It's automated like the Frosty Foam we visited earlier in the day. A few seconds after we each punch in our orders—and pay with our fake IDs, courtesy of Wombat—it pops out hot burgers and fries, along with sodas and warm, sugary funnel cake. We grab our food and sit at a long wooden table that's still damp from the earlier rain.

"So, do you think this plan will work?" Chris asks as he unwraps his burger.

"Hey, no talking about that now," Trent says, waving a fry around. "We're supposed to be having fun, remember?"

"Fine." Chris snorts but drops it. For a few minutes we just eat, everyone too hungry to talk. But as soon as most of the food has vanished, he starts up again with a new question. "All right, what are you all gonna do with your money from Aether Corp?"

I stare at my funnel cake as the wind spreads powdered sugar all over the table. Chris's words assume that we're going to make it out of this mess alive and that Aether is still going to pay us even if we blackmail them. But I guess for the moment we're pretending that everything is going to work out.

When no one responds, Chris keeps talking. "Guess I'll go first. Like I said before, I signed up for this thing for my son. I wanna marry my girl, do it right, be a real father. None of this shit I went through growing up with a crack whore for a mom who didn't even know which john knocked her up. My son is gonna have two parents and a house. He won't be sent to juvie at fourteen for jacking cars like I was. He's gonna go to college one day." He bunches up the empty hamburger wrapper, crumpling it in his fist. "And he sure as hell won't go to prison. Not if his father is around. I'll make sure of it."

"You'll be a good dad," Zoe says.

"Maybe. First step is being there, right?"

I don't know if that's true. My life wasn't that great when Papá was around. But I do admire Chris's devotion to his family.

Zoe takes a breath and goes next. "I want to get my sister—get custody of her when I turn eighteen in a few months, find us a place to live. It's...it's my fault she doesn't have a family. I thought I was protecting her by reporting my parents for...what they did to me, but then we got split up." Her voice falters, her lower lip trembling. "I don't want her to grow up alone like she did in this future."

Adam puts his arm around her. "It's not your fault, Zoe."

I nod. "You did what you could to keep her safe."

"I guess so. And..." Zoe shakes the ice in her soda as she stalls. "And I'd like to go to art school. Aether said they could help me with that too."

I smile at her. "You'll be a great artist."

"I hope so." She turns to Trent, who's next in the circle around the table. "What about you?"

"I have some uh…Well, I got caught stealing at a convenience store. Twice. Not a big deal, but Aether said they'd help me get rid of the charges. And with the money…" Trent digs around in his jacket, then pulls out what must be his last cigarette. "Well, it'd be nice to not sleep on the streets anymore."

"How long have you been on the streets?" Adam asks.

"Just the past year or so. The guy in my last foster home thought I was hitting on his wife, which was gross 'cause she was totally old. He told the social worker I stole from him, and I figured I was better off on my own. But shelter-hopping and squatting in abandoned buildings gets old after a while." He lights his cigarette and inhales sharply. "Aether can set me up for life. Freedom and security. That's what I want."

I totally understand that desire—it's behind everything I do too. The others look at me, waiting for my answer, but I pick at the edge of my cake. My plans seem so insignificant compared to all of theirs. And I've spent the last ten years keeping myself hidden, keeping everything personal tucked deep inside me where no one can see it. I don't know how to show that side of myself now.

"I want to go to college and become a social worker," I say. Zoe jerks her head up, and Chris raises his eyebrows.

"Why?" Trent asks, incredulous.

I know why they're so surprised. Most social workers are dicks or, worse, idiots. They don't give a shit about the kids they're supposed to help, or maybe they're just so overworked they can't actually find time to give a shit. But they're not all like that.

"When I was seven I was put in foster care. I was scared and injured, and I had no one. But the social worker who helped me, she actually cared. She made sure I was safe, set me up in a good home. She promised nothing bad would happen to me, and when she was around, nothing did." My eyes tear up a little—from the wind, I tell myself—and I blink the water away. "Of course, it didn't last. She disappeared, maybe got transferred or had a baby or something. But if it weren't for her, I don't know what would have happened to me. I just want to be that person for some other kid."

My head drops. I'm suddenly exhausted by laying my soul out on the table like that. The others are silent, all staring at me. I'm sure they're going to tell me I'm stupid for having a dream like that, but instead Chris lifts his soda in a toast.

"You'll be a great social worker," he says, and Zoe nods. Adam squeezes my hand under the table.

"Yeah, that's an awesome goal," Trent adds.

Their words make my chest ache, and I duck my head so they can't see the emotion in my eyes or the redness of my cheeks.

"What about you, Adam?" Chris asks, leaning forward. "Why are *you* here?"

It's the question I've been pondering myself, ever since I first saw Adam. I asked him the same thing before and he never answered me. Then once we got to the future I was too distracted with everything else going on to ask him again. But I can tell it's been on Chris's mind this entire time—and with the way he's looking at Adam now, I wonder if he started this conversation just to get to this point.

Adam pulls his hand away from mine and adjusts his glasses. "My mom. She's…she's having a hard time right now, and I've been working two jobs to pay the bills. I've had to postpone going back to school and gave up my scholarships so I could take care of her. But Aether said they'd get her some help, pay off our debt, and let me go back to school. They even offered me an internship with them while I'm in school or a job once I finish…which I guess my future self took, since he began working for them."

Sounds like his mom has a problem—an illness? Alcohol? Drugs? I guess it makes sense he wouldn't want to talk about it before. I remember his story of how she taught him origami. She clearly means a lot to him, and it must hurt a lot to see her like that.

"What about your father?" Chris asks.

"He left when I was five, started a new family in Florida. I'm the only one my mom has."

Chris studies Adam for a minute and then nods. I can't tell if he's still suspicious of Adam, but for now he seems to be letting it go.

There's a long moment of tense silence until Trent bundles up all his trash. "We still have a few hours to kill," he says. "We should check out the rides. I want to get on that new roller coaster."

"I'm going to take a walk on the beach, clear my head," I say, getting up from the table.

Adam jumps up a little too quickly. "I'll go with you."

Chris smirks, and he and Trent exchange a look that says they know exactly what's going on. But they're wrong. I'm not planning on a make-out session.

I'm going to find the spot where I'll die.

15:43

Dark waves hit the shore, lit by faint moonlight and the lights from the pier. My shoes sink into the sand as I start toward the first lifeguard tower. It would be romantic except I walk a bit too quickly, just a step or two in front of Adam.

"Where are we going?" he asks, struggling to keep up.

"This way." My pace increases with each tower we pass. Each step becomes harder, but I keep going.

By the third tower, Adam's breathing hard. "What's the rush?"

This is probably not what he expected when he said he wanted to walk on the beach with me. But honestly, I was hoping to do this alone. "I just want to look at something."

We pass the fourth tower. Almost there. The lights from the pier are distant now, the sand below me gray, the water pitch-black.

Adam catches up to me and bumps my shoulder with his. "Are you dragging me off somewhere so you can have your way with me?"

I can't help but smile. "Yeah, you'd like that."

"Very much."

I wish I *were* leading him on some romantic rendezvous. But now we're in sight of the fifth lifeguard tower and I slow, my steps faltering. The tower is empty, and the only thing around us is sand. Far at the back of the beach is an empty parking lot. The pier is a distant vision of twinkling stars. All I hear are the waves and Adam's heavy breathing beside me.

I walk around the tower slowly, but there's nothing here. I don't know what I expected. Some clue to tell me why my life will end here. Some explanation. A puzzle piece. But I'm just as confused as before we got here.

Adam watches me, his forehead creased with worry. "Elena, what is it?"

"This is where I'm supposed to die tomorrow. The place where I…" My voice trails off. "I guess I just wanted to see it."

"Have you ever been here before?"

"No. I can't figure out why this is the spot I'd choose. But the file in your future house said it was here by the fifth lifeguard tower north of the pier."

He takes my hand and pulls me toward him. "It doesn't matter, because that's not going to happen. We're changing the future. I promise."

"I know," I say, although I wish I felt as confident as he is. We have a plan, and I think it will work, but doubt still creeps in. The future is a noose around my neck that gets tighter with each passing minute.

"C'mon," he says, dragging me back toward the pier. "Didn't you say we should do something fun?"

I suppose he's right. If this is my last day alive, I should really *live* it. Up ahead, I see the faint lights of the Ferris wheel changing colors as it spins, and I let Adam lead me toward it.

A few minutes later, a safety bar drops down across our laps, trapping us in the car. It's barely big enough for the two of us and we're squished together, our arms and thighs pressed against each other's. Despite the icy wind tangling my hair, I'm warm all over.

The Ferris wheel lifts up with a jerk, and Adam lets out a little "Aah!"

"Are you okay?" I ask.

He looks a little sick but turns to face me, pointedly not looking down. "Sure, sure, just fine. Why are we doing this again?"

"Don't tell me you're afraid of heights."

"No, of course not." He peers down for a quick second and then jerks back. "Okay, maybe a little."

"You'll be fine. I rode this thing when I was a kid. If it's been here for thirty-plus years, I'm sure it's safe."

"Or it's a decrepit old machine that should have been replaced years ago."

"You're right. That must be it."

I lean against him, watching our breath make clouds in the air as we climb higher into the sky. From up here we can see every-thing—the black water and gray sand, the roller coasters with peo-ple screaming as they ride them, the stretch of boardwalk with all its colors and movement and life.

"My parents took me here for my birthday when I was a kid," I say. "One of my few happy memories of the three of us. Mamá and I rode this Ferris wheel together, and afterward I ate cotton candy and got it stuck in my hair. We watched people fish and we played in the sand. It was my one truly perfect day."

Adam is silent for a minute, while cheesy carnival music plays in the background. "What happened to your parents?" he finally asks.

I close my eyes, the memories replaced with much darker ones. I never talk about what happened, and I don't know if I can find the words to do so now. But I've told Adam everything else, and maybe with this one last piece, he'll finally understand.

"Papá drank a lot, and he was angry all the time. Some nights he'd come home and take it out on me and Mamá. Mostly my mother. Mamá tried to protect me, and most of the time she could, but…"

I rub the face of my mother's watch, blinking rapidly to fight back tears. "One night he—he wouldn't stop, and he had a golf club, and there was blood everywhere." Now that I've started, I can't hold back, the words bursting out of me like water from a broken dam. "I thought he was going to kill her. I jumped in front of her and yelled at him to stop. I tried to fight him, but I was only seven, and he hit me with the club. I fell, and he—he kept—"

My body shudders from the vibrant memory and Adam wraps his arm around me. His warmth at my side spurs me to keep going. "Mamá stopped him. She wouldn't let him hurt me. I ran to the phone and dialed 911, screaming the entire time. The dispatcher could barely understand me. But in that minute it took me to call, he hit her in the head, over and over. The police came, but they were too late. She was gone."

I bury my face against Adam's shoulder, struggling to breathe, and let the pain wash through me until it subsides. Adam holds me close, his hand rubbing my back. "It's not your fault," he says into my hair.

I pull back and meet his eyes. "Adam, I'm just like him. I lose control and hurt people too. I've tried my entire life to bury that part of myself, but the anger *always* comes back. It's in my blood."

"You're nothing like him," he says, resting his forehead against mine. His hand slides up to brush a stray tear off my cheek.

Our lips touch, and the kiss starts soft and slow, but then it grows stronger, our hands clinging to each other. We kiss like we only have seconds left in this world, like we're running out of time and this moment has to last for an eternity.

"Hey, lovebirds, ride's over," a man yells behind us.

We're back on the ground, the carriage rocking slightly. I unpeel myself from Adam and stumble out, dazed. Adam grabs my hand as soon as we're both out and flashes me a smile.

We reach the end of the pier where three old men sit with lines hanging over the side. We lean against the railing across from them, listening to the sound of the water lapping against the pier. The Pacific Ocean stretches before us but I can't see the horizon, only darkness and then a sprinkle of stars.

"Why would anyone fish here?" Adam asks as one of the men tosses his line.

He's probably trying to distract me from our earlier conversation, but I go with it anyway. "I don't know. It has to be toxic."

"Maybe the beach is cleaner now?"

"Yeah, right."

The wind picks up, tangling my hair in front of my face. Adam brushes it back, staring into my eyes. "You're so beautiful."

"You're pretty cute with those glasses too." As soon as I say it, I realize *I'm* the girl Future-Adam was referring to earlier in the day. Adam's eyes widen and he laughs, and I know he remembers that moment too.

He wraps an arm around me, and I lean against him as we watch the fishermen. Adam doesn't recoil from my touch, doesn't run away or look at me like I'm a monster. I can't believe he would accept me, knowing what's in my past and what I have the potential to become tomorrow—but somehow he does.

17:30

We return to Future-Adam's house and spread our supplies across his massive kitchen island. An assortment of cleaning products. Baking soda and sugar. A party-sized bag of ice. I lean against the counter and try to imagine what we'll use them for but come up blank.

"Now what?" Chris asks.

Adam takes off his jacket and hangs it on the back of a chair. "Now we put those chemistry classes to good use."

"Uh, I failed chemistry," Trent says.

"That's okay. We'll need your cooking skills too."

Over the next hour, Adam puts all of us to work. With Trent, he makes smoke bombs by cooking sugar and baking soda in a skillet with some other chemicals. This makes a smooth, brown mixture that they form into little round blobs and bake in the oven like cookie dough.

Meanwhile, Adam and Chris make chloroform using the cleaning products and all of the ice we bought. They work so fast I can barely keep up, but Zoe and I assist them with whatever they need, providing an extra hand or bringing them more supplies. In the downtime, we sketch a map of the building's lobby and sixth floor, using my memory and her drawing skills to create a rough estimate of the layout.

When we're finished, we have eight caramel-colored blobs and five wet rags doused in chloroform. Adam swears they'll all work. I just hope it will be enough to get us inside.

I check my watch. "We still have a few hours before we meet Lynne. We should get some sleep."

"Not sure I can sleep," Chris says. "I'm too amped up."

"Me too." Trent says, but he yawns. "Okay, maybe sleep does sound pretty good."

We split up and shuffle off to different bedrooms. Adam and I lock eyes, and without a word, he slips his fingers into mine. We don't speak as we walk down the hallway and find an empty room with a queen-sized bed, then shut the door.

I remove my jacket and slip off my shoes. My clothes are still damp underneath, as are Adam's. There's no way we can sleep in them.

I'm not shy. I slide off my shirt, leaving me in only my bra and jeans, and hear his sharp intake of breath. He removes his own shirt and tosses it aside, giving me another look at his toned chest.

I lead him to the bed and sit on the edge, looking up at him. I'm tired and I know I should rest, but now that we're alone, the last thing I want to do is sleep. These might be my last few hours alive. My last few hours with Adam.

He stands in front of me and runs his hands through my hair before touching my cheek, my chin, my neck. My muscles tense with anticipation but not fear. Never fear, not with Adam. I close my eyes and let him explore. I expect him to kiss me, but his fingers brush my arms. When I open my eyes, he's staring at the ink on them.

"I love your tattoos." He traces the vines running down my

forearm that wrap around a pink flower, a dahlia, with a name written below the petals. "'Esperanza,'" he reads. "What does it mean?"

"It's my mother's name. It means 'hope' in Spanish."

"Hope." He touches the other tattoos on my arms—the spi-
derwebs, the black stars, the blue waves. His hands trail across my
shoulders and to my back, finding the last of my tattoos. A flock of
birds, inked across my back as though they are flying up into the
sky. "And this one?"

"It symbolizes freedom." Turning eighteen and escaping the
foster care system. Being free and independent. Being able to live
without fear.

He leans down and presses his lips to my back, over the lowest
bird on my spine, and I gasp. I'm frozen in place as he kisses each
of the birds, moving up to my neck.

I can't take it anymore. I turn around and pull his mouth to
mine. Our lips meet and fire dances between us. We fall back on
the bed, our legs twisting together, my bare skin pressing against
his. Somehow his glasses come off. I kiss his face, his neck, his
shoulders, and everything in between. His hands tangle in my long
hair, his hips rub against mine, and I moan against his mouth.

I might be dead tomorrow, but I have tonight with Adam. I
want to make it count.

I roll on top of him and reach for the front of his jeans to undo
the fly. As I pop open the top button, his mouth tears away from
mine. "Elena—" He breathes heavily. "I can't…I mean, I've never—"

I freeze with my hand on his jeans. "Never?"

"No. But I want to. Now. With you." He looks away, clearing
his throat. "I just…wanted you to know. In case it wasn't good or
something."

Oh my God, I'm such an idiot. We're moving way too fast. I

don't want Adam's first time to be rushed and desperate and in some strange place. My first time was like that, in the back of some guy's car. With Adam, I want it to be special.

I might never get that chance with him. But he still deserves better than this.

I climb off him reluctantly. "I'm sorry. I got carried away."

"Elena…" He sits up and reaches for me, sliding his arm around my waist.

"We'll have time later," I say and hope it's true.

"Will we?" He stares off into the distance, then meets my eyes. "Elena, I don't want to go back to our time."

"You don't?" Adam has every reason to go back. Why would he give up his future?

"We could stay in the future. Not go into the aperture. Live the rest of our lives here like this, together."

It's tempting, so tempting, but I shake my head. I might not be giving up much by staying here, but Adam will lose everything. "Your mom needs you. And the cure—you have to develop that someday."

"I know." His head drops. "I just…my future self said he never saw you again after we got back."

I touch his chin and lift his head up. "You'll see me again. I promise."

But the same fear is inside me. Why *didn't* we contact each other after we got back? Was it future shock, making us forget this moment ever happened? Or was there just no time between when we got back and my death?

"Good, because I'm not going anywhere." He smiles and he's so cute, with or without his glasses. And far too good to be with someone like me. "I said I'd protect you after all."

I curl up beside him, resting my head on his shoulder. He wraps his arms around me and holds me against him. I can hear his heart pounding and place my hand on his chest, feeling his life pulse beneath me.

For the first time all day, I relax. I forget everything that's happened, and everything yet to come, and savor this moment. I might only have a few precious hours left alive, but in Adam's arms, I feel immortal.

20:59

The car drives itself into Aether Corporation's underground garage and parks in Future-Adam's spot. We jump out and slip on our backpacks, now filled with our added supplies from Aid-Mart. I have the gun with me too, even though I pray I won't have to use it. My insides dance with nerves and anxious energy, but I'm ready. We're actually doing something to change our future.

"Everyone knows what to do?" Chris asks.

We all nod and mutter "yeah." Zoe's eyes are wide, her hands tightly gripping the straps on her backpack, while Trent rocks back and forth on his heels with a grin. Adam pulls out the jammer and flips it on, the light changing to green. I check both my watches, counting the seconds as they tick by.

At precisely 3:35 a.m. the door to the stairs opens and Lynne peeks her head out. Emotion crosses her face when she sees us, but I can't tell if it's relief or worry. "You're here." She steps back so we can enter the stairwell. "There are two guards in the lobby, but otherwise the building seems empty. Good luck."

"Thanks again for your help," Adam says.

Trent hands her a walkie-talkie headset like we're all wearing. "If you see or hear anything, let us know with this."

Lynne disappears up the stairs to head back to her office as part of our plan. I count two minutes on my watch, then nod at the others. We crowd together and start up the stairs, the jammer in Adam's hands keeping us off the cameras.

Once on the sixth floor, I lead the way through the hallway, tracing the steps from my memory. We pass the door to the lab and creep past empty cubicles, listening for sounds of anyone else on the floor until we reach Future-Adam's office. Adam lets us in with a scan of his hand, and we quietly shut the door behind us. I let out a long breath. So far, so good—but now the real work begins.

"Which panel was it?" Chris asks as he drags a chair over.

"This one," I say, pointing to the spot in the ceiling that Future-Adam poked at.

Chris steps onto the chair and nudges the panel loose. He peeks his head inside and then turns back to us. "Looks good. Zoe, you ready?"

She's biting her nails again, staring up at the dark space over Chris's head. "I guess."

"You can do this," I say.

Adam pats Zoe on the arm. "Don't worry. I'll be right here if anything happens."

"Okay." She looks up at the ceiling and then takes a deep breath. "Ready."

She climbs onto the chair with Chris, and he lifts her into the crawl space in the ceiling. Her neon-green kneepads flash as she pulls her legs inside, and then she vanishes in the darkness. There's a long bout of coughing, but then I see a bright beam from her flashlight. Her blue-haired head pokes out again. "Ugh, it's really nasty up here."

"You won't be up there long," Chris says, hopping off the chair.

"You know where to go?" I ask Zoe.

She waves the map she and I made in her sketchbook. "Got it. I'll let you know when I'm over the lab."

After she takes off, Adam hands Chris the jammer. We each check our supplies again, and then Chris heads to the door. "All right, let's go."

He and Trent step outside, but I turn back to Adam. "Will you be okay here?"

"I'll be fine." He kisses me quickly, but I can see the worry in his eyes. "Be careful."

"I will," I say and then join the others in the hallway. I hate leaving Adam behind, but he's much safer staying in the office than with us. Besides, his presence there will make Zoe feel better, even if she doesn't actually need him.

"So you and Adam, huh?" Chris asks as we head to the elevator.

"Guess so." I haven't exactly been *hiding* whatever this is with Adam, but that doesn't mean I want to talk to these guys about it either. Things are still a bit too new and uncertain, and I'm not about to try to explain it, especially not to Chris of all people.

"Doesn't seem like your type."

"He's not, but…" I shrug, hoping he drops it.

"Just keep your eyes open. Something doesn't add up about him."

A dash of doubt trickles back in, but I shove it away. Yes, we still don't know why Adam is the only one not "purged" by Dr. Kapur and Aether Corp, but maybe we'll find out once we get into the lab and find the old files.

"Enough girl talk," Trent says as the elevator opens and we step inside.

We snap on thin surgical masks and yank on latex gloves. From a plastic bag, I remove two of the chloroform rags and hand one to Chris, while Trent grabs a caramel-colored smoke bomb from his backpack.

As the elevator nears the lobby, I press my back against the side wall. My heart pounds, adrenaline making me jumpy. I'm tempted to get the gun out, but I have to hope that Adam's magic rags will work. Chris checks the jammer one last time and then shoves it back in his jacket. Trent flicks his lighter on and off.

The door opens with a loud *ping*. Trent lights up the smoke bomb, then tosses it into the lobby. We rush forward after it, following the trail of smoke rapidly billowing out, which oddly smells of burnt sugar. I dart behind the front desk with Trent at my side. Together we grab the guard there, who's just getting up, and hold him while I shove the wet rag over his mouth. He struggles against us, but we manage to keep him still long enough for the chemicals to take effect. His body sags to the floor as he passes out.

Through the smoke, the hazy figure of Chris fights the second guard. Trent joins him, and they bring the guy down. I'm breathing hard through my mask, my eyes watering from the smoke, but I say a silent thanks to Adam for giving us a way to take out the guards without actually hurting them.

We drag both limp bodies behind the desk and then survey the empty, smoke-filled lobby. The guards are each wearing two flexis, just as Lynne said they would—one for their personal use, and one with the Aether logo on it to control the security systems here. Chris rips off one of the Aether flexis and puts it on himself, while Trent and I spread through the screen of smoke, keeping watch.

I hit the button on the side of my walkie-talkie headset. "The lobby is secure. How's it going, Zoe?"

Her voice crackles through the speaker. "Don't. Even. Ask."

"What, you're not having fun in there?" Trent asks.

"Very funny," she says.

Chris looks like he's staring at the floor, but he must be doing something on his flexi. "Like Lynne said, I can't open the lab from here, but I'm disabling all cameras in the building and cutting the alarms so they can't alert the police or fire department. I'll need, like, two minutes."

"Not a problem," Trent says.

The seconds crawl by as we wait. Every muscle in my body is tense, waiting for another threat. Trent's disappeared into the smoke. Chris sits behind the front desk, his eyes unfocused.

I hear a soft footstep behind me and spin around. Something hits my arm and my entire body jerks and spasms like I've been electrocuted. Sharp pain shocks through me and then I'm on the ground, looking up at a guard with one of those electrified batons. Karma's come to bite me in the ass.

The guard kicks me in the side and I scream. Or I try to, but no sound comes out. My body won't work. I can't move my arms or my legs. I gulp down air, panic rising in my chest. I have to get up. I have to *fight*.

A figure moves in the smoke, silent as a shadow, creeping up behind the guard. Trent bashes the guard in the back of the head with his flashlight, but it's not enough to knock him out. They fight, their figures hazy, while the numbness in my body fades enough for me to move again.

With a shaking hand, I grab the plastic bag in my pocket and pull out another of the chloroform rags. With my other hand, I try to push myself to my feet. One of my legs works, but the left one still feels like it's asleep, all painful tingles and weakness. I lunge at the guard as I topple over, pulling him down with me. We hit the floor hard, and I jab my elbow onto his chest, then press the cloth against his mouth. Trent helps me hold the guard down until he collapses.

I drop the rag and fall back on the cool floor, struggling to catch my breath. Tremors of pain echo through my chest where the guard kicked me. I shake my leg out, trying to get some feeling back into it.

"You okay?" Trent asks, helping me up.

Each inhalation feels like someone's poking my lungs with a butter knife. My ankle hurts too; I probably twisted it when I took the guard down. But I just say, "Yeah. Thanks for the help."

"Hey, I owed you one."

We drag the unconscious guard through the dissipating smoke to the front desk to stash his body with the other two. Each movement sends hot flashes of pain through me, and I have to lean on the desk for a moment until they pass.

"We're done here," Chris says into his headset. "You in position, Zoe?"

"Yep, I'm over the lab now."

"All right, we're heading back up."

We get back in the elevator and exit on the sixth floor. I limp a step behind Trent and Chris, cursing my throbbing ankle and ribs. I do *not* have time to be injured right now.

We stop to get Adam from his office, and as soon as he sees me clutching my side, he rushes over. "Are you hurt? What happened?"

I shrug. "Got in a fight with a guard. I'm okay."

Adam gives me a wary look like he's going to argue, but Chris speaks into his headset. "We're ready, Zoe."

"Okay, lighting it up now," she says.

We move down the hall to the lab and wait in front of the door. I lean against the wall to ease the pressure on my ankle and toss the bag of chloroform rags to Chris. There are only two left, but we shouldn't need more than one.

Zoe's voice crackles in our headsets. "Fire in the hole."

She's got one of the smoke bombs Adam made and should be setting it off in the air duct above the lab. Once the smoke enters the room, the guard will think there's a fire, hit the alarm (which Chris cut off), and run out—giving us the perfect moment to douse him with chloroform and then sneak in.

We gather around the door, listening, but I don't hear anything. No smoke creeps out from under the door. Did she actually set it off? Maybe the smoke bomb isn't strong enough, or the guard doesn't think it's a big enough threat to leave.

The door clicks. It flies open, and there's the guard, running out. He jumps when he sees us waiting for him, and Chris and Trent easily force the rag over his mouth. He falls limp, and they drag his body inside while Adam wedges something in the door to stop it from closing.

We're in.

21:46

The fire alarm blares, the red lights flashing through the haze of smoke. We enter a large space that looks like a chemistry class-room, with countertops and glass cabinets full of beakers, flasks, and brown bottles with red warning labels. A huge whiteboard on the wall is covered in precisely drawn equations—maybe Future-Adam's writing? There are no windows, but a hallway leads off to other rooms.

Adam moves to the counters and inspects the equipment there, his face set in something like awe or wonder. He must love all this science stuff.

I scan the room for any sign of evidence, while Chris pops open a panel in the ceiling and helps Zoe out. She coughs from the smoke, but her eyes dance with excitement as she hops to the floor.

I nudge her with my elbow. "See, I knew you could do it."

She dusts cobwebs off her blue hair and grins. "Piece of cake."

"So we're inside. Now what?" Trent asks.

"We need to hurry," I say, checking my watch. There's no telling if another guard will show up or if one of the guards will wake early. And we only have a little over two hours left in the future.

Adam puts down the beaker he's been examining. "It'll be faster if we split up to search."

We each pick a room, and I'm hit with a blast of cool air as soon as I enter mine, which has row after row of tall, blinking electronic equipment. Probably not the room we're looking for, but I spot a desk in the corner and riffle through it, just in case. Finding nothing, I check another room, but it's just a small kitchen and break room.

Back in the hallway, I study the door at the end that no one picked, with a big orange sign that reads CAUTION: BIOHAZARD. I can't imagine Future-Adam putting the evidence we need in a room like that. I'm not even sure it's safe for us to go in there without some sort of protective suit.

"Found something," Trent yells from another room. I rush inside with Chris and Zoe following at my heels. Trent's standing in the middle of a room full of dusty, old metal filing cabinets. None of them are labeled, but it's a good bet that Future-Adam stored the information about the old projects here.

"This has to be it," Chris says.

"What are we looking for?" Zoe asks.

I head for the filing cabinet closest to me and pull open a drawer. "Anything labeled 'Project Chronos.'"

For a few minutes we search in silence, and the entire time I feel like there's a ticking clock hanging over us, nudging me to hurry. I quickly skim through the files, my eye catching a Project Lethe and a Project Athena, but I don't see the one we need.

"Sorry. What'd I miss?" Adam asks as he slips through the doorway. He probably got distracted by more science stuff in another room. This is his lab in the future, so I can't blame him for being curious about it. It's another glimpse into his future life. We briefly explain, and he starts searching another filing cabinet.

"Here!" Chris says a minute later. "Project Chronos."

We crowd around him as he pulls out four thick files and lays them on top of the cabinet. The first one is about the original group of people who went to the future and is dated two years before we signed up. There's a ton of data about who they were—a mix of scientists and private security—but we flip through to the end, where we find brain scans, medical exams, and a report from Dr. Kapur about the mental state of the patients.

Chris reads a few lines:

> Two of the subjects never returned from the future.
> The three subjects who did return suffered severe
> memory loss, confusion, and paranoia.

Adam points to something farther down on the page. "It says here the original team was in the future for seventy-two hours, and they thought that might be the cause of their future shock."

We check the next file and find similar results, although the time in the future was reduced to twenty-four hours to see if that made a difference. Only one person went missing that time, but everyone else returned with the same problems as the first group. For the third group, they kept the length to twenty-four hours but only sent them ten years into the future instead of thirty, in case that was the problem.

I skim over Chris's shoulder as he reads Dr. Kapur's report out loud:

> Three of the subjects returned with the full effects of
> future shock and remembered nothing of their time in
> the future. But two of the subjects returned with lesser
> memory loss and were able to give us vague information

about their experiences. It should be noted that these two subjects were the youngest, at only twenty-two and twenty-three years of age. From the tests we've conducted, it appears that the time dilation is too difficult for the adult brain to overcome, even with only a ten-year jump. However, since teenage brains are still developing, they may not have these problems. It is my recommendation that younger subjects be found for the next trial. Ideally below the age of thirteen, though it may be difficult to control subjects of that age or obtain valuable information from them.

"This is it!" Trent says. "We can use this as evidence."

"Hang on to this." Chris hands me the report and then opens the last file: our file. And it's all there—our bios, our medical records, brain scans from before and after, and finally Dr. Kapur's report from after we returned.

Despite the normal brain scans, all five subjects claim to remember nothing from their time in the future. However, none of them suffer from the confusion and paranoia common in the previous subjects, and they appear to retain their memories from before their visit to the future. This seems to prove the hypothesis that the younger the subject, the fewer effects of future shock they will experience. As such, I recommend conducting the experiment again with younger subjects...

"Normal brain scans," Trent says. "Maybe we did *lie* about forgetting everything."

Zoe nods. "Keep going."

We flip through the report, but there's nothing about Dr. Kapur or Aether planning to kill us. If they did it, they didn't leave a record of it behind. I pocket the report anyway.

Chris turns to the last report in the file, written by Lynne about our deaths. I suck in a breath, knowing what's coming, what the others will learn, but it's too late to stop them now.

> Dr. Kapur theorizes that Elena—possibly due to her eidetic memory—suffered the strongest effects of future shock, yet also remembered brief flashes of her time in the future, resulting in extreme paranoia and confusion. With her history of violent behavior, it seems likely she turned on the other subjects in this confused state and then took her own life once she realized what she had done. We are unsure why the final subject, Adam O'Neill, was unharmed. With this unfortunate turn of events and the loss of the accelerator due to Dr. Walters's outburst, it is my recommendation that Project Chronos be concluded.

"Elena, what is this?" Zoe asks, her voice high-pitched.

Trent shakes his head. "I don't understand. *Elena* killed us?"

Chris doesn't say anything, but his head swivels slowly toward me, and I see murder in his eyes. The files drop back onto the cabinet, and then he lunges for me. I stumble back, my ankle and side screaming, as his hands rush toward me—to hit me or grab me, I don't know. Adam jumps between us, pushing Chris back, and then everyone starts shouting.

"Stop!" Zoe yells.

Trent holds Chris back by the arm. "Dude, let's hear what she has to say first!"

"Is. This. True?" Chris gets out between clenched teeth.

I don't know how to answer. I don't think it's true, I don't want it to be true, but maybe Dr. Kapur is right about future shock and its effect on me. Maybe I will lose my mind when we return and take the others' lives. And now I understand why I'll spare Adam's life. My feelings for him must have stopped me from hurting him, even in my confusion.

"No," Adam says when I can't speak. "Aether must be setting her up."

Chris's death glare switches to him. "Your knew about this too?" And then back to me. "You both *knew*?"

"I found out at the library," I say. "But I didn't think it was true. I don't have any reason to kill all of you."

Trent drops Chris's arm and gapes at me. "You knew about this and you didn't *tell* us?"

"Because I knew you'd freak out like this!"

"Yeah, no shit!" Chris yells. "All this time, *all this time*, we've been trying to find the killer, and all along it was *you*!"

Adam stands in front of me, shielding me with his body. He holds up his hands, looking back and forth between the others. "She's not the killer, guys. Aether just wants us to think that. We already know we won't suffer from future shock."

Chris snorts. "What, you think they planted this report in case we happened to find it in thirty years? No fucking way."

Trent shakes his head. "We know that Adam doesn't suffer future shock, but that's it. Sorry, Elena, but Chris is right. There's nothing in these files that even hints that Aether is going to kill us."

Zoe looks unsure, her face turned down to the floor. She sighs.

"If this is true, then it's not your fault, Elena. You can't do anything about future shock. But…you really should have told us."

"I know," I say. "I *know*. I just thought I could fix it or find out more before—"

Our headsets suddenly buzz, and then Lynne's voice says, "The police are in the lobby. Get out now!"

22:18

We burst out of the lab. Lynne is already in the hallway, waiting. She grabs Adam's arm. "Did you get it?"

"Yeah, we got it."

There's no time to say anything else. We rush down the hall and into the stairwell. My ankle throbs as I limp down the stairs behind the others, and after six flights, my ribs hurt so bad I almost want to lie down and die right there. Chris throws open the door to the parking garage and we dart inside.

"Freeze!" the police yell. "Hands up!"

Two cops stand in front of a police car, their guns pointed at us. No batons this time. Panic spikes in my blood. There's no way out of this without getting arrested or shot. But with our time in the future running out, we can't afford to do either.

A lighter flicks, and then Trent lobs one of the smoke bombs at the cops. They duck just long enough for us to start running in different directions as thick, white smoke begins to fill the air. I head toward Future-Adam's parking spot, while fumbling for the gun in my backpack. I don't want to use it, but if it's the only way out of this mess…

Then I hear the unmistakable roar of gunfire and the *plink* of bullets on metal. I drop down, using a car for cover, and my own gun clatters to the ground. Shit, these cops are not messing around.

Lynne crouches next to me, her face pale. I forgot she was still with us. I don't see any of the others or Future-Adam's car. I grope around for the gun but can't find it.

Adam's voice cries out and my head jerks up. One of the cops twists Adam's arm back, and when he struggles, the cop bashes him in the face with the butt of his gun. Adam falls, and a guttural scream erupts from my mouth. I grab the edge of the car to haul myself up, but then I hear Lynne yell, "No!"

There's a loud bang next to me, and everything seems to shift into slow motion. Lynne's arm jerks back from the recoil of the gun—my gun, now in her hands somehow—at the same time as the cop standing over Adam is knocked back. The cop bounces off the side of a car and then hits the ground with a *thud*. Before I can even process what Lynne has done, another shot fires. She collapses beside me.

For a second I can't move. She shot him, she killed that cop, and then—oh God, no. I hunch close to the ground, hands trembling as I check her body. Blood gushes out of a hole in her chest and she's not breathing. She's already gone. I feel faint. Lynne's *dead*, and my hands are covered with her blood, and I don't know where anyone else is or if Adam's okay, and I have to get out of here, *we* have to get out of here, *right now.*

Zoe appears in the smoke, tears running down her face as she hovers over Lynne's body. Seeing her clears my head a little. I need to get Adam. We can't leave without him.

I grab the gun and push myself to my feet, fighting through the pain. Adam's sprawled on the ground a few feet away, smoke curling around his body. I can't tell if he's breathing or not, but he must be alive. He has to be.

The other cop sees me, but Chris and Trent rush him from behind. They knock off his helmet and force the last chloroform rag over his mouth. While they take him out, I kneel beside Adam. He's breathing but unconscious, and a long gash on his forehead spurts blood. The other cop lies next to him, but he's definitely not breathing. A dark pool of blood spreads below his back. I'm paralyzed at the sight, my mind replaying the jerk of Lynne's arm as she fired the gun. I still can't believe she did it, that she shot this cop to make sure we could get away, and the price she paid for it.

"Elena, get the car!" Chris yells.

I don't want to leave Adam, but I don't know how to help him either. We need to get out of here before more police arrive—they're probably already in the lobby. I scramble off in the direction of the car, stumbling around on my injured ankle until I find it in the smoke.

I collapse into the car and drive to the others. I'm so exhausted my limbs are shaking, but I find them in the smoke somehow. The boys haul Adam's body into the backseat, while Zoe slips in beside me. As soon as the doors slam shut, I switch the car to manual and peel out of the garage, tires screeching.

"What about Lynne?" Zoe asks. "We just left her there!"

"She's dead," I say. My voice sounds harsh, but I can't think about her sacrifice without my throat tightening up. We screwed up and she died, but we don't have time to dwell on that right now. We need to get back to the research facility in the desert before the aperture opens. Once we return to the present, we can fix everything.

I hope.

23:41

Adam's awake by the time the car parks in front of the abandoned research facility. It took us about an hour to get here, leaving only nineteen minutes before the aperture opens. While we drove, Trent used the laser pen on Adam's forehead and the skin magically stitched itself together—too bad it won't work on most of my injuries, though Trent did fix the cut on my face from before.

We haven't told Adam about Lynne yet. Maybe because we're all in shock and can't talk about it, or maybe because, like me, the others have realized that we can stop her death from happening once we return to the present. We'll tell him later, after we sort everything else out.

The sky is lightening to sapphire blue as we get out of the car, but the sun hasn't popped up yet. The cool desert air slaps me in the face as we slip through the hole in the chain-link fence, me hobbling like an old lady, Adam stumbling like a zombie. We're a mess, but at least we made it back.

Once inside the building, we snap on our flashlights. Everything looks the same as when we left, but it's hard to believe we were here only twenty-four hours ago. We head to the basement level—down more stairs, my body protesting the entire time—and scan the room with our flashlights. Still empty. I check my watch—seven minutes to go.

I'm anxious to go back to the present, to get out of this nightmare that is the future, but another part of me is scared to face what might happen when we return. And what I might do.

"What's the plan?" Trent asks, his eyes shifting to me. "Now that we know Elena's going to kill us…"

I open my mouth to protest, but Adam cuts in. "Hey, we can't rule out the possibility that Elena was set up."

"It seems pretty clear," Zoe says with a sigh. "Sorry, Elena."

"It's okay," I say. "I wish I knew what to do or how to stop it…"

Chris crosses his arms, and his voice sounds reluctant. "There's only one solution. We can't let Elena go back to the present with us."

"No!" Adam says, stepping forward.

My first instinct is to argue—I can't give up my life, my dreams, my *future*—but then I nod slowly. This *is* the only solution. Deep down, I think I've known for some time that this would have to be my fate. It's the only way to keep them safe. I just didn't want to accept it.

"Chris is right," I say. "I have to stay here."

Adam takes my hand, pleading with his blue eyes. "Elena, no! This—you can't do this! I need you, I…"

I gulp, swallowing the emotion building in my chest. If I stay here, I'll never see Adam again—not the Adam of my time anyway. Future-Adam is the same person, but he's thirty years older than me, and it just isn't the same somehow. I'll never have a future with *this* Adam. But it's worth it to save the others. And if I go back and then kill myself, I won't have a future with Adam anyway. At least this way we'll all live.

I touch Adam's face softly, memorizing the curve of his jaw, the feel of the stubble on his chin, the way his eyes shine in the darkness. "I'm sorry, Adam. I wish it didn't have to come to this, but it's the only way the others will be safe. I won't risk killing them."

Zoe gives me a quick hug, and Trent slaps me on the back. Chris shakes my hand. "You're doing the right thing," he says.

"I know," I say, even if my gut is screaming *no, no, no*. Adam looks heartbroken, but there are no words that can fix this. It's better if he just lets me go.

"Elena, you can't do this," he says. "You have a life in the present. You can't give it up now. And I can't lose you."

"It's okay," I tell him quietly. "I'll go to your future self and he'll help me out. You'll see me in thirty years."

"We still need a plan," Chris interrupts. "If we're not suffering from future shock, we should pretend like we don't remember anything from the future. And if we are suffering from it...then we won't remember this conversation anyway. Either way, we don't want Aether to know what we did in the future or what we found. We need to leave behind everything we bought in the future...and your sketchbook too, Zoe."

She bites her lip but removes the sketchbook from her bag and hands it to me. I hold it close to my chest, grateful I'll have this one piece of her to keep.

They remove everything from their backpacks that wasn't originally in them—flashlights, walkie-talkies, the laser pen, the jammer—and even peel off their fake fingerprints. There's no reason for me to do the same. I just watch, trying to detach myself from the situation and convince myself I don't care. Even Adam finally sighs and starts dropping things on the floor, and the sound kills me.

Something heavy and metallic clatters to the ground by Adam.

We all swing our lights over, right as he reaches for it. It's a silver case with the word BIOHAZARD written all over it, popped open to reveal six vials full of yellow liquid. I can't make out the label from here, but I see a *G*.

Chris shines his light on Adam's face. "What. The fuck. Is that?"

Adam quickly snaps the case shut. "It's nothing. Just something I grabbed from the lab."

"What—" I ask, my brain working fast. I remember when Adam disappeared in the lab. He must have taken this case then. But why would he want it? And why keep it a secret from us? There's only one thing it could be. "Is that genicote?"

"The cure for cancer?" Trent asks.

"Yeah, it's the cure," Adam says as he shoves the case in his backpack.

I scramble for words, but all I can get out is, "Why?"

"I…" He hesitates and then takes a long breath. "This is why I was recruited. To bring the cure back to the present."

His words are like a blow to my gut. He knew about the cure all along. Why didn't he tell us? And that means Aether knew about the cure too. Is this the real reason we were sent to the future?

Chris lets out a string of obscurities. "I was right! You've been working for Aether this entire time!"

"Wait, let me explain—"

"Your future self set us up!" Chris starts toward Adam. "He convinced us to break into the lab just so you could grab that, didn't he?"

"Stop!" I yell. "Let's listen to what he has to say!" I turn to Zoe, who's been quiet this entire time, her face twisted in shock. "Zoe, tell them!" But she just shakes her head slowly and backs away.

Chris grabs Adam's jacket and shakes him. "Is that why you live and we die? Because you're working for Aether?"

While Chris is holding him, Trent grabs Adam's backpack, ripping it off him. "No!" Adam yells, but Chris shoves him away. I know I should help Adam, but a trace of doubt has crept inside me, and I stand there, frozen.

"Let me see that," Chris says.

Trent hands it over, and Chris yanks the case out before dropping the backpack on the floor. Adam dives for the bag and pulls a gun out of it. He aims it at Chris and Trent, and he's holding it more confidently than I ever did.

"Drop it!" he yells.

"You—you have a gun," I blurt out. And not just any gun, but a gun identical to mine. The same type of gun that is going to kill us tomorrow. Does that mean…Is Adam…*No*. It can't be.

His eyes flick to me for a second and then back to Chris and Trent. "I don't want to hurt you guys, but I need that case. Put it down now."

Chris slides the case across the floor to Adam. "It was you all along," he growls. "I knew it."

I don't want to believe it, but the evidence doesn't lie. Adam is the only one who is alive in the future. Adam has the gun that is going to kill us. And Adam had an ulterior motive all along.

Was everything he said to me—everything his future self said— a lie? Did he trick me into caring for him just so he could set me up later? My heart twists, but my inner voice says, *I told you so*. I can't believe I let my feelings for Adam blind me. I trusted him, against my instincts, against my nature, but I should have known better. The only person I can ever trust is myself.

Adam picks up the case right as a bright light appears. The faint golden dust floats in the air, forming a dome in the center of the room. The aperture!

Sixty seconds starts counting down in my head. Adam keeps the gun pointed at Chris and Trent, but he keeps glancing at the light. Chris looks like he wants to fight, but then he makes a break for the light, and a second later Zoe and Trent follow. All three of them enter the light and vanish.

Adam stuffs the case in his backpack. He steps toward the aperture, but then turns to me. "Elena…" He shakes his head. "I'm sorry."

He disappears into the light, leaving me alone in the future.

Fifteen seconds left. I should stay here in this time. That was the plan—to protect the others—but everything's changed now and I don't know what to believe. Was everything I learned in the last twenty-four hours a lie? Did Adam and Future-Adam plan all of it? Or will I really lose my mind and turn on the others? I still have the gun, so there's still a small possibility I'm the killer. If I go back, I might murder them all.

But if I'm not really the killer, if Adam and Aether set all of this up, then the others are still in danger.

Ten seconds. I dash toward the aperture, my ankle throbbing and slowing me down, pain shooting through me with each step.

Five seconds. I enter the aperture, and the golden flecks surround me, filling my vision. I'm in the sun, blinded, the white light searing my eyes.

And then, nothing.

THURSDAY

I blink to clear my vision, but for a moment I can only hear distant voices and machinery around me. My body thrums, a slight vibration running through it from the floor. Something loud *thuds* nearby. Am I back in the present? Did it work?

Slowly, the world comes into focus. Adam, Trent, Zoe, and Chris all stand nearby, looking as dazed as I am. The walls of the metal dome stretch around me, and the door's already open. That must have been the sound I heard. The others stumble through, and the people outside cheer. Bright-white spots still cover my vision, but I take a step toward the door, legs wobbling.

Outside, scientists in lab coats gather around the accelerator, clapping. In front, Dr. Kapur stares at us with eager eyes, like he's excited to pick apart our brains. Above him, I spot the giant clock on the wall. Only thirteen minutes have passed since we went to the future. And yet, in those few minutes we were gone, I lived an entire day.

Dr. Walters gives us all a proud smile. "You're back," he says, and he sounds relieved. I picture his older self, frail and trapped in his bed, racked by coughing fits and regret. I can't look at him the same now that I've seen the man he becomes.

Lynne beams at us like a proud mother, and my mind flashes back to her body lying on the ground, gushing blood from the hole in her chest. I just watched her die and yet here she is, alive and unaware of her fate in thirty years.

Chris glares at everyone, while Trent and Zoe just look around like they're lost. Adam takes off his glasses and rubs his eyes, standing a little apart from the others. He slips his glasses back on and meets my gaze. He mouths my name, but I look away quickly, his betrayal still as sharp as the pain in my ribs.

Some of the scientists rush forward to take our backpacks. They yank mine off before I can stop them, and only then do I realize I never emptied mine out. There shouldn't be anything too bad in there, but I hide my hands behind my back and peel off my fake fingerprints. I don't know if they'd still work now (are they electronic?) but they'd lead to too many questions. I slip them into my pocket, and my fingers brush over paper—the reports we stole from Aether's headquarters. I dropped Zoe's sketchbook during the fight over the case, but I still have these.

The case! I glance over, but Adam's backpack is gone, taken away like the others. Aether has the cure now, and there's nothing we can do about it.

And that's when it hits me: I remember everything. I'm not suffering from future shock—which means I'm *not* the killer and we're all still in danger. I can't tell if I'm relieved or even more scared now, knowing it isn't me. Mostly, I feel like I'm going to throw up.

"You all did such a great job," Lynne says. "We know you must be tired, but we have to send you to medical quickly to make sure you're okay, and then we'll debrief you. We want to know about everything you saw in the future."

"Please follow me," Dr. Kapur says, suddenly at my side. He

herds me like a sheep into the elevator. The others are split up too, following scientists in different directions. Chris shoots daggers at me with his eyes, but I don't see Adam anywhere.

In the elevator I lean against the walls, clutching my side and trying to breathe. Time must have finally caught up to me, because I feel like I could sleep for days. Hell, maybe I should after this is all over. Assuming I'm still alive, that is.

A part of me can't believe I'm in the present again. Everything I experienced in the last twenty-four hours, everything I saw and heard and lived through, hasn't actually happened yet. And yet it feels just as real as this moment now.

I limp into the medical area and the nurses descend on me, taking my blood pressure, draining my blood, and checking my heartbeat. I barely notice any of it. I rub my eyes, trying to snap out of the daze I'm in, but it's like I've been drugged or something. Is this future shock? I still remember everything, but the world around me is just a little bit fizzy, like I can't quite grasp on to it. Like my brain is out of sync. But maybe I'm just exhausted.

The nurses cluck at my ankle and aching ribs, taking x-rays of both. There's nothing broken, so they wrap me in bandages and give me some pain meds. None of them ask me what happened.

When they finish, I'm carted off for an MRI scan so they can study my brain. I understand now why they're doing all this. They want to see if I'm messed up like the other people who went to the future. But I already know the brain scans will come back normal.

They make me change into a hospital robe for the tests, and I hide the reports from the future and the fake fingerprints in the changing room, stashed between the pages of a magazine. The entire time they run the scans I worry someone will find the evidence. But when I get back, the reports and fingerprints are still hidden there, even though they've taken the clothes I wore in the future. I stash the evidence inside my own clothes, which they've left for me.

I'm given food and water, then left in a small room and told to wait. It's like an interrogation room, with a mirror on one wall and a table with two chairs in the middle. I sit in one of those chairs and get that creepy tingling on the back of my neck like I'm being watched. I feel like I should be in an orange prison suit with my hands cuffed to the table.

Dr. Kapur walks in, frowning, with his clipboard under his arm. "Elena Martinez," he says. I'm not sure if he's just saying my name or expects an answer. He studies me for a moment and then sits across from me. "How do you feel?"

"Tired and sore."

He nods and jots something down on the clipboard. "Any... confusion? Memory loss?"

"I..." I have to pretend like I don't know anything, to stick to the plan Chris laid out, even if I wasn't intended to be a part of it. I drop my gaze to the table. "I remember entering the accelerator and the light...but that's it." I squish my face up like I'm confused. "Did it work? Did we actually go to the future?"

His frown deepens and he taps his pen against his clipboard. "So you remember the moments before you entered the accelerator?"

"Yes."

"And you remember the time before that—the medical exam, the lunch with the others, and so forth?"

"Yes..."

"Hmm." He marks things down on the clipboard. "But you don't remember anything between the moment you entered the accelerator and when you walked out?"

"No, I don't." I rub my eyes and try to look pained. It isn't a struggle since my side still burns with each breath. "So we *did* go to the future?"

He ignores my question again and leans forward. "How did you get your injuries?"

"I-I don't know."

His eyes narrow. "You have a cracked rib, a sprained ankle, and a bruise on your face, and you *don't know*?"

I didn't realize my face was bruised too, but I guess it's been a while since I checked a mirror. Probably from when Chris punched me. I make my voice go higher like I'm starting to panic. "No—what's going on? Why don't I remember?"

He puts his hands on the table, his eyes boring into me. "Elena, are you telling me that you, with your eidetic memory, can't remember *anything* from your time in the future?"

"No." I stare down at my hands in my lap. "I've never experienced this before. It's like I was asleep or something. Big black patches of nothing. I wish I could remember."

He leans back. "We might have some things that will jog your memory."

The door opens and a man in a lab coat comes in and drops a black plastic bag on the table. Now I definitely know there are people on the other side of the mirror.

Dr. Kapur removes the walkie-talkie headset and the flashlight from my backpack. "Do you remember buying these? Or why you bought them?"

"No. Sorry." Seeing the items sitting there makes me squirm. Like at any moment he'll find a hole in my story or somehow get me to slip up and reveal that I do remember something.

He asks a few more questions about the items and why there was no money in my bag, but I play dumb. But then he removes a crumpled piece of silver paper, and I have to stop myself from showing the emotions flickering through me. Because as he starts to unfold it, I know exactly what it is: Future-Adam's origami unicorn.

"We also found this in your bag." He slaps it on the table so that the matte-white side is face up. "What do these numbers mean?"

"I don't know." Seeing it again brings back everything—the lies Future-Adam told me, the evidence I found in his house, the memory of Adam and the origami boats in the rain. I swallow hard, fighting the sting in my throat. Was everything we shared in the future a lie? The things he said, the moments we spent together…I thought he was sincere at the time, but maybe I was wrong. Maybe it was all an act and he never cared for me at all.

I can't help but wonder—if Adam is working for Aether, will he tell them what the numbers mean? Will he tell him that we're all faking our memory loss?

The interrogation continues for hours. Sometimes Dr. Kapur leaves and Lynne comes in to ask me the same questions in different ways. But eventually they let me go, after explaining that I should contact them if I remember anything and saying that they want to follow up with me in a week.

I'm sent to the lobby, where I'm given an envelope. I rip it open, and my hand trembles as I stare at the check inside. So many zeroes. This money is my future.

And what I'm about to do might jeopardize it all.

I check my pocket again to touch the edge of the papers inside and reassure myself they're still there. The receptionist tells me a car is waiting to take me home. I smile and ask where the nearest bathroom is.

Once inside, I hide in the handicapped stall, unfold the reports Trent gave me, and lay them out on the black-and-white tile. I dig my phone out of my bag and take photos of each one. The lighting in here isn't great, and my phone's camera sucks, but I make sure the important parts of the report are clear. Then I email all the photos to my roommate, Katie, with instructions on what to do if something happens to me. I don't know if this will do any good, but it's the only thing I can think to do. And I don't know anyone else I can send them to.

When I step into the hallway, I hear nearby voices and I freeze.

"Did you tell them anything?" Chris whispers.

"Nope, nothing," Trent says.

I sneak a quick peek around the corner. The two of them, plus Zoe, are huddling together like they're exchanging secrets. Their eyes look tired, their movements jerky. I'm only a few feet away, close enough I'm sure they'll be able to hear my quick breaths or the loud pounding of my heart. I flatten my back against the wall.

"What do we do now?" Zoe asks.

"We get the hell out of here," Chris says. "And be careful tomorrow. If Adam or Elena show up, I'll be prepared."

"What about Aether? Do you think they'll come after us?"

"Nah," Trent says. "I swiped something from Lynne's office we can use as leverage."

"What—" Chris starts, but he's interrupted by footsteps down the hall. Damn, I wanted to know what Trent stole.

"How are you all feeling?" Lynne asks, her voice cheerful. "Do you need help with anything?"

"No, we were just leaving," Chris says.

I hear more footsteps, and when I check again, they've scattered like cockroaches, leaving only Lynne standing in front of the elevator.

Lynne might know about Adam's secret mission to get the cure, but she also gave her life to save us. She might be the only one I can trust with the truth. And a part of me still can't believe Adam would actually kill us, despite what I've seen. I limp over to her.

She turns and flashes me her bright white smile. "Elena, is everything all right? I thought you'd left already."

"Can I talk to you for a minute? Somewhere private?"

Her eyebrows lift in surprise. "Of course. I'm here to address all of your concerns. We can chat in my office."

We take the elevator up a floor and walk down soft carpet to an office with a view of the desert outside. I rub my sweaty hands on my jeans. I thought I had this all figured out, but now I'm doubting my plan. Maybe this isn't such a good idea. What if she won't help me? What if she's in on it all?

She broke into her employer's office for us. She shot a cop for us. She took a bullet for us. I have to believe she wants to keep us safe and that she wants to do the right thing.

Lynne sits behind her desk and folds her hands on top. "What is it you want to talk about?"

I remain standing, my legs itching to bolt out of the room. But I spit out, "I think Aether is going to kill us."

She blinks quickly, her smile dropping. "Why would you think that?"

I hesitate, debating how much to tell her. I still don't know if I can trust her, even though her older self helped us get the evidence, even died for us. "I…remember some things from the future."

"You—what?" Her mouth drops open, but she quickly recovers. "So back there, you lied? Why?"

"Because in the future we learned about future shock." I pause, watching my words register on her face. "We have evidence of what Aether has done. And proof that we're all going to die tomorrow."

I remove the papers and unfold them, laying them on the table. She leans forward and scans them. Her head jerks up. "How did you get this? Where?"

"We got it in the future. You helped us get it."

Her eyes widen. "You—you saw me in the future? You talked to me?"

"Yeah. You said you overheard Dr. Kapur telling Dr. Walters they should 'purge us' before we died. You said you'd help us stop them."

"Of course I'll help you. But what…what was I like? Did you see my daughter by any chance?"

"You felt guilty about what happened to us. About not being able to stop our deaths. And your daughter is married with two kids. She's a pediatrician." I pause. I should tell her about her own death, but this might be my one bargaining chip. "I promise to tell you more once I know we're safe…including how you died."

She gasps. "I died? While you were in the future?"

But I just raise an eyebrow and wait.

She purses her lips and sits back in her chair, considering. "What can I do to help?"

I collect the papers off the table and shove them in my bag. "I've already emailed copies of these reports to a friend. If something happens to me, she'll go public with them. If something happens to the others, I'll do the same. Aether's experiments and the effects of future shock—and how they want to use little kids next—will be all over the Internet. But if Aether leaves us alone, this will never get out. We'll keep it a secret if you let us live our lives in peace."

"I see…" She drums her fingers against the table. "I find it hard to believe Aether would have you killed, but I'll make sure you're safe from them. I guarantee they'll leave you all alone—but in return, I want to know *everything* that happened to you in the future."

"If we make it out of this alive, I'll tell you everything, I swear."

"Good." She stands up and sets her hand on my arm. "Elena, you don't need to worry. Nothing is going to happen to you or your friends. I promise."

It's hard to tell if she believes me or if she's just telling me what I want to hear. Maybe she thinks I'm suffering the paranoia side effect of future shock. Either way, I believe she'll honestly try to help us and will do everything she can to keep us safe. That's no guarantee we'll live past tomorrow, but it's the best I can do.

FRIDAY

I don't go to school the next day. I plead to Mrs. Robertson that I'm sick and show her my bandaged ribs, and she takes pity on me and lets me stay in bed. I sleep for hours, longer than I have in years. Making up for lost time, I suppose.

When I wake, it's already 1:00 p.m. Katie's at school, so I'm alone in our room. I pack a bag, throwing my meager belongings into it. It's strange, being back in my bedroom after everything I've lived through. It feels too normal and I…am not.

My mind keeps replaying everything that happened yesterday. I can't stop thinking about the future, and how in a few hours I'll be dead—or not. By coming back to the present, did I kill the others and myself? Did I change the future and save our lives when I took the evidence to Lynne? Or was this how it happened all along, in one never-ending loop?

Did we change our fate? Or did we make it happen?

Either way, I'm not going to sit around and let death find me. I grab my bag and sneak out of the house.

First, I go to a nearby bank and open a checking account—I never needed one before today. They deposit my check from Aether and I ask for $5,000 in cash from the teller. It barely makes a dent in all the money in my account.

I should feel free now. I don't have to worry about what will happen after I turn eighteen. I can go to college, find a place to live. My future looks bright for the first time in my life, but I still feel like I shouldn't be here in the present. And thinking of how I almost stayed in the future brings back memories of Adam and how he betrayed us. A part of me wishes I could talk to him. A part of me wants to strangle him.

I take a bus downtown to Union Station. The crowd surges around me as I check the train times on the screen. This is the last part of my plan to keep us all alive. If I'm gone, I can't kill anyone. If I disappear, Aether won't be able to find me. And since they know I have evidence against them, they won't kill the others—not unless they want me to go public with it.

I buy a ticket to New Orleans, the farthest city available. I check my watch. Thirteen minutes until the train arrives. Thirty-six minutes until the window for Trent's death begins. He's supposed to be killed sometime between 3:00 and 4:30 p.m. But I've done everything I could to make sure we'll all be safe. *We're not going to die*, I tell myself over and over.

But I can't help feeling like I missed something, like I forgot something, some piece of the puzzle, some part of the equation. But that's impossible. I never forget anything. Everything is stored away in my head. I just can't see how it all fits together.

Maybe I can text Trent, tell him to be careful or to get out of town, just in case. But as I grab my phone I realize I don't have his number. I don't even know if he *has* a phone.

But I remember the location where he was killed. I could go there, make sure he's still alive...

No, I have to get on this train. It's the only way to guarantee I won't kill the others. The only way I'll know for sure that I'll be alive tomorrow.

But with each passing minute the feeling that something's wrong grows. It gnaws at me, itching underneath my skin, begging me to scratch at it. My gut tells me none of us are safe, and I can't ignore it.

The train arrives, but I can't get on. I have to know if Trent is okay. Even if it might lead to my own death.

I bolt out of the station and run to the nearest bus stop, but the bus isn't there yet. I pace back and forth under the hot, relentless sun. The future was so cold and wet that I forgot we were having a heat wave in the present.

Finally, the bus arrives. I jump inside, swipe my pass, and rush to the back. It takes about a million years for everyone to load onto the bus, and then we're moving, but we're still too slow. I grip the back of the seat in front of me, willing the bus to go faster, but there's traffic. Of course there's traffic; we're in LA.

It's a long ride to Trent's part of the city. I keep muttering, "C'mon, c'mon." People around me give me looks and move to different seats. They probably think I'm crazy or looking to pick a fight. I check the map on my phone, memorizing the route I need to take as soon as I get off. I just pray I'm not too late.

We finally reach my stop, and I jump out the side door and race down the street. I don't know this area, but the map is burned into my mind and I remember exactly where to go. Turn right here. Then left there. My ankle and side begin to throb, but adrenaline and fear keep me going. I have to make sure Trent is safe before I can get on with my life. I have to make sure the future we saw isn't starting.

By the time I find the address, sweat has soaked through my

tank top and my entire body aches. A chain-link fence surrounds a rundown building covered in graffiti. I can't tell if it used to be an apartment or something else, but it's clearly abandoned now. I find a gap in the fence to duck through and slowly walk to the entrance, eyes darting around for a sign of anything suspicious.

The front door is unlocked. It creaks open, and the room inside is dark, with only pinpricks of light bursting through the boarded-up windows. A musty old smell fills my nose.

"Trent?" I call out from the doorway. Shivers creep up my spine despite the heat. There could be someone hiding inside, watching me, or a dead body at my feet, and I wouldn't know it.

I turn on my phone's flashlight and wave it around. The place is empty and gutted, just wooden planks and chipped pieces of tile, with bits of plaster and foam scattered around the floor. My heart pounds as I scan the space, but I don't see any dead bodies or any movement.

"Trent?" I take a step forward, the floor groaning under my weight. A thick layer of dust and cobwebs hangs over everything, and I imagine there must be rats and spiders and God knows what else living here. But I don't see any sign of Trent. Maybe this isn't the place.

I creep farther inside and swing the light—and see a shape in the corner. A lump.

I hold my breath, terrified of what I might be looking at, but it's just a pile of blankets surrounded by trash. But as I get closer, I realize it's not trash. It's clothes and library books and empty packs of cigarettes. Something shiny and metallic catches the light from within the blankets. I bend down and pick it up. Trent's silver lighter.

This is the place. Trent must be squatting here—but where is he? I can't imagine he'd leave his lighter behind, not when he played with it constantly. This is wrong, all wrong. I shouldn't be here. I need to get the hell out of this place, but I have to know what happened to Trent. I have to know he's okay.

A creak behind me makes me drop the lighter and spin around, heart pounding. I wave the flashlight all over the place but don't see anything in the darkness. I do another sweep, just to be sure.

The light flashes over a tiny, dark spot on the wall across from me that seems out of place somehow. I inch closer, both drawn to the spot and repulsed by it. As I move my light, I see more tiny spots across the wall…and some of them are dripping.

My mind screams, *No, no, no*, but I keep moving the light down, following the trail to a puddle of inky wet darkness at my feet.

I jump back, crying out. It's blood; it has to be. Panic makes my legs move, and then I'm in front of the building on the other side of the fence—with no idea how I got there. I bend over, clutching my side and trying not to vomit on my shoes. I can't breathe, can't think, can't stop shaking.

Because even though there was no body, I know, *I know* in my heart that Trent is dead.

* * *

The dumpster is a few blocks away, behind a Thai restaurant. I remember the location from the reports in Future-Adam's safe. Maybe I should have come here first, but I have to believe that Trent is still alive. I have to hang on to the shred of hope that his body won't be in the dumpster or that he'll be injured and not dead, and I can somehow still save him. Otherwise it will all be for nothing.

And I'm not ready to give up yet.

I drag over a wooden crate and stand on it to lift off the dumpster's cover. It hits the back of the restaurant with a loud *bang*, and the smell assaults my nose: trash, rotten food, and something else I don't want to identify. For a second I keep my eyes closed, unable to look. Because if I look and see what I know will be in there, then it will be real.

I open my eyes. At first I don't see anything unusual. Trash bags, discarded boxes and containers, moldy fruit.

But then I see it. A pale hand.

I choke back a sob and lean into the dumpster to shove trash out of the way with my bare hands. I barely even notice how disgusting it is. I find Trent's blond hair and wrap my arms around his chest to pull him free. His head flops to the side, and there's blood all over his clothes, and his skin is weird, and I know he's gone, but I can't, I can't, I can't—

"Hey, what are you doing?" a voice yells. I jerk up, dropping Trent's body back into the dumpster. A guy in a white apron stands at the back door of the restaurant, glaring at me.

"I-I, um…" I stumble to the ground, tripping on the edge of the crate. I can't explain this, can't even comprehend what is happening right now, but I know how this must look.

I run.

When my head clears, I'm leaning against a wall, clutching my side and gasping for air. Sweat drips from my forehead, mixing with the tears streaking down my face. Tremors of pain and grief shoot through me as I picture Trent's lifeless body, dumped with the trash. I remember how he cooked for us and bargained for our IDs with his last pack of cigarettes. How he saved me from the guard in Aether's lobby. I think of how he wanted a second chance to turn his life around. Now that chance has been stolen from him.

Why didn't he run? Why didn't he stay away from the place where he knew he would be killed?

Except…he didn't know. He knew the approximate time of his death and where his body was found and how he died, but he didn't see the crime scene photos or read the reports. He didn't know the specifics. None of them did. I'm the only one who knew all the details of their murders.

I've made a terrible mistake. I should have told them everything. If I had been honest with them, maybe Trent would be alive now.

I may not have pulled the trigger, but his death is my fault.

But I still have a chance to stop the other murders. I consider calling the police, but they'll think I did it or want to take me in for questioning—especially after that guy saw me with Trent's body. Maybe Lynne can help me if I tell her what's going on. She promised me we'd be safe, but Trent is dead, so obviously that was a big, fat lie.

My one comfort is that I know now I'm not the killer.

My heart refuses to believe Adam would shoot Trent and leave his body in a dumpster. But my head says I can't trust him either, even though I don't think he's a murderer.

Aether gave us the guns in our backpacks—it *must* be them, trying to get rid of us and set me up as the murderer. Either Lynne failed to help us, or she lied to me and is in on it. Maybe, by trying to blackmail Aether, I'm the reason we're being killed—although it would make more sense for them to just kill me then.

Oh God, I don't know what to do. I don't know if anything I've done has changed the future, or only made it worse. Or if it's impossible to change our fate at all. Maybe all we can do is let fate carry us toward our grim destiny.

No. Screw that. I grab my phone and dial Aether's number with trembling fingers and ask for Lynne.

"I'm sorry," the receptionist says. "She's out of the office at the moment. Can I take a message?"

"No, just…tell her to call me."

Damn. What else can I do? I don't have Zoe or Chris's number—but I do remember Chris saying he works for Downey Automotive. I call the shop, but some other guy answers. When I ask for Chris he puts me on hold for a good five minutes then says Chris isn't there. I get the feeling he's lying, but I give him my number and tell him it's urgent.

I doubt Chris will call me. Not if he thinks there's a chance I might be the killer. My only choice is to find Zoe. I know that by going to the crime scenes I might be helping them frame me for these murders, but I push off the wall and start toward the bus stop anyway. Because if Trent is dead, then we haven't changed the future and we're all going to die in the next few hours. And Zoe is next.

* * *

I leap off the bus and dash down the street toward the address memorized in my head. It's like déjà vu, except the sun is lower and the neighborhood is nicer and there are tears in my eyes that won't fall, not yet, because I refuse to believe Zoe's already dead.

It took me two different buses to get to the area where Zoe's girlfriend lives. I check my watch as I near the boxy, gray apartment building—5:46 p.m., and the police report said she died sometime between four thirty and six. I might still have time.

I circle the building until I find the right unit, then stand in front of the door listening, afraid to do anything else. I don't want to see what's inside, because a part of me already knows what I'll find.

Finally, I knock. No answer.

I wait a moment and then knock again, harder. Still nothing. Why isn't she answering? Is she already—?

"Zoe?" I yell through the door, pounding on it with my fists.

My inner voice is telling me to run, yelling that I'm setting myself up, but I don't know what else to do. If there's a chance Zoe is alive in there I have to try to save her.

I check the doorknob, using my shirt so I don't leave fingerprints this time. It opens easily—the door isn't locked.

"Zoe?" I step inside a small studio apartment with drab gray carpet. There's a queen-size bed with a yellow comforter, a small TV, and a desk. Art decorates the walls, plastering them with sketches, paintings, charcoal drawings. I recognize it as Zoe's work.

But the place has been trashed—drawers and cabinets open everywhere, clothes thrown across the floor, a broken lamp in the corner. Whoever was here must have been looking for something, but they're already gone.

I hear the sound of running water from behind a closed door. I try to convince myself that Zoe is just taking a shower, but I remember the crime scene photos and I know what's coming. I'm already crying as I open the door.

The shower's on and the room is like a sauna, full of hot, moist air. I smell something metallic that sends waves of primal horror through me. I choke and cover my mouth with my shirt. It's a tiny bathroom, just a sink, a toilet, and a tub crammed together. I force myself to push aside the shower curtain.

Zoe's lying in the tub with the shower's spray directly above her head. It drips down onto her blue hair and over her limp body, the water mixing with the blood and turning pink before washing down the drain. There's more blood on the wall where the water doesn't reach, and bullet holes in the tile behind her. My mind processes all of this and files it away before I can react, before I drop to my knees beside her and clutch my head, hyperventilating and making little gasping sounds.

I squeeze my eyes shut, wishing I could scrub the image of her body from my brain. I already saw it once in the photos, but it's a thousand times worse in person. I didn't know Zoe long, but in those few short hours, she became my friend. She proved to be braver than I originally thought when she convinced Wombat to help us and later when she crawled through those ducts and set off the smoke bomb. She wanted to go to art school and to be reunited with her little sister and give her a better life. But I failed her and now she's dead like Trent.

Maybe Future-Adam was right, and we can't change the future. Maybe, no matter what happens, our fate is already written and we're just puppets being pulled along by strings. And by traveling to the future, the five of us are forced to relive this loop over and over.

I switch off the water and briefly touch her blue hair to say good-bye. I might have failed Zoe and Trent, but I still have a few hours until my own clock runs out. I can still escape, get out of the city, try to flee my fate.

But what about Chris? He has a kid on the way—I can't abandon him. I need to tell him the others are dead at the very least, but he won't answer my calls.

I have to track him down in person.

* * *

Downey Automotive is a hole-in-the-wall mechanic shop that fixes banged-up cars that were in accidents and fender benders. They're scattered across the lot behind a chain-link fence. As I approach, a big black dog barks at me from the other side. A guy looks up from the hood of one of the cars, but he's not Chris.

The inside of the shop is hot enough to melt your skin off, with one wimpy fan blowing in the corner. Sweat rolls down my back, hot and slick under my tank top. Behind the counter is a guy in his twenties who's completely covered in tattoos, even along his neck and hands. Three days ago he totally would have been my type.

He gives me a slow once-over with a grin. "Hey, mami, con que te ayudo?" I get the feeling he's asking if I need help with more than just my car.

"I'm looking for Chris."

"He's gone." The guy leans back and crosses his arms. "You the one who called earlier?"

"Yeah. Could you give me his number, por favor?"

He rubs the back of his neck. "I don't know. I can't just hand out his number to some random hyna."

"It's an emergency." I lean on the counter and give him my best pleading look. The guy's eyes immediately dart down to my chest. He's not exactly subtle. But he isn't budging either. "It's about Shawnda," I add.

He gives my boobs another long appraisal and clears his throat. "Yeah, okay. But don't tell him you got it from me."

"Gracias." I glance at my watch while he scribbles numbers on a Post-it. Chris only has an hour before the window of his death begins. This is my one chance to warn him before then, and if this number doesn't work, if this guy is playing me, there's nothing else I can do.

But just as I'm slipping the number in my pocket, Chris walks into the shop. "Cortez, give us a minute," he says, and the guy behind the counter disappears into the back.

I almost want to hug Chris it's such a relief to see him alive. But he glares at me, the muscles in his neck twitching, a heavy wrench clutched in his hand.

"What the hell are you doing here?" he asks.

"Trent and Zoe are dead," I say quickly. "I think you're next. You have to get out of here. You have to—"

"What?" His eyes bulge a little. "How do you know they're dead?"

"I-I went to see them and found their bodies."

He grips the wrench harder and growls, "Get out of here. Now."

"Chris, listen to me. I'm not the killer. I don't even have a gun!"

"Yeah? And where's your boyfriend?"

"I don't know! But I don't think he's the killer either."

"No, course not. 'Cause he tricked you, and now he's going to set you up." He shakes his head. "You're the one who should run."

"But Shawnda and your son—"

"I don't need your help!" he yells, getting right up in my face. "I have it under control! Now get out of here before I call the cops!"

I step back, stunned by his outburst. I don't think he'll hurt me, but then again, he had no problem punching me before. The fan whizzes behind us as I stand there, staring at him and willing him to listen to me. But he just smacks the wrench against his palm, his eyes hard, and I finally turn around and walk out.

I can't believe he's so stubborn. I did everything I could—I called, I tracked him down, I tried to help him—but I guess he can take care of himself. If he would just *listen* to me, we could work something out to save both of us. But as usual, I'm on my own.

I don't know where to go or what to do next. My body moves mechanically, my brain completely shut down. I only snap out of it when I realize I've walked five blocks under the relentless sun and I'm dying of thirst.

I stop at a convenience store to buy some water and then get the bathroom key from the manager. Once inside, I take a minute to dig the blood out from under my nails, but the sight of it flaking into the sink brings back all the images of Trent and Zoe. Everything hits me again—the bodies, the smell, the lifeless look in their eyes—and I rush to the toilet to throw up.

Once my entire stomach is empty and my throat burns, I slump next to the toilet. The floor's covered in piss and a cockroach skitters by, but I can't find the will to get up. My gut aches from the vomiting and my cracked rib, and now that I've stopped moving, my ankle feels like it's on fire. But the real pain is from knowing my friends are dead, and there's nothing I can do to fix it. I wish I could go back and do everything over, but the only time travel to the past is regret.

No, dammit, I'm not dead yet. I heave myself off the disgusting floor and clean myself up in the sink. I need another plan.

I call Aether again, but Lynne is still out of the office. I scramble for other ideas. The evidence from the future is still in my bag. I said I'd go public with it if any of us were killed, but the truth is, I'm not exactly sure how to do that. I was hoping Katie could help me—she's a bit more computer savvy than I am—but when I text her, she says she's about to meet with her social worker. I'm hesitant to involve her in this anyway. I don't need anyone else to get killed because of me.

Maybe I should enlist my foster mother for help. I don't want to put her in danger either, but at least she could hang on to the hard copies of the reports, in case something happens to me.

I dig through my bag for the reports and my hand brushes something else made of paper: Adam's origami unicorn, the one he made from a napkin at that first lunch together. It's a bit crushed and rumpled now, but as I run my hands over the folds, all the memories of Adam that I've tried to repress flood my brain.

My feelings for him made me blind, made me go against everything I've learned in my seventeen years: to not trust anyone but myself. But despite everything that happened, despite the fact he lied to me and betrayed our team, I still can't believe he's a murderer.

He may have been working for Aether, but the way I found Trent and Zoe…Adam could never have done that. I don't know if anything between us was real, but I *know* him on some level, and he's not a killer.

It doesn't matter. I'm done with Adam. We had a brief fling, but it's over now. If he cared for me at all, he would have been honest with me about what he was doing. I crumple the unicorn into a ball and throw it across the bathroom.

Future-Adam's words come back to me, telling me to trust his younger self when the time came. I thought he meant that moment in the rain when Adam asked me to open up to him, but maybe I was wrong. Maybe he meant before the aperture opened, when Adam said he was recruited to get the cure. He never got the chance to explain, and I never gave him another one. And like Future-Adam said, we're never going to see each other again.

I head for the door, but as I step over the crumpled unicorn I pause. Wait. Future-Adam said he never saw any of us after we got back. Does that mean if I go to Adam now I'll be doing something different, something that didn't happen in the other timeline? Or did he lie to me about that too?

I have to make a decision. But whatever I choose, there's no way to know if I'm changing my fate or just following through with it.

The first path is the one the normal Elena would follow, the one my head says to follow now—to forget Adam and go through with my plan to use the evidence against Aether.

But the other path is a complete shift from everything I know, the opposite of what I'd normally do, and the thing my heart desperately wants me to do: to trust Adam.

I pick up the origami unicorn and make my choice.

* * *

Adam lives near LAX—I saw his address in our file, when we broke into Aether headquarters—on a street of identical one-story houses. The grass hasn't been mowed in a while, and there's an older Toyota sitting in the driveway. I check the numbers on the porch again. This is it.

I can turn around now. I can run away, escape down to Mexico or something, and try to save myself. But I can't shake the feeling there's something I missed, some clue I can't put together, and Adam is the key. I don't know how, but he is. And though every thought, every nerve, every muscle is yelling at me to turn around, I ring the doorbell.

Adam opens the door in a button-down shirt and jeans. His hair is messy, his eyes are tired and his glasses slightly askew, but he's more handsome than ever. He sucks in a breath at the sight of me. "Elena."

I don't know what to say. There's too much to explain, too many words between us, too many questions and explanations and apologies. I'm torn between wanting to throw myself into his arms and trying to shake the answers out of him. Instead I blurt out, "Trent and Zoe are dead."

"What? Dead—are you sure?"

"I saw them. They were shot, just like Future-Adam's files said."

Before I can say anything else, a brown dog pokes his head around Adam, tongue panting. The dog tries to lurch past Adam to get to me, but Adam pulls him back. This must be the dog Adam told me about.

"Sorry about Max," Adam says. "Do you want to come in?"

I step into a small living room with striped furniture and a table with a huge stack of untouched mail on it. Max spins in circles, tail wagging, butt wiggling, a big doggy grin on his face. I kneel down and wrap my arms around his neck, burying my face in his warm fur and happy body. It's exactly what I need right now.

"Are you okay?" Adam asks. "Sorry, that's a stupid question. Of course you're not okay. But I mean, you're not hurt, right?"

"I'm fine." I reluctantly stand up, and Max bounds off to do laps around the sofa. "But Trent and Zoe are both dead, and someone saw me with Trent's body, and I tried to warn Chris but he wouldn't listen, and I only have a few hours left before I'm going to die, but I don't know what to do, and—"

He stops my rambling by putting his hands on my shoulders. "Elena, it's okay. Slow down, and we'll figure it out."

Footsteps sound down the hall, and we both jump back like we've been caught kissing. An older woman in a green robe and fuzzy slippers stands in the doorway. She has a scarf wrapped around her head.

"Adam, is everything okay?" she asks, eyeing me. Not in a suspicious or hostile way, the way some parents might look when confronted with a tatted-up Mexican girl in their living room, but with curiosity. I imagine Adam doesn't bring many girls home.

"Yeah, Mom. This is Elena…She's a friend."

I can't help feeling like I don't belong here, but I step forward and offer her my hand. "Nice to meet you, Mrs. O'Neill."

"Very nice to meet you too, Elena." She grips my hand and I'm shocked by how bony hers is, how thin her fingers are. She looks older than she probably is, her skin sallow and hanging from her bones. There are bruises along her arm, like she's been injected or had blood drawn many times. She takes her hand away and adjusts the scarf, and I realize she has no hair.

I flash back to Adam saying his mom was "having a hard time." *Of course.* She has cancer. That's why he develops the cure in the first place, why he brought it back from the future, and why he couldn't let the others take it.

He did everything to save her life.

His mom gives us a tiny smile, like she knows what we're up to. "I'm going to get some water and then I'll leave you two alone."

"I'll get it for you," Adam says, already moving toward the kitchen. "You should go back to bed."

When he's gone, there's a second of awkward silence as I stand there with his mom. But she keeps smiling at me. "Adam's a good son."

"I know." I rub a finger over my mother's watch, missing her all over again. If I'd had a chance to save her, I would have taken it too. Even if it meant lying or stealing or betraying someone close to me.

Adam returns with some water and helps his mom back to her room, Max bouncing behind him. I hear Adam say something about giving her another shot soon, and then he tells her to rest.

He returns to the living room, his hands shoved in his pockets. "Elena—"

"Your mom," I interrupt. "She has cancer."

"Yeah." He stares at the floor. "That's why I took the cure. But I was never working for Aether, I swear."

"Then who recruited you to steal the cure?"

"It was Lynne. Aether never knew about it."

Lynne—so she *was* in on it the entire time. A memory floats to the surface, from in front of the lab when Lynne asked Adam, "Did you get it?" She wasn't asking if we got evidence—she was asking if he got the cure.

"Why didn't you tell me?" I ask, the question that's been eating me up ever since I saw him drop the case.

He sighs. "I hated lying to you, but I couldn't tell anyone about my true mission. I knew you would all think I was working for Aether and was somehow behind all of your deaths. And I didn't trust the others with the cure—especially once I found out what it did to people without cancer. But I'm not a killer. You must know that."

"I do. That's why I'm here."

A sad smile crosses his face. "I wanted to call you, but I didn't have your number, and I've been taking care of my mom all day. And…I didn't think you wanted to hear from me."

"No, I should have trusted you. I should have listened to you or come here sooner or…"

"Maybe. But I should have fought harder for you."

We move together at the same time, our lips meeting in a desperate kiss. His hands slide down my arms, along my tattoos, and I dig my fingers in his hair, pulling him closer. I'm afraid to let go, afraid to let the kiss end, afraid to face what's coming in the next few hours. Because for the first time since we returned to the present, I feel like I'm exactly where I'm supposed to be.

When the kiss ends, he rests his forehead against mine. "I'm really glad you came to see me."

"Me too. I wasn't going to, but…I changed my mind."

"I didn't think I'd ever see you again. I knew I wasn't suffering from future shock, but I didn't know about the rest of you."

"Wait," I say, pulling back. "If Lynne knew about future shock, wasn't she worried you'd come back crazy?"

"Not really. Dr. Kapur was pretty confident that none of us would suffer from it. Plus, she was desperate. Her daughter is dying from leukemia, so she needed the cure right away."

"Her daughter…" The photos I saw in the future, of Lynne's daughter in a hospital bed.

"That's how I met Lynne. Her daughter is in the children's ward of the hospital where my mom gets her treatments. Lynne was always there, and we talked about my mom and my studies and this scholarship I got…"

"But how did Lynne know about the cure?"

"When she sent the third group of people to the future, the ones who remembered some things, one of them told her I'd just developed a cure. I didn't believe her at first, but she convinced me that if I brought the cure back, we could save both my mom and her daughter. That's why I signed up. Well, that and I was desperate for money. We were about to sell this house to pay off the medical bills before Aether came along with their offer." He looks down at the floor, sucking in a long breath. "I'm sorry I didn't tell you. I wanted to, but I couldn't risk not being able to bring back the cure."

But as he speaks, I'm not really listening anymore, because his words are like a puzzle piece fitting everything together. Memories flash in rapid succession: the moment before the aperture opened, when Trent reached for the case of genicote. Back in the present, when he told the others, "I swiped something from Lynne's office we can use as leverage." Zoe's girlfriend's apartment, ransacked as though someone was looking for something. Lynne being out of the office all day.

"Did Lynne call you today?" I ask slowly, not wanting to believe the theory forming in my head.

"Yeah, she called me this morning. She asked if I had any extra doses of the cure, but I didn't. I asked her if there was a problem. She said no, and then she hung up. Why?"

It's not Aether Corp trying to kill us. I was wrong this entire time. Lynne is the killer.

I can't believe it. I trusted Lynne. She wanted to help us. She *saved* us in the future.

No, she saved *Adam*. The one person who could cure her

daughter. She never cared about the rest of us. She just needed to make sure Adam brought the cure back. And she had to make sure he returned to the present to develop the cure in the first place. The rest of us were disposable.

In the future, she lied to us about Dr. Kapur wanting to "purge" us. She's the one who recruited us in the first place. It all makes sense. Perfect, horrible sense.

Trent must have stolen the cure from her to try to use it to protect us, but Lynne needed that to save her daughter's life. She must have tracked him down, and when he wouldn't give it to her, she killed him. The others must have been in on it too, which is why she searched Zoe's place. Does that mean she didn't find the cure—does Chris have it? Is that what he meant when he said he was handling it?

I would never believe Lynne could kill someone, but I saw her shoot that cop. She had zero hesitation with the gun. Her aim was perfect. And if she would kill an innocent cop to save her daughter, I can believe she'd kill us too.

"Elena?" Adam asks, searching my face. "Why do you ask?"

"Um. I was just curious because I tried to call her earlier. But she wasn't in the office."

"Oh." He runs a finger along my arm, staring into the distance. "I talked to her when we got back from the future and told her that you thought Aether was going to kill us. She said she'd protect us, but if the others are dead, then…" He trails off and shakes his head. "But it doesn't matter, because by coming here you've already changed the timeline, right?"

"I don't know." Chris could already be dead by now. There's nothing I can do for him or for the others, but I might have time to stop Lynne from pinning the murders on me and getting away with it. It makes me sick, knowing that in the future she's friends with Adam and he had no idea she was the one behind our murders. That is not going to happen this time.

Adam's right—I changed the future by coming here, and I can change it again now.

But I can't call the police. I have no real evidence Lynne is the killer, and I can't tell them some crazy story about the future and the cure for cancer. I don't even know where Lynne is right now.

But I know where she *will* be.

"We'll figure it out." Adam breaks through my thoughts again, giving me a grin. "Hey, I said I was going to protect you and I meant it."

I force a smile. "I thought I was the one protecting you."

"Not this time." He wraps his arms around me and I breathe in his warmth, wishing I could freeze this instant forever. This memory, this is the one I want to remember. Because I have to lie to Adam to save him.

I can't tell him about Lynne. He'll want to come with me, and I care too much about him and his future to risk his life. I have to know that even if I fail, Adam will live to develop the cure and save millions of lives.

"Do you have any food?" I ask. "I haven't eaten anything all day."

"Oh, yeah. We have some pasta leftover from dinner. I'll go fix some for you."

"Thanks."

He kisses me quickly and then heads into the kitchen. I watch him as he disappears, memorizing every movement, every line of his body, every strand of his hair. And then I silently slip out the front door.

* * *

There's a message waiting for me when I leave Adam's. I pace at the empty bus stop while I listen to it.

"Elena, I got your message," Lynne says, sounding worried. "Call me back right away."

This is it. I can confront her right now about being the killer, about shooting the others and setting me up...but there's still a slight chance I'm wrong. I *want* to be wrong.

I dial the number she gave me, and she picks up on the first ring.

"Oh, Elena, thank goodness. Are you okay?"

I sit down hard on the bus stop bench, gripping the phone. For a second I can't speak, can't decide what to say to her. "I'm okay. But the others...they're dead."

"What? Are you sure?"

"Yeah. I saw them. I-I think Aether killed them."

She sucks in a breath. "I tried to stop them. I told my boss you had evidence and would use it if something happened, but...No, we shouldn't talk about this over the phone. They could be listening. I can help you, but we need to need to meet in person."

A chill creeps along my bare skin. "Where?"

"Somewhere we can talk in private. Aether is looking for you, and I'm sure they're watching me. We need to be careful."

"How about...the beach?"

"Oh—I was just about to suggest that. Perfect. Maybe at the fifth lifeguard tower north of the pier?"

I close my eyes, all my suspicions confirmed with those few words. There's no way Lynne could know my body was found there. She *is* the killer.

If I hadn't gone to see Adam, I would have trusted Lynne in this moment. I would have met her at the beach, hoping she would help me, never suspecting she was the killer. No wonder she was able to take me down so easily. She used my trust and my desperation against me.

"Elena…are you there?" Lynne sounds so worried that I almost believe she actually cares.

"Yeah. That place sounds good."

"Perfect. Can you be there around eleven thirty?"

"I'll be there."

"I'll see you then." Lynne pauses. "And, Elena, be careful."

"I will."

The call ends, and I clutch my phone in my lap. In a few minutes this will all be over, one way or another.

I check my watch. It's after ten, near the end of Chris's window. For all I know he's already dead, but I have to try to warn him one last time.

I dial his number, the one the guy at Downey Automotive wrote on the Post-it. It rings twice and then clicks to voice mail. As soon as it beeps, the words rush out of me. "Chris, this is Elena. The killer is Lynne. Stay away from her. Get Shawnda and run—just whatever you do, don't meet with Lynne. I know you don't trust me, but please, *please* believe me about this."

There's nothing more I can say, so I hang up. Dammit. I'm too late. If only he had listened to me earlier, if only I had been up-front with him from the beginning…but he's probably already dead, and now his son will grow up without a father. Lynne's taken both of their futures.

I don't need to see Chris's body to know how he died. I remember the crime scene photos perfectly. Shot like the other two and ditched on a street corner two blocks from Downey Automotive. I clench my fists, white-hot anger building at the thought of what she's done. Of how she almost got away with it.

Not this time.

* * *

The fifth lifeguard tower stands alone before the waves, a raised white box against the dark sea. I make my way toward it, shoes sinking in the sand, and each step reminds me of when I came here with Adam. I couldn't understand then why I would kill myself in this spot, but now it seems like I was fated to come here to fight for my future.

By the time I reach the tower, I'm clutching my side and breathing heavily, and I've stumbled twice on my weak ankle. Everything hurts, but I can't lose focus now. I'm early—it's only eleven—and I check the voice recorder app I downloaded on the bus. I switch it on and then stuff my phone in my underwear, a place I figure Lynne won't search me if I die. But the police will find it. I just have to get Lynne to confess, so that she won't get away with our murders. I won't let Adam spend the rest of his life trusting a murderer.

I lean against the side of the lifeguard tower, scanning the beach around me. It's pitch-black except for the faint sliver of the moon and the dim light on the sand. Everything here is in black and white—the sand, the water, the sky, the few stars visible over the light of the city. The only thing with any color is the Ferris wheel in the distance.

After some time, a slim figure approaches from the parking lot, moving quickly over the sand. As it gets closer I make out the shape of a woman in a suit. Lynne.

I wait for her to come to me, knowing this has to end here, tonight. I wish I had a weapon or something, but without a gun of my own I'd always be at a disadvantage. She's probably never been in a real fight before though. My best chance is to get her to confess, distract her, and then attack.

When she's only a few feet away, she raises the gun with a gloved hand. "Hello, Elena."

I don't see any regret or hesitation in her eyes. Her hand is steady as she aims at me. And that certainty, that confidence scares me more than anything else. I *trusted* her. We all did, and now she's aiming a gun at me like it's no big deal. How could she lie to our faces, both now and in the future? How could she swear she would help us and then kill us all?

"You don't seem surprised to see the gun," she says. "But I had a feeling you knew when you suggested the beach. Did you see that in the future?"

I step back quickly, my feet slow and catching in the sand. Suddenly I doubt my plan. Why did I think I could fight against a woman with a gun? The recording, I remind myself. I have to get her to talk.

"You lied to us all along, both you and your future self," I say. "Our entire trip to the future was set up just so you could get the cure, wasn't it?"

"That's true. Dr. Kapur *did* want to use teenagers, but I had to convince Aether to go along with it so I could recruit Adam. I figured he had the best chance of getting the cure, and I didn't have time to send multiple teams. And I chose the rest of you to assist him, even if you didn't know that's what you were doing. You, in particular, were chosen to protect Adam. From your files I knew you liked to fight for the underdog. That's why I gave you a gun."

All this time I thought I was chosen for my memory, but that was another lie. I flash back to the first time I met Lynne. She asked me if I liked to fight and I said, "No, but I will if I have to." I remember her smile at hearing those words.

And on that first day at the Aether facility, they'd left the five of us alone, probably to see what we did and how we interacted. Only after I defended Adam from Chris did Lynne walk in and start talking about the project. Even my feelings for Adam were manipulated from the very beginning.

I glance around, looking for help or a way out. I have to keep her talking. "And you sent us thirty years into the future instead of ten, didn't you?"

"I had to. Adam discovered the cure ten years from now, but it was still brand-new and untested and not available to the public yet. I wasn't sure how many years it would take for it to be safe to use and widely available, so I secretly set the accelerator back to its previous setting. I figured in thirty years it should be easy for Adam—or his future self—to get the cure."

"But why kill us?" I ask, inching closer to her. "You got your cure!"

She sighs, and I hear the first hint of emotion in her voice. "I never planned for any of this to happen, truly. Trent stole my doses of the cure, and when I went to talk to him, he said he didn't have them. But then he attacked me and I shot him. It was an accident, I swear. After that…well, I had to deal with the others too."

"You *killed* them," I spit out. "They trusted you, and you killed them!"

"I just wanted the cure back! My daughter…she only has weeks left to live. Maybe *days*. Do you know what it's like, watching your four-year-old child wither away in a hospital bed, and there's nothing you can do? The cure was the *only* way to save her life!"

"But you have the cure now. I won't tell anyone about this," I lie as the wind twists my hair behind me. "You don't need to do this!"

"I'm sorry, Elena. I like you. I really do. But once you came to me with the evidence, I had to stop you from going public with it. I don't want to kill you, but this is the only way to tie up all the loose ends."

My life is just a loose end to her. I want to shout at her that I'm a person, just like the others she killed, with goals and dreams and a future of my own. But something catches her gaze along the beach, and for a second the gun dips down. This is my chance.

I rush her, slamming against her with my weight. A sharp cry escapes me as the pain in my side spikes from the impact. We go down and struggle in the sand, wrestling for the gun. But then she hits me in the ribs and I scream, pain crashing through me like a tidal wave. She whips the gun against my face, and I'm knocked on my back, momentarily stunned.

She kneels over me, pressing the gun to my temple. I dig my fingers in the sand, but my head spins and everything hurts, and I know this is the end, this is how she'll make it look like I killed myself.

"Lynne—" I start, but then I see someone behind her, a dark figure against the dark sky.

"Lynne!" Adam says. "What—"

"Adam?" Her head turns at the sound of his voice.

No! What is he doing here? He shouldn't be here!

Adam smashes into Lynne, forcing the gun away from my head. And suddenly I can breathe again, my mind clearing. I scramble to my knees, fighting to move through the pain. I have to get up. I have to help Adam. I have to save him.

Lynne brings the gun up to point at Adam and icy dread freezes my heart. I launch myself at her in a red haze of pain and anger. I steal the gun from her hands and slam it against her face, like she did to me only minutes earlier. She falls and I move in close, gun gripped tightly in my hand.

I want to hit her again, over and over and over. I want to unleash my rage on her, to make her pay for all the deaths she's caused—but I stop myself. I'm not that person anymore. Adam convinced me I don't have to be like my father. I can control my anger and keep it from taking over.

I am *not* a killer.

I take a long breath, aiming the gun at Lynne. "Call the police," I tell Adam.

"Already did."

"No!" Lynne yells and knocks my arm away. She brings me down in the sand, a tangle of legs and arms and bodies as her hands reach for the trigger. I feel her grasp it, and I pull back just as an incredibly loud bang goes off.

The air smells of gunpowder, and I don't think I'll hear anything ever again. The gun went off—am I shot?

Lynne goes limp against me. I roll off her and quickly check myself, but I'm not hurt. She doesn't move, her glassy eyes staring up at the sky. A dark stain creeps out of her shirt and spreads to the sand, black on white, like the rest of the beach.

I scramble back and kick the gun away. Lynne is dead, but this time, I don't feel the same shock and grief as when I saw her die before. Only relief. It's over.

"Elena, are you okay? Elena!" Adam's hands travel over my body, inspecting me for injury.

"I'm okay." I grab on to his shoulders to steady myself and he wraps me in his arms. I bury my face in his neck, breathing him in to reassure myself that he's really here, that we're both still alive. "You came for me."

"I knew you'd be here. And I said I'd protect you, didn't I?"

"Yeah, you did." I tilt my head up and he kisses me, his mouth gentle, sharing his warmth and strength until I can stand on my own again.

I pull back and check my mother's watch. It's 11:38 p.m., the time of my death. I stare at the watch, holding my breath, until the minute hand moves past, ticking over to 11:39.

We did it. We changed the future.

We're free.

TUESDAY

The last time I was in the hospital was after Mamá was killed. I don't have fond memories of it, but this place is different. There are murals on the walls of dancing animals, and the floor is decorated with colorful stars. The elevator door is even bright purple.

Adam leans against the nurse's desk, smiling at the girl behind it as they chat. They all love him here, which somehow doesn't surprise me. They give him two blue volunteer jackets, and he slips one on.

"This way," he says once he's back at my side.

He hands me the second volunteer jacket, and I put it on as he leads me down the hallway. Each door is painted a different color. We stop in front of an orange one, and Adam knocks twice. When there's no response, he pushes it open.

A tiny girl lies in a hospital bed with a dozen tubes coming out of her. Her head is shiny and smooth. Her eyes are closed, her pink lips just slightly open. Her small hands grip the edge of the covers as she breathes slowly. My heart clenches; she's so young, so tiny, so innocent. I'll never forgive Lynne for what she's done, but seeing her daughter like this helps me understand why she fought so hard to save her.

Adam moves beside the bed and opens the Doctor Who lunch box he brought. He pulls out one of the three doses of the cure we found on Lynne's body and hooks it up to the girl's IV.

"I'll have to come back tomorrow night to do the second one," he says as he steps back. "It has to be delivered over three days, one dose every twenty-four hours."

"But it'll work?" I ask. "She'll be cured?"

"I think so. It seemed to work for my mom. We won't know for sure till she goes back in for tests, but I can already tell she's a lot better."

"Good." Lynne's daughter shouldn't have to pay for her mother's mistakes. And once Adam figures out how to make the cure, he'll be able to save even more lives. It took Adam ten years in that other future, but now he won't be burdened by grief or trying to figure out who killed us. He can focus on his destiny.

"How much does your mom know about the cure?" I ask.

"Not much. I told her I got an experimental drug and she wasn't allowed to ask how. I'm sure she thinks I did something illegal, but so far she hasn't asked too many questions."

The door opens and an older woman asks, "Who are you?" Her eyes are red, like she's been crying, but she looks exactly like an older version of Lynne with darker hair. Her mother, I guess.

"We're volunteers," Adam says with a warm smile. "Just checking on her."

The woman nods, and we slip past her and out the door. As it shuts, I see her take the girl's hand, and I breathe a little easier knowing Lynne's daughter won't grow up alone. I hope she still becomes a pediatrician and a mom, like I saw in Lynne's photos.

We take the elevator down a floor and find room D117. Chris opens his eyes when we enter, his face ashen. My heart lifts seeing him alive. Those pictures I saw of his body are only memories of a future that will never happen, not anymore.

"Hey," he says, sitting up. The blanket slips down, revealing a large bandage on his side. "Didn't think I'd see you two again."

"Had to come see how you're holding up," Adam says. "How are you feeling?"

"Like hell, but I'll live."

"What happened?" I ask.

"Trent gave me the cure to hide, but Lynne threatened to go after Shawnda if I didn't give it to her. I got your message right before meeting with her, but I had to hand the cure over. Barely got away in time. Still took a bullet to the chest, but I'm alive, thanks to you. I won't forget that."

My throat tightens up with emotion, knowing he trusted me enough in the end to listen to my warning. I manage to get out, "Glad you made it."

"And the two of you took her down." He whistles, which dissolves into a short round of coughing. He clutches his side and then takes a deep breath. "I just wish…Zoe and Trent…"

"Me too." I bow my head, and Adam squeezes my hand.

"I'm sorry about before and everything I said. I was wrong about both of you." Chris clasps my hand and then Adam's. "Although you're still the biggest nerd around."

"I'm okay with that," Adam says with a grin.

We chat for a few minutes about Chris's plans for the future and promise to keep in touch. As we leave, we pass Shawnda in the hall, and I smile knowing her son will grow up with a father now. Hopefully he won't end up in prison this time.

But Zoe's sister isn't so lucky. The only thing Adam and I could do was take the recording of Lynne's final words to Aether. When they offered us more money to keep quiet about it, we convinced them to set up a trust fund for Zoe's sister instead. Maybe that will be enough to give her a better future than the one we saw. And since Trent didn't have any family, we had them donate money to a homeless shelter instead. He would appreciate that, I think.

Dr. Walters told us he plans to destroy the accelerator to prevent Aether from sending anyone else to the future. I hope he succeeds, but I'm not convinced it will stop them. They may not have been behind our deaths, but they weren't exactly innocent either. I plan to keep a close eye on them.

And in thirty years, Adam and I will be ready for our younger selves. We'll find a way to save Trent and Zoe—maybe in an alternate timeline, maybe in this one.

This time, we know we can change the future.

I take Adam's hand as we leave the hospital, as we take our first steps into our new, unknown future. Together.

* * *

Adam pulls into the restaurant's parking lot, and my stomach twists when I see where we are. Seriously, of all the places to eat in LA, he had to pick this one?

"We're eating here?" I ask as he shuts off the car.

"Is that okay? I know it's not fancy, but they have great burgers…" He studies my face with a frown. "We can go somewhere else if you want."

I'm tempted to suggest another place, somewhere that won't bring back bad memories, but no, I'm being silly. I smile at him. "This is great."

He opens the door to the restaurant for me, and I take a deep breath to steel myself before walking in. Everything is exactly as I remember it. The NOW HIRING sign in the window. The smell of fried food. The waitress in a red skirt the size of a belt. Oh God, it's even the same waitress.

Her eyes pass over us and I wonder if she'll recognize me as the weird girl with the freaky memory. But then it hits me—I don't care if she does. I'm not ashamed of my eidetic memory anymore. My gift helped me stop Lynne and save Chris and myself. I'll never forget the terrible things I've seen, but I'll always remember the good things too. Zoe's smile and Trent's laugh. That first kiss with Adam in the rain. My mother's voice.

We sit at one of the tables with the hard, wooden seats and checkered tablecloth. It was Adam's idea to go on a real date like a normal couple. I'm not sure we can ever be normal, not after what we've been through together, but I'd like to try.

"I interviewed here for a job last week," I say after we look through our menus. "Didn't get it, obviously."

"Really? No wonder you wanted to eat somewhere else." He adjusts his glasses, looking worried. "We can still go…"

"No, it's fine. And it's not like I need the job anymore." Thanks to Aether, I don't need to worry about that. A few days ago I didn't even think I had a future. Now the possibilities seem almost endless.

Adam begins folding one of the paper napkins in front of him. "So what will you do now?"

I watch his long fingers work, the movements almost hypnotic. "I'm going to get my own place after I turn eighteen. I'm going to start college in the fall to become a social worker. And"—I look up to meet his gaze—"I'm going to help you develop the cure."

His eyebrows shoot up. "You are?"

"If you want my help, that is. I'm not a genius like you and don't know all that chemistry stuff, but I thought I might be able to help with the business side of things or something…"

"I would love your help, Elena." He gives a little laugh. "No, I *need* your help. I'm supposed to do all these great things in the future, but I have no idea where to even begin."

"You'll figure it out."

"Maybe. I'm just glad I won't have to do it alone this time." He slides an origami rose across to me and I smile, gently touching the soft edges.

"I was also thinking about getting another tattoo," I say.

"Oh yeah? Of what?"

"An origami unicorn."

A wide grin spreads across his face. "I can't wait to see it."

The air-conditioning kicks on overhead with a loud rumble, blasting cold air down on us. A dusty, round clock ticks overhead. 7:44 p.m. Two minutes faster than the watch on my wrist. But I don't need to count minutes or hours or days—not anymore. Adam and I have plenty of time.

The future is no longer a threat but a promise of things to come. For once, I look forward to it.

ACKNOWLEDGMENTS

This book would not exist without the help of so many people, to whom I owe my endless thanks.

To my husband, Gary Briggs, for being my inspiration, my best friend, and my number-one fan. The future seems bright as long as you're at my side.

To the Adams and Briggs families for always believing in me and supporting my dreams, and especially my parents, Gaylene and Peter Adams, for raising me as a reader and a geek.

To my awesome agent, Kate Testerman, who never gave up on this book or on me, along with everyone else at KT Literary.

To Wendy McClure and everyone at Albert Whitman for giving this story a home, making it even better, and then sharing it with the world.

To Rachel Searles, who helped me figure out this book's plot at Panera and over many emails; Cortney Pearson, who read each chapter the second I finished it and cheered for me to keep writing; and Stephanie Garber, who helped me figure out a tricky plot point and always made me smile.

To the other author friends who kept me going and helped me

in various ways through the years: Susan Adrian, Karen Akins, Riley Edgewood, Dana Elmendorf, Amaris Glass, Jessica Love, Kathryn Rose, and Krista Van Dolzer.

To my Latina readers for helping with the Spanish and making Elena more authentic: Nancy Unruh Berumen and Aline Strickler; with additional thanks to Zoraida Córdova and Mónica Bustamante Wagner, who answered some of my questions.

To everyone who has followed me on my path to publication and offered me a kind word, a smile, or a congrats along the way—I truly appreciate all of you.

And finally to all of the readers and bloggers who take the time to read my books and help spread the word about them. You make being an author the best job in the entire world.